MW01076962

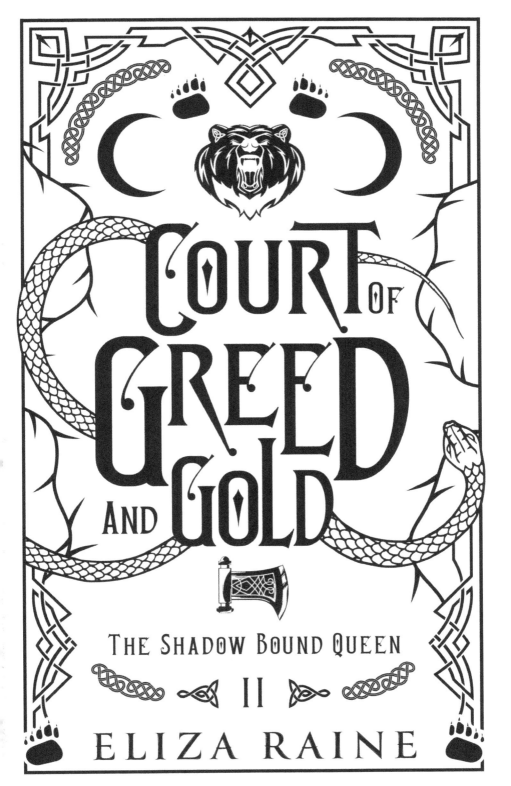

# COURT OF GREED AND GOLD

## THE SHADOW BOUND QUEEN

### II

# ELIZA RAINE

*For everyone who never gives up.*
*For the love of Odin, you've got this.*

SHADOW
COURT
PALACE

SHRINE

ROCK
STAIRCASE
INSIDE
MOUNTAIN

YGGDRASIL

THE
AXEMAN
STATUE

CAVE
FOREST

ROOT
RIVER

# Ansuz

## MESSAGE

REVELATIONS · VISIONS · INSIGHT

# I

## REYNA

I scrambled back down the tree, my heart hammering so hard against my ribs they ached.

"Voror, are any of those things still alive?" I asked as my feet touched the ground and I reluctantly looked over the mass of body parts.

The owl swooped low over the carnage. "They were not alive to begin with," the owl said drily. The fear I'd heard in his voice before was gone. "Their smell is incredibly offensive."

"It's safe?" Energy was beginning to surge through me, washing away the paralyzing fear.

"They will reform, but not for some hours, I think."

"Is that Arthur? The bear from the palace?"

"Yes."

On cue, the bear looked up from where it was ripping apart the body of the Starved One who had spoken. Its eyes fell on me, but it didn't move.

ELIZA RAINE

Gingerly, I picked my way through the bodies toward the Prince.

Voror hadn't been lying. The smell was worse than offensive. Trying to take shallow breaths through my mouth, I kept my sights fixed on the Prince's slumped body.

"Reyna, he said the Queen was coming. He told you to run for good reason. If she finds you out here, her behavior may be unpredictable." Voror's tone was measured, but urgent.

"He saved me. I need to make sure he's..." I trailed off as I got closer.

He's what? Alive? Safe?

*What the fuck was I thinking? Why wasn't I running?*

I reached his body and crouched quickly, brushing loose hair from his face.

His eyes flickered open.

"You're alive," I breathed.

"You will not be if she finds you. Take Arthur and run." His voice was a strained hiss, and the light in his eyes was dim. Blood trickled from the corner of his mouth, and his eyelids fluttered closed.

"Shit."

"Leave him," Voror said, the urgency increased. "The Queen will be able to help him. We must leave. I hear horses."

I shook my head, staring at the scars on Mazrith's face, and the small stream of bright blood running along his jaw. "No. I saw the tension between them. I don't believe she would hesitate to finish the job the Starved Ones started."

Voror's wings beat loudly in the silence as he landed beside me. "You think she would kill her own son?"

"Her stepson. And yes. And I think he knows that, too."

"Then why did he come here? Why did he weaken himself like this?"

It was a good question. Could he have come for me?

I moved his fur cloak, looking for his staff.

The top of it was completely smashed, the silver skull in bits.

A frisson of fear and an innate sense of wrongness whirled through my gut. I scooped up the bits I could find, shoving them in my pocket, then looked over at the bear. He stared back at me, jaw working as he chewed on something.

"Voror, can you communicate with the bear?"

"I shall find out."

The owl took, off, hooting softly. The bear gave a quiet growl, then lumbered toward us.

I got to my feet, trying not to back away as Voror swooped back. "I need him to carry the Prince. Can you ask him to do that?"

The owl blinked at me. "I can try. He is not very bright."

"Try."

The owl and the bear exchanged a few more noises. I held my ground when Arthur reached us, dipped his head, and nudged the Prince's still form with his nose. With a bleak wail, the bear looked straight into my face.

I swallowed, then nodded. "I know. He needs our help."

"And quickly. You have about five minutes before the Queen and her guards reach us."

Panic at the owl's words made me move, my nervousness of the huge bear lessening.

"I'm going to lift him onto your back," I told Arthur. He blinked back at me, then slowly lowered himself to the ground. Relief washed over me, and I dropped into a crouch.

As soon as I tried to push one hand under the Prince's prostrate form, he stiffened.

"Oh, thank Odin," I muttered as his eyelids flickered open. "Get up. You need to get up." I pulled at his huge chest.

Fresh panic set in as I realized that there was no way in *Valhalla* I would be able to lift him. He was twice my weight, at least.

"Why aren't you running?" His voice was even weaker than last time, and more blood ran from his lips when he spoke.

"Get the fuck up!" I heaved at him, trying to pull him to a sitting position. "Just as far as Arthur!" His face paled, then set firm as he glanced to the side, seeing the huge bear right next to him.

"On three," I gasped, winding my arms as tightly around his fur-clad chest as I could, and rocking back on my heels. "One, two, three!"

He lost consciousness halfway through the move, but not before he was able to lift most of his own weight.

It was enough.

He toppled onto the bear's back, taking me with him, and I let out a small hiss as I slid straight off the other side, almost landing in the remains of something I didn't even want to think about. I scrambled back up, worried Mazrith would slide off too, but he was a dead weight across Arthur's huge form. Voror swooped low to the ground, rising a second later with the rod of the Prince's broken staff in his beak.

"You will need to ride Arthur. You can't outrun a horse on human legs. And you must keep him from falling."

The sound of hooves in the distance removed any argument or reluctance I may have had about mounting the huge creature.

Throwing one leg over the bear, and then tugging the Prince's massive weight across me, I wound one hand into his black fur.

"Let's go, Arthur."

With unexpected speed, the bear stood up straight and took off.

Riding a giant bear, I quickly discovered, was not the same as riding on the Prince's horse.

There was an equal amount of exhilaration, but for all the wrong reasons. His back was too wide, and staying on at the same time as keeping the Prince on was nearly impossible.

"Voror, please tell me he knows where he's going?" I called as we smashed through the undergrowth, trees passing us by in a blur. Flashes of white in my peripheral vision confirmed the owl was keeping pace.

"Somewhere safe, he says." Voror sounded doubtful.

Anywhere was safer than wherever the Queen was. What would she make of the decimated Starved Ones?

How had the Prince killed so many of them, and was that what had caused his staff to break?

More to the point, *why*? Why had he come?

There was absolutely no question in my mind that I would be dead if he hadn't.

Worse than dead. Pulled apart and stitched back together, to live an endless life as an undead, unsated monster.

The thought made me feel sick as we flew through the forest, and I clutched at the fur-clad Prince even tighter. The memory of my vision swam before me.

When he awoke, I was getting to the bottom of Prince Mazrith's secrets.

*If* he awoke.

After what was probably fifteen minutes, but felt like hours of tense sliding and slipping and clutching, the bear slowed down. We had reached the edge of the forest, and the dark, rocky mountainside loomed before us. The silver band around the bear's huge shoulders began to glow, and then he picked up pace again. My thighs squeezed hard around his haunches as we accelerated toward the solid mossy rock.

"Arthur!" I yelled, just before a shallow cave became apparent in the hill-face. The bear slowed to a stop in the mouth of the cave, dropping his back haunches and I slid off his back, Mazrith still across my lap. We landed on the cave floor softly, but in a heap.

Before I could say or do anything, Arthur turned and

galloped out of the cave, facing the trees. The silver bands around his limbs and chest glowed even brighter, and he reared up on his back legs. Silver runes sparked to life inside the bands—hundreds of them—rushing from the creature and coming together to form a beautiful, glittering shield. The runes danced and shimmered but held together, making a perfect oval decorated with a fierce bear-head. It rivaled anything I had ever seen a warrior carry, and my breath caught as I stared.

As Arthur dropped back onto all four paws the shield spun in the air, sending sparks of glowing runes in an arc around the front of the cave. The bear ambled over, sniffing at the slightly scorched line they had made in the ground. Nodding with what I could only assume was satisfaction, he glanced up at the shield. It vanished with a shimmer, and the glow died away from the bear's silver bands.

Voror swooped into the cave beside me. "It seems the stupid bear has some uses," he said, with a tone of approval. "He is adamant the shield will hide us from view. But do not cross the line the runes have made."

I nodded in amazement, then remembered I had a severely wounded male across my lap.

To be precise, a severely wounded shadow-fae prince, who had risked his own life to save mine.

I stared down at him. His face was white, and being tipped off the bear's back hadn't even caused him to stir.

What in the name of Freya was I supposed to do now?

# 2

## REYNA

"Fire."

I dragged my gaze from Prince Mazrith's face at the owl's single word. "What?"

"You need to make a fire. Healing requires energy, and you will both use all of yours keeping warm if you have no fire."

I nodded and gently extricated myself from under the Prince's huge weight. I made him as comfortable as I could on the cave floor before pushing myself to my feet. A throbbing ache pulsed from the snakebite on my foot, and I did my best to ignore it. "Fire. Wood," I muttered to myself, trying to focus.

When I left the cave mouth, I took careful note of the scorched line of runes marking our invisible shield. There were plenty of trees and drift-piles of twigs and dry leaves on the ground within the boundary, and I set to gathering them up.

My mind raced as I worked, the adrenaline draining away, and a tell-tale shake beginning in my limbs.

The Starved Ones had come for *me*.

Bile surged up my throat as I crouched to break up a fallen branch.

The visions I'd suffered of the hideous creatures all my life could not be coincidence.

They knew me.

*We'll give her back when we're done with her.*

That's what she had said, the female who had stayed back in the trees. I'd never heard of a Starved One speaking.

The memory of her hideously creepy song floated back to me. Starved Ones were supposed to be mindless, hungry, undead monsters, not whatever the fates she had been. But there was no doubt in my mind she had been one of them. I shuddered as I rose, arms full of wood, unable to stop myself picturing Arthur pulling her to pieces.

Would she reform?

I sent a prayer to Freya that I would never, ever lay eyes on her again. She would feature in my nightmares, I had no doubt, but the gods might be kind enough to never let me see her in the flesh again.

I set the wood down in the cave mouth, then scrabbled around for a suitable rock to use for flint. I did what I could to avoid looking at the unconscious Prince.

"Fire first. Half-dead enemy fae captor second," I told myself. "Voror?" The owl was perched on a boulder near the very back of the shallow cave, his white feathers shining in the gloom.

"Yes?"

I swallowed, then forced the question out. "Why would the Starved Ones come for me?"

The owl clicked his beak. "I do not know."

"What do you know about them?" I sat on the ground, concentrating on lighting the fire, trying to keep my shaking hands busy.

"Only what legend says. They were once living, healthy humans, and then they turned on each other, and ate the flesh of their kin. The gods punished them by making them endlessly hungry."

"But doesn't that also punish the people they now prey on?"

"Yes. The gods will have had their justifications, I am sure."

"I didn't think Starved Ones could speak. But that female - she *sang*. Have you heard of that before?"

"I believe she was an Elder."

I paused and looked at him. "An Elder?"

"One of the original clan."

My mouth fell open in horror. "Wait, the *original* clan? Who ate each other? Who were punished by the gods?"

"Yes. They began to stitch together the remains of those they preyed on, creating new creatures, but the original clan live on, in as much capacity as those creatures can live."

I let out a long breath, and my shaking fingers dropped the rock on the ground.

That made her ancient. More ancient possibly than the fae who ruled the five Courts. "Why do they want me?" My words were a whisper.

"I imagine for the same reason that the Prince wants

you. The same reason I was sent to help you. The one we are both currently unaware of."

I bit back a retort with an effort. Voror was my ally. If I'd had any doubt before I was pushed off the edge of the shrine, then that had been expelled utterly.

My eyes fell on Mazrith. Could the inscription on his shrine be connected to the Starved Ones? I wasn't sure even he knew why he was supposed seek the 'copper-haired *gold-giver*', past those ancient scrawls.

The scars on his face looked clearer, now his skin was so pale. One long, broken one dragged all the way from the corner of his brow, across his raised cheekbone, then finished over his sharp jaw.

Had he sustained them fighting?

Had a woman cut him, defending herself?

I knew instantly that wasn't the case. *Because he has honor.*

Whether I trusted him or not, I couldn't deny it. Could it be that the Shadow Court Prince was different than the fae who had abused and disrespected me and my kind my whole life?

A fresh trickle of blood welled at his lips, making more shivers roll through my gut.

"I don't know how to help him." My words came out a mumble, and Voror flew toward us, landing on the cave floor and poking his beak at the thick furs swaddling the Prince's body.

"He usually wears many belt pouches. He may have medicine or magic in them."

I nodded, giving myself a mental shake.

*Come on, Reyna. Get yourself together. He saved your life. Now you need to save his.*

I moved to his side, abandoning the unlit fire. My hands were still shaking too much to strike a light, so it would have to wait.

First gently, and then with more force, I tugged away his huge cloak. My shaking hands stilled completely when I saw his bare chest beneath the furs.

"Shit."

"That explains his unconsciousness," Voror said quietly.

A wound gaped in the very center of his sternum.

As wide as my palm and roughly circular, there was no blood or bone visible. It was as though he had been burned, a black, stone-like substance seared into his flesh, tinged red in places. As I stared, I thought I could see the ghostly shapes of runes dancing in and out of focus in the cracked surface.

My hand moved unbidden, reaching out to touch it.

"I would not do that, if I were you," the owl said.

I stopped moving. "Did the Starved Ones do that?" I asked, even though I knew they couldn't have. Surely only magic could have inflicted a wound like that?

"I do not know. Search his belt."

I forced my gaze off the wound and moved my hands instead to his belt. Voror had been right, there were lots of pouches. Delving into the first one with only a modicum of awkwardness about being so close to his trousers, my fingers closed around something cool and hard.

I pulled out a small stone object I didn't recognize.

Dropping it on the ground next to me, I continued my search.

Small knives and throwing stars, three small, complicated objects made of stone and wood, a few tightly-wound scrolls, and two horn-shaped flasks lay on the ground before me when I was done.

I picked up the first flask, removed the stopper and sniffed. Mead. I tried the second and recoiled at the pungent smell. "I don't know what that is, but it smells disgusting. The other is mead," I told Voror.

A memory swam back to me. When the Prince had thought I was about to go hysterical on him, he had forced me to drink mead. He had said it was restorative.

It was better than nothing, I decided.

Leaning over him, I carefully pulled his jaw open a little, and tipped a bit of the mead between his lips. It dribbled over them and into his mouth. Nothing happened.

"Normally, his magic would heal him," I muttered, thinking aloud. "What about his staff?" I pulled all the bits of the broken skull and thorns I'd picked up out of my pocket. Like a puzzle, I began fitting them back together, and as I turned over the strangely cool broken pieces, I realized my hands had stopped shaking.

"I think I left a piece behind," I said a few minutes later as I surveyed my handiwork. I had sort of managed to put the skull back together, but with nothing to bind the pieces, it would not stay that way. And there was a large gap in the right-hand side.

Voror clicked and flew back to his perch at the back of

the cave. "You would need a *shadow-spinner* to restore the magic anyway."

"Maybe that's what I should do? Ride Arthur to where Tait lives and bring him back here?"

I glanced out of the cave to where Arthur was, flat on his belly by the rune-line, eyes closed.

"I fear that is a long ride, even on the stupid bear."

"He's not stupid."

"You haven't tried to talk to him," Voror muttered.

"Hush, he saved our lives."

He clicked his beak again. "The bear's intelligence notwithstanding, I'm not sure Prince Mazrith will survive that long. That is no ordinary wound."

I looked from the bear to the owl, fear making my stomach clench.

Just a few days earlier, I would have killed him myself.

"Mead." The Prince's rasped voice shocked me so much that I dropped the skull I'd just put back together.

# 3

## REYNA

"Mazrith?"

"More mead."

Nothing but his lips and his eyelids were moving. I rushed to pour more mead into his mouth. This time, he swallowed.

"More?"

"More. But slowly."

I nodded and carefully poured small measures into his mouth.

Color began to seep back into his face, and by the time the flask was empty, he was shifting on the hard floor.

Slowly, he pushed himself into a sitting position, his face giving away his pain.

"Lean against the wall," I said, moving to help him. He stiffened when I stood and gripped his shoulders, but let me help guide him backward so that the side of the cave could take his weight and keep him upright.

"Tell me what happened," he croaked, eyes fixing on me. The blue light was gone, the icy gray dull but intense.

"We got on Arthur's back, he ran, and now we're in a cave."

"No. Tell me how you ended up outside the palace."

"Oh. Somebody pushed me off the edge of the shrine."

Darkness flickered through his eyes, and the wound in his chest flashed brightly. His face screwed up in pain, forcing his eyes closed.

"How did that happen?" I whispered, pointing to his chest.

"Who?" His burning eyes flicked open again as he gritted out the word.

"What?"

"Who pushed you?"

"I-I don't know. I guess the same person who put the snake in my rooms."

"I will find them," he growled.

"Not like this, you won't. How did that happen to your chest?" I asked again, struggling not to look at the wound.

"Reyna Thorvald." My eyebrows raised in surprise at his use of my full name.

I stared at him, unsure what to say. Anger was written over his face, and I didn't know if it was directed at me.

"I find myself forced to be at your mercy, and I need to know if you are as honorable as your namesake."

*At my mercy?* He really was in a bad way. "I could have left you there," I said quietly.

He stared back at me, the anger softening. "I told you to leave me there. Why did you not?"

I tipped my chin back. "Because I am as *honorable as my namesake*." He said nothing, so I carried on. "You saved my life. Now I'm saving yours."

"And when we are even?"

"We can work that out if you make it." I shrugged. His eyes bored into mine.

Eventually, he spoke. "The power needed to kill that many Starved Ones caused damage to my staff."

I glanced down at the remnants of his staff. "I think damage is an understatement. It was destroyed."

He followed my look. "You... You picked up the pieces?"

"I think I missed one or two. But I got most of it. Wait, are you saying the Starved Ones didn't break your staff, but *you* did?"

He nodded slowly. "Yes. The power overwhelmed the staff. And its destruction wounded me."

"What?" I couldn't keep my astonishment from my voice as I looked between him and the black hole in his chest. "Your own magic did that to you?" In all my life working with magic and staffs, I had never heard of such a thing.

A dark look crossed his face. "The staff needs repairing if I am to heal."

"You need Tait?"

"Yes. And my warriors."

"Did they come with you? Where are they?" I glanced instinctively over my shoulder, out of the cave, even though I knew full well that we were alone.

"No. We must make our way back to the palace, as fast as we can."

I let out a small snort of disbelief before I could stop myself. "You're not exactly fit to travel."

"My enemies are out there. I will not wait here, with no magic, to die in a fucking cave," he hissed.

"Hey, I don't want to be here anymore than you do. If you know a way out of here, please share."

"This is my land. My Court. My mountain. I take care of her, and she takes care of me."

I blinked at him. "Did you hit your head on the way down? What are you talking about?"

He glowered at me, then turned his head to look out of the cave, to where the huge bear was sprawled on the ground, just inside the line of runes marking the shield.

He let out a low whistle, and Arthur lifted his head lazily, blinking toward the cave. With effort, he heaved himself up onto all four paws.

"Know that you are only seeing the secrets my Court hides because I have no choice," Mazrith said, as the bear lumbered into the cave.

"You're not the only one with no choice, *your highness.*"

Arthur reached him, dipping his head and nudging his nose at the side of his pale face. Slowly, the Prince wound his hands into the bear's fur, and pulled himself up. Even more color drained from his skin, his pain evident. I moved to help him, cursing quietly.

"Are you sure we shouldn't rest first? The Starved Ones could still be out there, and let me tell you, it was not easy keeping you on this bear the last time you passed out."

He cast a sideways glance at me as together we managed to get him up onto Arthur's back, one leg either side of the beast's colossal shoulders. "We are not going out into the forest. Please, gather up the things from my belt."

"Where are we going?"

"Get the things from my belt," he repeated. "We will need them."

I put my hands on my hips. "Tell me where we're going, and I'll pick up your things."

His eyes flashed as he glared at me. "Odin's raven, you are impossible."

"I'm not impossible. In fact, it's very simple. You do something for me, I do something for you."

His expression hardened, his jaw tensing. "Like I save your life, you save mine?"

I held his granite gaze. "Just like that, yes."

"We are going into the mountain," he snapped after an awkward second or two of silence. "There are hidden ways to the palace throughout the Shadow Court."

I had been inside the mountain more than I cared to already, but I supposed anything was better than the forest. The memory of the scattered bodies of the Starved Ones littering the forest floor spurred me to collect up all the Prince's items even faster.

Voror could fly through the rock, as he had when I'd worked in the shrine, so moving through the mountain wouldn't be a problem for him. I hadn't seen any sign of him since the Prince awoke, but I knew he would be nearby, no doubt listening.

I handed the Prince his belt, all the pouches refilled.

"Thank you. Get on."

"What?"

"Get on Arthur. It is a day's ride, and we will need to rest frequently. We need to start moving."

"How did you get here so fast if it's a day's ride? In fact, how did you even find me?"

"Magic." He ground his teeth, his face still pale. "Will you please get on the bear? You can ask your endless accursed questions once we are moving."

I did as I was told, pulling myself onto Arthur behind the Prince. It was actually a relief to be off my feet, a slight pulsing from my injured foot reminding me I wasn't in great shape myself.

The bear began to move, not out of the cave, but further into it. His pace was slow and gentle, another relief compared with the breakneck speed we'd galloped through the trees.

I watched in wonder as we reached the back of the cave and seemed to walk straight into solid rock.

"It's an illusion," I murmured.

"Yes. There are many gaps in the rocks all over the mountain, but they are incredibly difficult to see."

The dim light from the forest vanished as we rounded a corner, and fear instantly gripped me.

*What if the Starved Ones could get inside the mountain too?*

We would have no hope, trapped inside the rock, in the dark.

"Voror?" I whispered, fear overriding my previous decision to keep my animal friend a secret.

I felt the Prince tense in front of me in the dark. "Who is Voror?"

I heard a soft hoot in the distance, then the owl's voice in my mind. "I am here."

"Are there any Starved Ones near us?"

"I can sense only the fairly disgusting creatures that dwell naturally within the structure," he answered.

I sagged in relief. "Thanks."

"Who are you talking to?" Mazrith growled in the darkness, louder.

I sighed. "You wouldn't believe me if I told you."

"Try me."

"He's... he's an owl."

There was a long silence as we rocked gently from side to side with Arthur's rolling gait.

"An owl?" Mazrith said eventually.

"Yes. An owl with..." I trailed off and Voror's voice entered my mind.

"Choose your words carefully, *heimskr*," he said.

"Almighty intellect and enormous bravery," I finished. "And *he* thinks I'm an idiot, too."

"You can speak with this owl." It was more of a statement than a question.

"Yes, if I keep one of his feathers on me." I had no intention of telling the Prince how Voror had come to be with me, sent by a mysterious fae. To my relief, he didn't ask.

"Why do you ask this owl if there are enemies nearby?"

"He smelled, or heard, the Starved Ones coming before. He says he has excellent senses."

Mazrith grunted. "Owls have no sense of smell."

"I beg to differ," said Voror, haughtily in my mind.

Despite everything, my lips quirked in a smile. "Well,

you two can argue that out later. The point is, if Voror says there are no Starved Ones in here with us, then I believe him."

I got no answer, and we lapsed into silence.

The only light in the tunnel was coming from the faintly glowing silver runes in Arthur's fur.

"How long will it be this dark?" I asked. The idea of resting here, or even of getting down from the bear's back, made me nervous.

"Not much longer. Commence asking your infernal questions."

# 4

## REYNA

I glowered pointlessly at the Prince's back in the darkness.

"You would have questions too if you were in my position, you know," I said.

"I will only answer what I deem necessary."

"No doubt," I muttered. Choosing a question I was pretty sure I already knew the answer to, I started hesitantly. "What would have happened if I had left you in the forest?"

He shifted in front of me. "You mean if the Queen had found me before the Starved Ones reformed?"

"Yes."

"I am quite sure she would have taken an opportunity she has long awaited."

My suspicions that the two wanted each other dead confirmed, I frowned. "Why did she follow you to the forest?

"She was suspicious of me leaving the palace with such urgency. It roused her interest."

Something squirmed in the pit of my stomach.

*He had left the palace in a hurry to find me.*

"Why do you and your stepmother not openly oppose each other?"

"I am my father's son. The Court would be forced to choose sides, and she knows she is not as popular as my father was."

"Then why don't you overthrow her?"

There was a pause before he answered. "She has leverage."

Again, I'd suspected as much. He was clearly stronger than she was; it made no sense that he tolerated her. "What does she have?"

"Something I do not."

I resisted the urge to thump his back. "That's a very vague answer."

"It is the only answer you are getting."

I ground my teeth. I couldn't expect to get all of his secrets right away.

"The Starved Ones," I said. "They wanted me. Why?"

"Because you are special."

My breath hitched. "How?"

"I don't know." His answer was soft and slow, and I sighed. He had no more idea who I was than I did. "You have no information about who your parents were?"

"I already told you I don't." Irritation, as well as discomfort, made my words sharp. I didn't talk to anyone but Lhoris about my fractured childhood.

I'd grown up different enough, I didn't need to add more fuel to the bully's fire by making it common knowledge that I had no memories prior to being what Lhoris and I guessed was about ten years old.

My building annoyance dissipated just as fast as it had come, though, as Arthur lumbered around a corner and out of the tunnel.

'Cave' did not do the space justice. Nor did 'cavern'.

It was more like an underground forest; every tree, leaf, and a stream breathtakingly lit by a dreamlike blue-green glow.

"Fates, it's beautiful," I breathed, as Arthur ambled over shining grass which glinted purple as his huge paws disturbed it.

A large, surreally silent waterfall streamed over a rocky outcrop, ending in a pool of crystal-clear water, and a few feet beyond that was a small glade, covered by the swooping, glowing branches of a weeping willow. More trees covered the huge area, some that looked familiar; oaks and yews and birches, and some that looked like they had been plucked from a painter's imagination; huge bulbous things that resembled the bodies of bugs and insects, standing ten feet tall.

I looked up, struggling to believe this could all be inside the mountain, but high above us was a ceiling of solid dark rock.

The glowing flora gave off plenty enough light to see around us, and when Arthur came to a stop by the pool, I slipped off his back quickly. It was a significantly more dignified dismount than the previous time, but my foot throbbed when it touched the ground. Ignoring it, I moved quickly to the water, pausing when I reached it.

I turned back to Mazrith. He looked down at me from Arthur's back.

"Is this safe to drink?"

He nodded. "Yes. But drink slowly, or you will make yourself sick."

I refrained from rolling my eyes at him. "You think I don't know about going hungry and thirsty?" I muttered instead, before turning back to the pool and scooping up a handful of deliciously cool water.

When I had taken a series of slow, deep sips, I turned back to the Prince. "You want some?"

He pulled the empty mead flask from his belt. "Fill this, and I will meet you at the willow glade."

Voror swooped down as soon as the Prince and Arthur moved off toward the glade, wings moving silently. I felt an unexpected rush of relief to see him as he landed on the edge of the pool and clicked his beak.

"Did you know this was here?" I whispered.

"No. But there is prey here." At my alarmed look, he blinked, then elaborated. "Rats."

"Ah."

"I will return when I am fed," he said, then took off.

Once the flask was filled, I took my time walking to the glade, taking in everything around me. It was quiet; no sound of leaves rustling in the wind, or the rats Voror claimed were around. The air smelled of soil, though I could see no dirt on the ground between the magical glowing plants.

Reaching the willow tree, I ducked under the twinkling curtain of leaves and saw the ground beneath its canopy was a carpet of shining purple-green grass. With light coming from both the ground and the leaves above, it was unexpectedly bright under the tree.

Mazrith was sitting beside an iron brazier, the huge bear on his haunches behind him. I passed him the water and wondered if it was the color of the light that was making him look so deathly pale, or if the ride had taken its toll on him.

"Arthur," Mazrith said. "If you would." His voice was hoarse.

I watched in delight for the second time as the bear reared up on his back haunches. His runes shone brightly, then rushed from his fur to form the stunning shield made from silver light. It spun in the air, before shooting out in a dome around the tree. I looked down at the ground for the little scorched rune marks I knew would be left, seeing them in a neat circle around us.

His job done, the bear tipped back onto all fours, strode around to the other side of the trunk, and slumped down to the ground, eyes closing.

"How long will Arthur's shield last?"

Mazrith looked at me. "As long as I am alive. We are bonded."

"Huh. So even if your staff is broken, the bear can use magic?"

"The only magic he has is his shield. But yes."

I stared at the huge dozing bear. "I didn't know fae could have magical pets."

Mazrith grunted. "Do not let him hear you call him a pet. And most fae can't. Only royalty. A gift bestowed by the gods, before they vanished." He dipped his hand into a pouch in his belt, then held it out to me. "Light the fire. Use this."

I took the little stone object from him, then looked at the brazier. "Now, I know there seems to be a common belief that I'm stupid, but there's no firewood or coal in the brazier. Secondly, starting a fire under a tree seems... unwise. Am I missing something?"

"There's a small trigger on the back of the clicker." He gestured at the thing in my hand. "Just hold it to the liquid in the bottom of the brazier. The tree will be fine."

With a shrug, I did as he said. When I pressed the little trigger on the back of the clicker, a tiny orange flame burst out of the end, and the dark liquid in the bottom of the dish flared warm orange. I moved my hand back quickly, and within seconds, a dancing fire filled the brazier.

As if responding to the new light, all the glowing around us dimmed.

"How..." I pointed at the tree, looking around slowly, frowning.

"Nobody can sleep with all the bright blue," the Prince muttered.

"What is this place?"

"A sanctuary."

I couldn't argue with that. Soft ground, clean water, and warm shelter were more than I could have hoped for.

"How long are we resting?"

"I need a few hours." His voice was strained, and I nodded.

Choosing deliberately to keep the fire between me and the Prince, I settled as comfortably as I could on the grassy carpet.

He watched me through the flames. "You are not stupid. You are belligerent. There is a difference."

"Is that right?"

"Yes. Belligerence is a choice. Stupidity is not."

I narrowed my eyes at him but said nothing.

He was right. I wasn't stupid. And I did choose to be belligerent. Because for most of my life, it had often been the only way to feel like I had any control over the vicious fae who owned me. My only thread of defiance in the face of endless incarceration.

When I didn't answer, he spoke again. "I was lured away from the shrine with false information of a raid, so that you would be alone and unprotected."

The memory of the cloaked figure, followed by the terrifying fall, made me shiver. I tugged my legs up to my chest. "Who lured you away?" I asked.

"I do not know. The message was passed through many clansmen and guards. A deliberate ploy to make it too convoluted to find the source."

"Oh."

"You did not see anything at all of who pushed you?"

I shook my head. "No. They were cloaked."

"Did they use magic?"

"No, I don't think so."

Anger played over his face, and he hesitated before speaking again. "How did you survive the fall?"

"Voror. He pushed me so that I landed on a big patch of water-moss, which broke the fall."

His head tilted ever so slightly. "Your owl knows of the shrine? How did he reach it without my knowledge?"

"He can, erm..." Unable to think of a feasible lie, I opted for the truth. "Fly through rock. And he follows me."

He frowned and started to speak, then winced in pain. "I am becoming very tired."

Annoyance that I hadn't asked half the questions I wanted to warred with genuine concern. "You should rest," I said reluctantly.

A faint groan escaped his lips as he moved to lie down, and I instinctively leaped up.

His skin was icy cold as I leaned over to help lay him back onto his furs. I found my eyes drawn to the wound on his chest, and the compulsion to touch it was almost overwhelming.

"Don't." His voice snapped my eyes to his face, only a foot from mine. Pale and pinched, but always intense.

So perfectly proportioned yet scarred.

Everything that was different from my world, yet somehow exactly as it should be.

"Are you in my mind?" I whispered, unexplained emotion gripping me.

"No. I have no magic. But even if I did, your mind is your own. I swear it."

My breath caught. "Really?"

"On Odin."

"Why? Why would you give up that power over me?"

"Honor. You could have left me to die. You *should* have left me to die." The Prince of the Shadow Court's grey eyes were so full of intensity, I could have stared into them forever and never seen their true depth.

"You know, you still might die," I said, trying to break the breathless intimacy that was threatening to take me under its spell.

The beautiful grey eyes narrowed, still searching mine, but I didn't know what for.

I forced myself to move back, my cheeks heating. "Rest. I'll keep watch."

"You don't need to keep watch. Arthur's protection is infallible. Sleep."

Before I could answer him, his eyes were closed.

# 5

## REYNA

Fatigue crashed over me as soon as I found a comfortable position on the soft grass. Expecting my tumbling thoughts to keep me awake, I had been ready to dissect what I knew and come up with a list of what I needed to know next. But before I'd replayed the conversation with the Prince even halfway, my drooping eyelids and aching body won out, and deep sleep took me.

Until the nightmares I expected to come did exactly that. She was everywhere: The Elder, with her hideous song.

I dreamed that the second Arthur had pulled her apart, the pieces jerked along the forest floor, stitching themselves back together in her awful impression of a human being. Wherever I ran, however far ahead I got, and wherever I hid in the dense woodland, she found me. Her face loomed out of the darkness, her singsong voice ringing loud in my ears.

"Reyna."

I gasped as a deep voice tugged me from my dream, groping for a weapon.

I blinked at Mazrith, still laid out by the fire. The remnants of my bad dream fled instantly.

"Oh fates."

The wound in his chest was glowing brightly, and his face was screwed up in pain.

I scrambled to my feet and swore loudly as the snakebite in my foot sent bolts of searing pain all the way up my shin as soon as I put my boot on the ground.

"Are you alright?" Mazrith gritted out.

"Me? Never mind me, why in the name of Odin is your chest glowing?"

I hopped to his side, dropping down beside him and staring at the wound. The hard black substance was cracking apart, revealing... *gold*.

"What..." My words died on my lips as I dragged my eyes from the gold glow and up to his face.

He had changed. The scars that had been more visible as he had paled now *dominated* it. My heart stuttered in my chest as I scanned his skin, trying to find an inch that didn't bear the marks of a blade. Even his screwed shut eyelids were covered.

"Freya help you, what happened?" I whispered.

His eye fluttered open. "The other flask. I need the other flask." When I didn't move, he hissed through his clenched teeth. "Now, Reyna."

I forced my gaze away, moving quickly on my knees to get his belt from where it lay. I found the flask and moved back to him. "What is in it?"

"You don't want to know."

I hesitated, before unstopping it. "Why not?" My voice was small, and I cursed my own curiosity.

"Just pour some in my mouth." A profound sense of wrongness washed over me as I pulled the stopper out, and I found myself staring at the criss-cross marred flesh of his face again. "Please, Reyna."

I moved my hand, making myself pour the foul-smelling stuff into his mouth.

He convulsed as soon as he swallowed, and I scrabbled backward, clutching the flask. A small black rune floated from the open neck of the bottle at the same time one drifted from the Prince's lips. Slowly, the scars on his face receded, and the cracked black flesh closed over the gold beneath, dimming, then extinguishing, the glow.

I was too stunned to move. To speak.

*How was I seeing black runes?*

I was a *gold-giver*. I saw *gold* runes. Nothing else.

The Prince drew long breaths, the tension that had been gripping his body relaxing even as my heart pounded faster.

"What are you?" I was barely even aware I said the words.

His deep breaths calmed, and his head slowly turned toward me. "What do you mean?" His words were granite.

"You are not what everyone thinks you are..." I trailed off, staring.

"I am the Prince of the Shadow Court. The Prince of Snakes." Somehow, even lying on his back with a gruesome wound in his chest, he oozed danger. Instinctively, I shuffled further away from him.

*He has no magic. His staff is broken,* I reminded myself.

Never mind that he could snap me in two if he wanted to.

*Be brave, Reyna. The brave earn their braids. They go to Valhalla.*

"That's not an answer," I said, as steadily as I could.

Slowly, he pushed himself up onto his elbows, then to a sitting position. He was swallowed in shadow as his huge chest blocked the orange glow of the fire behind him.

I forced myself to hold my ground, not to shuffle any further back on my backside. But my fingers were trembling around the flask.

"Put the stopper in that, and put it down. It must not spill." His voice rang through the silence.

As unsettling as it was to know he could see me shake, I did as he bid me.

When the flask was sealed and on the ground, he spoke again. "You fear me."

I swallowed hard. I didn't want to answer him. But he already knew. "Yes."

His face was too dark for me to make out an expression, but his body tensed. "Do my scars scare you?"

I faltered. "What?"

"Do my scars scare you?" he repeated, louder.

"N-no. You scare me," I spluttered. He was silent, and I shook my head, trying to clear it. "What are you?" I repeated my question, drawing on my courage. I wasn't going to tell him what I'd seen in my vision, tell him that I knew for certain that he wasn't what he seemed.

I didn't need to. The wound and the gold runes were enough.

"I am a fae Prince," he growled.

My pulse quickened. "You're not a shadow-fae?" I breathed.

He gave a mirthless laugh in the gloom. "Have you ever seen, or heard, of a fae able to manipulate shadow as I can?"

I remembered Lhoris' awe at his power on the boat. "No," I admitted.

"Do you believe that any other than a shadow-fae could perform such feats?"

*But what about the gold?*

"Why do gold runes float from you? Why is that wound concealing gold?" I raised my chin, taking a breath, trying to show him I wasn't backing down until he gave me an answer.

He hissed something in the ancient language, too fast for me to follow, then his shoulders dropped. He turned, the firelight catching his face as he moved.

"Sit. Over here, where I don't feel like a wolf with its prey."

His words making me feel weak, I pulled myself onto my knees and moved toward him. Keeping a few feet between us, I sat back on my behind, drawing my knees up.

Anger was dancing in his eyes. His face was pale again, but no longer the tapestry of scars it had been. I almost asked what was in the flask and how it had reversed whatever had just happened with his wound so quickly, but I

COURT OF GREED AND GOLD

stopped myself. The answer I needed from him was about the gold runes.

"The gold," I said, fixing my eyes on his. "Tell me about the gold."

His gaze flicked down to his chest, then back to my face. I watched his expression change, from quiet fury into resigned tension.

"I have been cursed," he said, eventually.

# 6

## REYNA

"Cursed? Cursed how? By a gold-fae?"

"I have no need to tell you more than I wish to. I do not trust you." His eyes narrowed, then he spoke again. "All you need know is that I have until my thirtieth birthday to find a way to break it."

I blinked at him. His mother's words in my vision came back to me.

*"Enough magic for five years. You must find the mist-staff by your thirtieth birthday."*

My mind whirred.

I already knew more than he wanted me to. I knew that to break his curse he needed to find whatever a mist-staff was.

He had said in the vision that he had no magic without his mother. I glanced down at his chest. Did that mean this curse had taken away his magic and his mother had given him hers instead?

"Your thirtieth birthday," I mumbled. "When is that?"

Firelight reflected off his face as he scowled. "Two months from now. When the last gold rune floats from my skin... Then it is over."

"And... That's why you took me? You think I can help break this curse?"

"Yes."

I tilted my head, trying to work through my tumbling thoughts. "I thought you wanted me for something to help overthrow your stepmother," I said, in an attempt to offer him some truth.

"When my curse is broken, that will not be far behind."

"Is that what she has on you? Does she know about your curse?"

"Absolutely not," he said sharply. "The only being alive who knows of it is Tait." His eyes flicked to the flask, but he didn't say any more.

So the *shadow-spinner* had given him whatever was in it.

"And that?" I pointed at his chest.

He glared. "As I told you. I used too much magic for the staff to handle. It exploded."

I was sure there was more to it, but I nodded. "Why are the runes gold? Was it a gold-fae who cursed you?" I asked again.

"You are obsessed with gold," he growled.

I raised my hands, glaring. "I'm a *gold-giver*. What do you expect?"

"Gold is in your blood," he muttered angrily.

"Hey, I'm human. There's nothing in my blood."

"You are rune-marked."

"I'm human."

He shifted his huge shoulders as he stared at me. "Chosen by the gods to work with magic."

"Human," I repeated, loudly.

He held my defiant gaze silently.

When it became clear he was saying nothing else, I spoke. "So, what is the curse? What happens if you don't break it? *How* do you break it?"

"You need know none of the answers to those questions. Only that the shrine holds the key. We must return to the statue, and you must finish your work as soon as we are able."

I swallowed awkwardly. "I, erm, broke the gold staff. When I fell."

"What?"

I fished the end of it out of my pocket. "I accidentally brought it with me."

He stared at the lump of gold. As my vision started to tinge, I set it down on the grass.

"It looks... repaired."

"Oh. Yes, I finished fixing the bent feather."

"And? Was there anything special about it?"

"I don't think so." I looked between him and the staff-top, worry washing through me. "Look, I'm willing to examine it further, but not now. Working with gold-"

He cut me off. "When you are rested and replenished, we will return to the shrine, and you will fix the statue and find out what secrets it holds."

Before I could respond, he gave a low whistle, and Arthur lifted his head.

"I have a short respite from my wound that I wish to take advantage of. We continue on to the palace now," he said.

Riding a giant bear through a glowing cave-forest with a fae Prince was not something I ever would have dreamed I would be doing. But the ethereal beauty surrounding us was lost on me, my mind stuck instead on trying to sort through what I had learned.

Prince Mazrith needed my help to lift a curse that *must* have been placed on him by a gold-fae.

Unbeknown to him, I also knew that he was using his mother's magic, not his own.

What would happen if he couldn't break this curse? Would he drop dead? Or would he just be magic-less? I supposed that for the heir to the throne of the Shadow Court, having no magic was as good as dropping dead. His Court would not accept a powerless King any more than the insane Queen vying for power would.

My thoughts flicked to the scars that had covered his face.

Had he been hiding them with magic? Whatever was in that flask had made them recede, and restored his strength, so why hadn't he drunk from it sooner?

I let out a long silent breath, awash with confusion and a raft of new questions.

The Prince was an enigma. Secrets and violence, power and magic.

He was shadow-fae royalty, a famously-feared living monster.

But he hid his wounds, believed fiercely in honor, and was living his life under a curse.

I knew I couldn't trust him.

So why in the name of Freya did I want to so badly?

It took a few hours to reach the other side of the glowing forest, where Arthur began to climb a set of steps carved into the rock-face.

I found myself drifting off frequently, the gentle rock of the huge creature lulling me to sleep.

After what must have been another few hours, the steps leveled out into a long ledge that looked over the glowing forest below. A trickle of shining water carved its way across our path, down the rock.

"Do you want to stop for water?"

"Yes," I said, needing to move my numb legs and backside.

The pain from my foot when it touched the ground was enough to take me to my knees though, and a string of curses flew from my lips.

Mazrith was off Arthur's back in a flash, kneeling before me. "The snakebite?"

"Yes. It's fine," I gritted out, even though I was pretty sure it wasn't fine. More swells of pain were washing up my whole shin, the intensity making my stomach churn.

"I will fetch you water," he growled.

I tipped back onto my behind, taking deep breaths and trying to focus on Mazrith filling the flask instead of the pain.

Whatever was in the other flask was clearly still working, as he was able to walk and bend, something he couldn't do at all before. But his huge, fur-covered shoulders were tense, and his body hunched awkwardly.

His face was a picture of barely contained fury when he returned, and I tried not to show my nervousness. "I won't slow us down, if that's what you're angry about," I breathed, taking the flask from him. "I just need a minute."

"I am angry with the person that did this to you," he hissed. "The power of all the ancient gods together will not save them from my wrath when I have them in my grasp."

I blinked up at him. "Why?" The word whispered from my mouth before I could stop it.

"Because-" he said, then stopped, his expression changing. Cool control slammed down in place of the raw fury. "I need you to break my curse."

Something fluttered in my stomach unpleasantly. "Of course."

I drank from the flask slowly.

"Are groups of Starved Ones like that that normal in the Shadow Court?" I asked, trying to break the awkward silence.

"They are vermin," he hissed, his face darkening. "To suggest they are welcome in my Court is an insult."

I held a defensive hand up. "I know nothing about your Court."

"You have made that clear since you arrived," he said quietly. "It's good to hear you finally admit it."

I glared at him. "That's not what I meant, and you know it."

He raised one brow. "But it is true. All that you know is rumor and slander from our oldest enemy."

"Hey, it's not just the Gold Court that hates you. Your Court has terrorized the Ice, Fire and Earth Courts continually."

"And I assume you heard this from the gold-fae?" Mazrith's face was set in stone, anger sparking in his eyes.

"Yes."

"Did they also tell you that the mighty gold-fae were the only ones *we* fear?"

"Yes," I said, less certain of myself as I remembered Ellisar's map on the boat. The map that - unlike the Gold Court maps - showed all five Courts equal in size, rather than the huge Gold Court in the center. And showed surrounding parts of *Yggdrasil* that the Gold Court maps had ignored.

I swallowed hard. Could it be possible that the Gold Court had lied about the Shadow Court all these years?

But the magic of the shadow-fae was mind control. *Inducing fear.* Images of the Queen with her red eyes and black teeth were enough for me to shake my head.

"There are bodies hanging from the ceiling in your palace, and I have seen those for myself."

The Prince dropped my gaze.

Shadow-fae were the literal embodiment of darkness, and all the humans killed in their raids over my lifetime were not lies.

Gold or Shadow, they were all fae. Which meant they were all greedy, twisted monsters.

# 7

## REYNA

The silence descended again, even more awkward than before.

"Voror said that the creature that sang that awful song was an Elder," I said, moving the subject back to the Starved Ones.

"Yes. I wish I knew how she gained access to my Court," Mazrith snarled.

"Are the Elders really the original clan that the Gods punished?" He nodded. "When did the gods vanish?"

He frowned at me. "How is it you do not know the answers to these questions?"

I snorted. "I'm a thrall." He stared at me, waiting for more. "I didn't have history lessons growing up."

"Then, you are more knowledgeable than you should be. You have given me the impression of one educated."

I felt my cheeks heat. "I've been lucky."

COURT OF GREED AND GOLD

He eyed me a second, then spoke. "The gods left six hundred years ago. They took the high fae and the dwarves with them and left the Starved Ones behind. Nobody knows why they left."

"Dwarves really existed?"

"My grandfather's best friend was a dwarf."

I cocked my head. "How old are you?"

"As I already told you, thirty in two months."

I frowned. "But your grandfather was alive six hundred years ago?"

"Fae live long lives."

I knew that, of course. But it had never really occurred to me what it must be like to live that long.

"How old was your father when he died?"

Mazrith's face flashed with anger at the mention of his father. "Enough questions. We must move on."

I cursed myself as I kept my face neutral. I'd pushed him too far.

"Is there anything to eat inside this mountain?" I asked, getting gently to my feet. He gripped my hand in his, helping me up, and a bolt of something tingly passed from him to me. We both froze, and two gold runes floated from his wrist.

I didn't have a chance to ask him what had just happened. He let go of my hand as though it were on fire and swung around to Arthur.

"Here, boy," he muttered, and the bear moved to his side, dropping low to the ground. I opened my mouth to speak, but he cut me off, climbing onto Arthur's back as he spoke. "There's plenty of edible prey inside the mountain, but we are not in a position to catch any of it. We must get back to the palace."

He held my gaze for a beat, my heart skipping fast in my chest. A dark braid fell forward over his face as Arthur shifted.

He was beautiful.

So accursedly beautiful, so fiercely powerful, even with the black, cracked hole in his chest.

"Reyna, we need to get back to the palace. Now."

Did he know what I had been thinking? Had I been staring up at him like a teenaged girl with a crush? Fates, I hoped not.

I shook my head, trying to clear whatever was muddying my thoughts as I rolled myself onto Arthur's back, waving away the Prince's reluctantly proffered hand. Mazrith was right, we needed to get back to the palace.

I needed to be out of his company long enough to get myself straight, get my thoughts under control. We needed to get out of this mountain.

"Reyna?"

I startled awake at the voice, unsure if it had been real or part of a dream. I realized that I had slumped forward, onto the Prince's back, properly asleep.

I blinked around, blearily. Arthur was still making his way up the winding staircase in the rock, though the path

COURT OF GREED AND GOLD

was wider and less steep now. Small caves dotted the rockface on our left, and the right was a sheer drop.

I pushed myself off Mazrith's back.

I felt sick, I realized as I moved my head gently. The headache I had was likely because I was thirsty, but when I thought of actually drinking or eating something, my stomach roiled.

"Reyna." The voice reached me again, inside my head.

"Voror?"

"There is something coming." Fear gripped me instantly.

"The Starved Ones?"

"No. They are creatures of the Shadow Court. I have not seen them before, but they do not look friendly. They are heading down the path toward you."

"Mazrith," I hissed, tapping the Prince's back.

In one slow movement, the Prince slid sideways off the bear's back.

I swore, trying to grab him. He was too heavy though, a dead weight. A cry escaped my lips as he crashed to the ground, his head bouncing hard against the rocky floor.

"Arthur, stop!" The bear did, and I slid from his back, taking care to keep my injured foot off the ground.

Dizziness swamped me, and I was forced to stop and lean on the bear, sucking in breaths.

"Mazrith," I groaned. When had he passed out? It was a miracle we'd both stayed on the bear as long as we had.

Arthur gave a low growl, his runes shining bright.

An answering growl drifted back from the gloom.

"Ohh fates," I muttered, and pushed myself off Arthur and moved to the Prince.

Voror swooped into view, landing next to him. "It is a long fall, with no water at the bottom. Take care," he said.

I rolled the Prince over, wincing at the blood on his temple, grasping at for the flask of disgusting smelling liquid.

Arthur roared, and I looked up from the Prince's belt.

My insides turned cold, fresh dizziness washing over me.

Two enormous wolf-like creatures were stalking around the bend in the path, toward the bear. They were ink-black in color, except for their shining red eyes and glistening white teeth. Wisps of shadow played over their long fur, making them look like they weren't solid, something from a dream. Or a nightmare.

"Shield!" I half-shrieked at Arthur.

But the runes didn't burst from his fur as they had before. In fact, their glow was dimming.

"The bear's energy is depleted. He has traveled for two days with a heavy burden," Voror said.

"Fuck." I moved back to Mazrith's belt, yanking the flask out of a pouch. I felt the same bone-deep unease I had last time I had handled the flask.

A snapping sound made me spin.

Voror was in the air, wings beating in the face of a third wolf I hadn't noticed, who had bypassed Arthur and made straight for me and the Prince.

The wolf jumped and whirled, chomping his lethal jaws at the owl.

"Leave him alone!" I yelled, looking for anything I could

use as a weapon. Finding a rock, I launched it at the wolf, catching him hard in the stomach. He backed up, teeth bared.

Arthur was circling with the other two, trying to keep himself between them and us.

Voror swooped again as the third one made another grab for me. The beasts tail whipped up, catching Voror and sending him spinning.

The wolf lunged for me.

I threw myself to the ground as it pounced, the flask tumbling from my hand. I kicked out hard with my good leg as it reached me, catching it in the air. It yelped loudly as it crashed into Arthur's side and the bear turned in surprise. It was the distraction the other two needed. As one, they pounced.

# 8

## REYNA

"Arthur! Voror!"

I tried to struggle to my feet, but the third wolf was back on all fours, snapping his teeth at me. Caution was keeping him at bay, but I didn't know for how long.

"My wing is damaged. I'm not sure I can help," the owls voice reached me. Relief that he was alive had no time to settle, as I watched Arthur desperately try to shake off the two relentless wolves.

Guilt consumed me. I'd given the things the chance to attack. The bear had been carrying us without food or rest, it was our fault he couldn't fight back.

In the distance, a new noise reached my ears. I sucked in a shaky breath and listened.

"Voror, can you hear that?"

"Yes. Horses."

I never would have believed that I would be happy to see

shadow magic. But the sight of a ribbon of black shooting around the corner and slamming into one of the wolves trying to tear chunks out of Arthur's back made me light-headed with relief.

Frima and Svangrior came galloping around the bend above us, shadows whipping around them.

I saw the fear fill the wolf's eyes before his tail tucked under his body and he turned and fled. I sank down to my knees, crawling to Arthur.

"Hey, boy, you did amazing," I croaked, trying to scan his massive body for serious injury.

Frima and Svangrior leaped off their mounts together, Frima rushing to the Prince. Svangrior moved to me, eyes glinting.

"What happened?" Frima asked as she dropped to her knees beside Mazrith.

I started to answer her, but a fresh bout of dizziness made me tip sideways. Svangrior caught me roughly. "We need to get them back to the palace. Now."

"Palace," I mumbled thickly. "Yes. Palace."

I had been holding on through sheer survival instinct, but with the responsibility of keeping myself and the Prince alive stripped from me, my faculties abandoned me too. Exhaustion took over.

I was barely aware of what was happening as Mazrith

and I were loaded onto the horses. Svangrior told me that Arthur was not seriously hurt and was following us, and Voror kept assuring me he was safe, but past that, I was too tired, confused, and in pain to care about anything else.

We weren't being eaten by shadow wolves. We were on our way to some sort of help. That was enough.

I flitted in and out of sleep as we rode, draped over Frima's horse like some sort of deer for dining on, but unlikely to fall off.

I was vaguely aware of entering a cave with a secret door like I'd seen before, and then of being transferred from the horse to a small food cart. Curtains dropped down either side of me, so I couldn't see out. Panic briefly tried to take hold but lost out to bone-deep fatigue. These fae would not hurt me, I knew. They were loyal to their Prince, and he had ordered them to keep me safe.

When the cart stopped moving and the curtains were lifted, I saw Ellisar heaving the Prince's still form off another cart, onto the thick fur rug covering the dark floorboards.

"Is he..."

"He's alive," Frima said, before crouching and helping me off the trolley I was on. My foot gave out instantly, and I dropped to my knees.

"Brynja," Frima barked, then moved to the Prince. Tait, the *shadow-spinner*, was leaning over him, muttering fast.

The maid crouched, looping one arm through mine. She helped me into the big upholstered chair.

"Are we in the Prince's rooms?" I mumbled, blinking around myself, trying to focus.

"The Serpent Suites, yes."

I recognized the wall color, I thought dimly. A door next to the fireplace opened, and I saw Kara's face, Lhoris right behind her.

"What the—" I started.

The girl rushed me, throwing herself into my lap to grip me in a tight hug. Tears of pain pricked my eyes, but it didn't stop me reveling in her incredibly welcome presence.

"Reyna, what in the name of Odin happened?"

The shock of seeing my friends lent me strength and I shifted in the chair. "It's just my foot. From the snakebite. And I'm very tired and hungry."

Kara shuddered as Lhoris reached us. "Brynja told us about the snake," he said. "I am glad to see you safe. Though I am not sure you are well." He frowned down at me, concern in his dark eyes.

Voror's voice sounded in my mind. "I am in the rafters. My wing will heal, but I need to rest here for now. And I must agree with the bearded man. Your complexion is green. I have not seen this in a human before," he said.

"Green?" I looked at Kara. "Am I green?"

She bit her lip, then nodded. "I'd say there's a green tinge, yes." She looked down at my feet. "We should probably have a look."

"Fine. Why are you two here?"

Kara looked at Brynja, then sideways at the fae crowded around Mazrith. "I don't know. They brought us here yesterday, and someone has been guarding us since." I noticed she had bags under her usually bright eyes. "We heard them talking about you and the Prince being missing."

Lhoris spoke gravely. "I think that in your absence, the

Prince's warriors wanted to keep their leverage on you safely where they could see it."

*And safe from the Queen's crazy appetite whilst Mazrith wasn't around to protect them.*

"Where have you been? What happened?" My mentor asked quietly.

"I can't tell you now," I whispered back.

"Reyna, we need to look at your foot, and make sure your wound is not infected," Kara said.

I could hear the doubt in her voice, and between the pain, the dizziness, and the nausea, I couldn't help agreeing with her.

"Brynja, bring hot water over here, now," Frima called, and the maid gave me an encouraging smile before hurrying away.

I nodded at Kara. "Let's get this over with."

"Okay. Tell us everything you can. It might help distract you from any pain," she said apprehensively, sitting down and reaching for my boot, then pausing. "Which one?"

I gestured at the wounded foot, then took a deep breath. "So, someone tried to kill me. Twice actually," I started, casting a suspicious glance over at the fae warriors. "The first time, with a snake."

Kara gently unlaced my boot as I spoke, and I only winced a little at the pain. "Erm, Reyna, this is going to need cutting off."

"What?"

"Your boot, not your foot!" she said in alarm.

I gave her a look. "But I need my boots. You can't cut one off."

"Well, I'm not going to be able to pull it off."

Reluctantly, I looked down.

She was right.

My ankle was so swollen, there was no way in *Yggdrasil* that my boot was coming off. Worse, the skin on my leg was actually green. Not sallow and sickly green like I imagined my face might be, but properly green, like a frog.

We all stared mutely a moment. "What kind of snake bit you?" Lhoris asked eventually.

"I don't know. I didn't ask."

Kara frowned at me. "Who doesn't ask that?"

"Someone terrified of being mind-controlled by a fae prince," I muttered.

Voices rose from the fae, and then Mazrith's voice boomed through the room.

"I told you to attend to *her*, now!" Everyone fell silent, then a flurry of movement began, Frima, Brynja, and Tait all moving toward me.

"I'm fine-" I started, but Kara's usually small voice was strong enough to cut me off.

"I think the snakebite is infected. She needs help."

I glared at her, but she held my look.

Brynja's sympathetic smile quickly turned to one of disgust as she saw my booted foot. "Oh fates, that doesn't look..." She trailed off, then crouched beside Kara.

Frima swooped down, a knife in her hand. "I'll cut your boot off. It will hurt, but I assure you I will do no damage to you with my blade." To my surprise, her matter-of-fact tone did something to soothe me, and I nodded. "Tait, give her something for the pain."

"Don't even think about refusing," Kara hissed at me, and I gave her a dry smile.

"I may be difficult, but I'm not a *heimskr*," I told her. "I'll take whatever they've got."

Tait rummaged in one of what must have been ten pouches on his belt, and then handed me a small vial with something honey-colored in it. I sniffed.

Mead and something else. Something stronger.

A wave of pain spread up my shin, making my breath short, and I knocked back whatever was in the vial.

"Odin's raven, that's good," I hissed as something fiery burned all the way down my chest.

"Do it now," Tait said, his voice tight.

Frima moved, her blade working across the tough leather of my boot.

A warm feeling washed over me, doing a fine job of blocking most of the pain.

I made myself watch as the boot was finally peeled away in pieces.

"Huh. I would say infected," I said, somewhat detachedly. It didn't really feel like my foot anymore. It certainly didn't look like my foot.

It was green, and huge, and had two very angry black dots where the snake's fangs had pierced my skin.

Frima sat back on her heels, looked at Tait, then over at Mazrith.

"How bad is it?" I heard the Prince ask.

She paused before answering. "It's not good."

"Tait, you fix her foot before you touch my staff," the Prince barked.

"But... you have an angry black hole in your chest that keeps making you pass out," I said mildly, a pleasant humming starting up in my head, forcing out the headache. "You should really fix that first."

Tait blinked down at me. "Mazrith said you have the pieces of his staff?" he asked me gently.

"Yes. But that has a hole in it now too. I missed a bit." My stomach churned, and a flash of pain made my whole body tense. "I... I feel sick," I said quietly, as new pain beat at the back of my head, making my vision blur.

Tait turned to the Prince. "I think, perhaps, we should sedate her."

A trickle of alarm tried to make itself present through my foggy thoughts, but a soothing squeeze on my arm from Kara made me ignore it. "We won't leave your side," she whispered.

I shrugged. "The Prince wants me alive. He needs me."

Kara raised a questioning eyebrow, but then Tait blocked my view of her, passing me a new vial.

"I'm afraid to say this one is not so pleasant," he said apologetically.

Pain was surging up from my foot again, and I took it from him. "Will it stop this hurting?"

"Yes. You will be unconscious, and as such, feel nothing, while..." He paused and looked round the room at the unlikely group. "While one of us, Odin-only-knows-who, tries to sort this out."

Being unconscious seemed infinitely preferable to the headache, nausea, and pain.

*And I knew he would keep me safe.*

I drained the vial and let the blackness come.

# 9

## REYNA

When I next woke, I had no headache at all. And no pain in my foot. It took a long time to force myself to open my eyes though.

When I finally did, I saw that I was still in the Prince's rooms. In fact, I was in his bed. Again.

Groaning, I rolled into a sitting position. *You have to stop making a habit of this, Reyna, He's going to think you want to be in his bed.*

Forcing out the flashes of the fae-wine dream that accompanied that thought, I pushed off the covers, noting that I appeared to be wearing a man's shirt that was much too large for me, but kept my modesty intact.

I looked down apprehensively at my foot, gut tightening.

The whole thing was bandaged in clean white gauze, halfway up my shin. The skin coming out of the top of the bandage was a normal color, which I supposed was good. I poked tentatively at it.

It felt okay.

"You are awake." The Prince's voice brought my head snapping up. He was standing in the open doorway, leaning hard against the frame.

"I am."

"Tait!" He called. The *shadow-spinner* appeared by his side, Kara hot on his heels.

"How are you feeling?" Tait asked as he came over and bent over my foot.

"Good. What did you do?"

"Not me, my lady," he said, shaking his head. "I make potions and spin shadows, I don't perform..." He looked pointedly at Kara. "Operations."

I looked at my protégé, brows rising. "Ellisar helped too," she said, blushing. "But it turned out that the books I read on venom were really quite useful. And Ellisar's father was an animal healer."

"An animal healer?"

She frowned at me, concerned. "Yes, you know, his job is to-"

"Yes, I know what one is, I just..." I trailed off, shaking my head. "Will it heal?"

Her smile didn't quite reach her eyes. "It might."

"Right."

"For now, we think we removed the venom, and we have tried to treat the infection with some potions Tait had."

Mazrith's deep voice made everyone look at him. "As soon as I can get a trustworthy Court healer to you, it will be done. But with the Queen suspecting I am weak, and numerous threats to your life already, I trust nobody right now."

"If we could get a trustworthy healer then they would need to attend to you," Tait muttered, looking at the Prince before turning back to me. "Do you need anything? Are you in pain?"

"No," I said. "Just hungry."

He nodded. "Good. Then I must return to my work with the staff before mead stops being so effective on the world's most stubborn fae Prince." He glared at Mazrith, then hurried from the room.

Brynja entered a second later, holding a plate covered in bread and cold meat cuts, and a large glass of what I hoped was mead.

"My lady," she said as she set them down, casting nervous glances at the Prince, still in the doorway. "Let me know if you want any more." She hurried out before I could thank her.

"Kara, go with her," Mazrith said.

I opened my mouth to protest, but the look on his face brooked no argument. Kara planted a fast kiss on my cheek, then left the room. He stepped in, closing the door behind him.

"What are you doing?"

"We need to talk. Eat first."

Slowly, he eased himself into the large chair by the fireplace at the end of the enormous four-poster bed. Ravens were embroidered across the big cushions. A door on his left was ajar and I assumed it was a bathing chamber.

Fixing his eyes on me, Mazrith folded his arms.

"I can't eat with you staring at me like that."

"You need to eat. You are weak."

"Just what every girl wants to hear," I said. "Stop staring at me."

"Fine." He turned to face the fire, and I shoveled slices of ham into my mouth.

"Are you in pain?" His voice was so soft I only just heard him.

"No. Are you?"

He continued to stare at the fire. "Yes."

"Oh."

"But Tait will repair my staff tonight, and then I can reverse some of the damage."

"Right."

"I-" he started, then stopped, shifting his weight in the black chair.

Dropping the chunk of bread I was holding, I selected a slice of roasted beef. "You what?"

He turned to me, and I caught a glimpse of unexpected emotion in his eyes.

"I mean to say, I did not know you were in such pain."

I put the meat back on the plate awkwardly, and pulled the tangle of blankets tighter around myself. "It's fine," I told him.

"It is not fine. I will find out who put that snake in your bedchambers, and I will tear them apart with my bare hands. Shadows are too good for them."

Fierce rage glinted in his eyes, and I had to remind

myself that he had no magic. The power was all coming from him.

I parted my lips, about to tell him he didn't need to be so protective over his toys, but the retort didn't come.

Why was he so angry that I had been hurt?

Because he needed me to save his life?

Or was it something more? Did I *want* to believe it was something more?

"It was barely days ago that you were threatening to do such terrible things to my only friends," I said quietly, as much to remind myself as him.

"It was the only way I could make you come with me. Make you assent to the binding."

I lifted my hand, the black binding rune burned into my skin. "So, you wouldn't have hurt them? It was a bluff?" I let my derision fill my tone. "Horseshit. You took what you wanted, by threat and force."

"As you would expect of my people," he snarled.

"Exactly."

Groping for resolve, I told myself it was true. Threat and force. Secrets and violence. That was his world.

But as I stared into those intense, beautiful eyes, I didn't fully believe it.

Would he truly have killed Kara and Lhoris?

I made myself go back to that day, when he'd exploded into the workshop in the gold palace, the glinting skull mask over his face. He had seemed every bit capable of slitting their throats, just as he had threatened to.

"The ring," he said abruptly.

"What?"

"The serpent betrothal ring. It has my magic in it. That's how I knew where you were when you were carried from the palace."

I blinked, my mind whirring. I'd jammed the ring in my pocket in case I was expected to wear it in the palace, and it had been there ever since.

Realization washed over me. If I had ever escaped, he would have found me instantly.

A creeping feeling of betrayal and anger, rose in my chest, and for a moment, I thought I could feel the binding rune burn hot on my hand.

Freedom truly was a long-lost dream.

My face hardened.

"I need you to finish your work in the shrine. As soon as possible. And I need your word that you will tell no-one about my curse."

I nodded, not trusting myself to speak. He continued to stare at me. "Your word, Reyna," he said eventually.

"On Odin," I ground out. I meant it. I would tell nobody about his curse. But I would do whatever I could to find out more. It might be the only thing to save me.

# 10

## MAZRITH

I knew she would be angry about the ring. Freedom was what her heart truly desired, I had seen that.

Freedom.

Something she, nor I, would ever experience.

She thought she knew more about me now. Thought she was working out my secrets. How wrong she was.

Her fierce green eyes were holding mine, and the more I stared into them, the more I marveled. How could a human woman, one ostracized and used her whole life, have so much fire left burning within her?

*You knew, Mazrith.* My mother's voice rang in my mind. *You knew this would happen.*

It was true, of course. I knew that if I ever found her, she would test everything. My entire being.

The copper-haired *gold-giver.*

The tool of my enemy.

*The haunter of my dreams.*

67

She was dangerous. She didn't know she was, but she had the power to change everything. The fate of *Yggdrasil*.

Yearning coiled in my gut, so powerful it almost broke me. I wanted her to know what she was. Wanted her to feel true power. To take her revenge on those who had wronged her.

*No.*

*Control her. Keep her close, but never let her in. She is the key.*

I had gone too far the night of the ball. That accursed dress, her beautiful body pressed against mine. Every male there staring, letting their every thought play out for anyone to see - it had been too much. I had almost gone to a place I could not return from.

And now, I had let my emotion show again. I had let her see the rage that overtook me when I thought of anyone causing her harm.

That's why she had to know about the ring. That's why I needed her scowling with hatred at me now, plotting behind those bright, defiant eyes. Those beautiful fucking eyes.

I couldn't be weak. *Odin, help me be strong. Mother, help me be strong.*

# II

## REYNA

"I must rest now. You should do the same." His words were as terse as I felt.

"You can have your bed back," I said, shifting to the side of the mattress.

"No."

"I don't want it." We locked eyes, and I knew my anger was seeping out of my expression. I did nothing to temper it.

"You need to rest," he ground out.

"I've been unconscious for hours. I do not want to sleep." It was true. As true as the fact that I didn't want to be in his bed anymore.

Another minute passed in silent battle, then he gave a slight shrug of his huge shoulders. "Fine. Ellisar!"

The door creaked open immediately, and the huge warrior poked his head through. "Maz?"

"Send someone to help her dress," he said, nodding his head back at me, then striding stiffly from the room.

"I can dress myself," I said, then remembered I wasn't in my own room so didn't have any of my own clothes. "If anyone has anything I can wear."

Ellisar gave me a grin, then ambled away. Brynja arrived a moment later with a clean shift and a plain green dress. I tried to convince her I could get ready myself, but she insisted on helping me. Relenting, I asked her to help fix my hair into the spelled headband, along with Voror's feather.

"Who, erm, bathed me?" I asked her awkwardly as she fiddled with my hair.

She gave me a reassuring squeeze on the shoulder. "Myself and Kara. Your modesty was protected, my lady. There, you are all ready now."

"Thank you," I said as she stepped out. "Could you tell the Prince I'll be out in a few minutes, and then the room is all his."

She bowed her head, then left the room.

"Voror?" I whispered as soon as she was gone.

"Reyna."

"I'm glad to hear we've moved on from *heimskr*. How is your wing?"

"Recovering well."

"Good. We need to talk."

There was a flurry of white, then he swooped silently down from the rafters. "About what?" he said, perching on the end of the massive bed. I looked him over briefly, satisfied I could see no sign of injury.

"I need to know how much of what happened inside the mountain you saw and heard."

"All of it. I am supremely stealthy and observant, with excellent hearing."

"Right." I refrained from rolling my eyes. I dropped my voice low. "So, what do you think about his curse?"

"There is plenty he is not telling you."

"I know." I bit my lip, unsure how much to admit to the owl.

He cocked his head. "There is plenty you are not telling me."

I nodded slowly. "And I can't tell you all of it. But I know that he is using his mother's magic."

Voror blinked. "His dead mother?"

"Yes."

His huge eyes bore into mine. "And?"

I took a breath, making a decision. "Have you heard of a mist-staff?"

"No."

My face screwed up in disappointment. "I had hoped you had."

"Why?"

"I think that's what the Prince wants me for. To help him find a mist-staff."

We both fell silent a moment. "I believe there is no change to the previous plan, other than you be highly alert for folk trying to kill you," Voror said eventually.

"Fix the statue?" I said.

"Yes. See if that takes you closer to any answers."

"Okay. Same plan. Fix the statue," I said with a firm nod.

"And don't get killed."

I gave him a look. "You're supposed to be lord of stealth

and observation. I task you with keeping an eye on everyone and working out who my mysterious assailant is."

His feathers bristled. "A task I am already taking seriously."

"I'm pleased to hear it." For all my flippancy, I was actually incredibly grateful to have the magical owl on my side. A bodyguard who could fly through walls and had already risked his own feathers to save me—twice— was pretty special. And the truth was, I was more alarmed by the cloaked assassin than I would admit.

I wouldn't be caught off guard like I had been in the shrine again though. Whoever it was had shown their hand, and now I would be ready for them.

When I left the Prince's bedroom I found myself in the main sitting room. The Prince was in the deep armchair with his back to the bedroom, Frima crouched beside him and talking quietly. When she saw me, she rose.

"Your friends are through there." She pointed to the closed door by the fireplace. Her tone was cool, and I wondered if she had given up her tactic of trying to make friends with me.

I nodded and opened the door, stepping into a short, narrow hallway that had one open door to my left, then turned sharply to the right. Weapons hung on walls: axes and daggers and throwing knives.

I peered through the open door. The walls of the large room were grey, like the sitting room and bedroom, and the drapes and soft furnishings all black. But there was an enormous round table dominating the center of the space that looked like it had been cut straight from a giant tree. It was beautiful, and I instantly wanted to run my hands over the rich wood, to feel the texture and age of the material. Half of it was covered in an interpretation of the Shadow Court, modelled from painted paper carefully laid out, and small carved wooden figures that reminded me of chess pieces.

Svangrior's large form stepped into the doorway, between me and the map. "Feeling better?" he asked, without a hint of warmth.

"Much."

"Reyna! Come and sit here," I heard Kara's voice. Svangrior held my gaze a moment, then stepped aside, revealing Kara and Lhoris sitting at a much smaller table under a large window at the back of the room. Ellisar was sitting at the other end of the giant table and gave me a cheery wave as I walked past him.

"I, erm, heard you helped with my foot," I said, pausing next to him. He nodded. "My dad was good with a scalpel. Turns out I'm not too bad either."

Feeling immensely grateful I was unconscious when this huge human had taken a scalpel to my flesh, I nodded. "Well, thanks."

"You're welcome."

When I reached Kara she shuffled down the bench she was sitting on to make room for me. "How's your foot?"

"Good. I can walk on it fine, now," I told her.

"Look." She pointed out of the window, and I leaned over to get a better view.

The Shadow Court really was nothing like I had imagined. The sky above the spindles of the gleaming black palace looked like somebody had taken a navy sheet of silk, pricked thousands of holes in it, then held it up to a star.

"It shines," Kara breathed. "My books said it did, but the descriptions don't do it justice."

"The Gold Court shines too," grunted Lhoris. "That doesn't mean there's any good in it."

I looked around the room, deciding not to let my mentor know how mesmerizing I found the view. "Is that a map of the Court?" I whispered, nodding my head at the pieces across the table.

Lhoris nodded. "I believe so."

"Tell us the rest of what happened," Kara said, pushing a glass of dark liquid toward me. "Ginger beer," she beamed. "It's delicious."

I took a sip, eyeing my young friend. Aside from how tired she looked, I had never seen her more alive. "You haven't been mistreated in my absence?" I already knew the answer was no.

She shook her head, eyes flicking briefly to Ellisar. "No. In fact, it's nicer in here than it is in the thrall quarters. There's a big bedroom along the hall that Lhoris and I slept in, and we have a bathing room to ourselves. Frima said these rooms are called the Serpent Suites."

I nodded. "Good."

"So, you got to the part about the snake in your room."

"Right." I told them about the snake biting me, and

about seeing the Prince torture the poor guard. Even though my voice was low, I knew that Ellisar and Svangrior could hear me, so I kept my recounting as neutral as possible.

"The Prince wanted me to visit a part of the Court that was… high up. He had to leave for a short while, and someone pushed me. Off the edge."

Kara's eyes were wide. "Off the edge of what?"

"It doesn't matter. But it was high. I was saved by landing on watergrass. But the current took me to the forests at the edge of the Shadow Court."

"Then what happened?"

Ellisar shuffled his chair closer to us, and Svangrior moved to lean against the nearest wall, watching. I turned, looking straight at the bad-tempered fae. "Has your Prince told you how he broke his staff?"

He nodded.

Confident I wasn't saying anything I shouldn't, I spoke. "Starved Ones." Kara's hand flew to her mouth and Lhoris swore.

I told them about Mazrith showing up, and about Arthur and our trek through the forest. "Then we journeyed as far as we could with our injuries until he and Frima found us and brought us back." I pointed at Svangrior.

"Tait said you picked up the pieces of Maz's staff," Ellisar said.

Realizing that I no longer had my trousers, and therefore my deep pockets and their contents, I started. *The gold staff-top had been in my trousers.* "Where are they?"

"The *shadow-spinner* has them. He says you have saved him many days work." Svangrior's voice was tight, like he hated admitting that I'd done something right. When I caught Lhoris' eyes though, I did not miss his disapproval.

"I had to," I said to him quietly. "It was him or the undead."

His jaw twitched, but his face softened. "I am sorry to hear what you have been forced to face. But pleased you are here now to tell the tale," he said gently.

"Me too." I reached over and squeezed the back of his hand gratefully. "Where is Tait?"

If the *shadow-spinner* had the contents of my pockets, then he also had the gold staff top, and I wanted that back in my possession as soon as possible.

"Why?"

"I want to ask him something."

"He is working."

"It's important. To the Prince." It wasn't a lie. Without the gold piece, I couldn't fix the statue, which was the only thing the accursed fae Prince wanted me for.

With a sigh, Svangrior pushed himself off the wall. "Come with me."

# 12

## REYNA

I followed Svangrior back into the sitting room. The Prince was nowhere to be seen, the only occupant Frima. She was sitting in the chair by the fire, staring at the flames and sipping a drink.

"She wants to talk to Tait. Says it's important," Svangrior growled.

Frima eyed me, then tilted her chin. "She saved Tait days of work. I'm sure he won't resent ten minutes. But if he's spinning, you'll have to wait."

Svangrior grunted, then moved the other side of the room, where a tapestry of a crown made of bone, threaded with deep grey vines was hanging. Shadows wisped from his staff, running over the tapestry before shooting underneath it. The fabric shimmered, then the soft glow of a door appeared within it.

"Secret doors everywhere," I muttered, eyes wide.

"And all will open only for shadow magic," Frima answered me, warning in her tone.

I gave her a look. "I didn't try to escape. In fact, I was going to try and get back on my own. Before the Prince found me."

She snorted and went back to her drink.

I wondered what had the Prince told them about the shrine. He didn't want anyone else to know the statues existed, he had made that clear, but he must have told them something about what had happened.

I stepped through the magical door behind the tapestry, and my wonderings vanished, replaced by burning curiosity.

Tait was standing over a huge spinning wheel on a table in the middle of a small workshop, surrounded by piles of spindles and wheels, and various small wooden parts.

The table and the wheel appeared to be as one, made from something that looked exactly like the substance the palace walls were made from. It was a deeply dark, smooth stone that shone with specks of light when I moved, and I could see no joins, as though it were completely organic rather than created by man or fae.

The parts of the skull I had retrieved were on the surface of the table, next to the needle-sharp spindle end of the wheel.

Tait looked up at us, his eyes flashing when he saw me. "Ah. Are you feeling better?"

"Yes. I hope I'm not disturbing you?"

"No. I could do with some help, actually."

Svangrior shifted beside me. "She belongs to our enemy," he barked.

Tait looked at him, then pointedly at the black rune on my wrist. "On the contrary, she belongs to your Prince."

"I'll belong to Odin's arse before I belong to your infernal Prince," I snapped, then instantly regretted my outburst.

A laugh bubbled out of Tait, and Svangrior hissed. "Blasphemy *and* idiocy. She's all yours," the fae snapped, before whirling from the room.

I looked apologetically at the *shadow-spinner*. He nodded sagely. "You've come for your gold?"

My pulse quickened. "Yes."

He pointed to where a belt was hanging on a cart covered in spindles and small pieces of dark wood. "I found it when I was looking for that," he pointed to the skull. "I didn't mean to pry. But of course, I had to ask Maz about it." He blinked at me through his thick glasses.

"And what did the Prince tell you?" I asked carefully.

"About the shrine. And the statues with their staffs."

I moved to the belt without saying anything, to rummage through the pouches for the staff top.

Tait was the only person aside from Mazrith to mention the shrine. Could he be lying about the Prince just telling him today? Could it have been him who pushed me?

My gut said he was more trustworthy than any of the fae. But he was still a slave to the Shadow Court.

"You know, he should have died from that wound. You did well to save him."

"Whatever was in that flask saved him," I said, finding

the gold staff-top. I plucked it out and slipped into the pocket of my dress with a sigh of relief, before turning back to Tait. "What was in the flask?" I didn't really mean to ask the question, but it popped out unbidden.

He pulled a face, eyes darkening. "Nothing you would want to concern yourself with."

"It felt wrong."

His eyes narrowed, and he peered at me. "It should not have," he said quietly. "Not to you."

I frowned. "What do you mean?"

"Come. Hold this for me." He pointed at the skull. "The gap I need to fill is awkward to reach."

Unable to resist the chance to see how a *shadow-spinner* might do their work, I left the belt and moved toward him.

Carefully, he picked up the pieces of the reassembled skull as one and passed them to me. He reached out and touched the end of the spindle, wincing as the end pierced his skin. I sucked in a breath of surprise, but when he pulled his finger away, a ribbon of inky shadow came with him, like a web from a spider.

He reached out his other hand and gestured at the spindle. "Slide the skull on. Don't let the pieces come apart," he said, voice low and intense.

A little hesitantly, I did as he bid. Thinking that there was no way that the stone spindle wouldn't just force all the pieces of silver metal apart again, I placed the base of the skull against the spindle tip, the web of shadow still streaming from it to Tait's finger.

Like a magnet, I felt the metal draw itself toward the

spindle. With ease, the skull slid down onto it, the stone moving through the metal like it didn't even exist.

"Thank you. You may let go now."

I realized I was still holding the skull, staring. I stepped back, fascinated, as the shadow from Tait's finger flew toward the wheel, looping itself all the way around it and back again.

Tait cast a sideways glance at me. "If you wish to stay, you can, but I must warn you, I will be here a few hours."

I glanced around me, spying a small wooden stool. I pulled it toward me and sat down. "If you don't mind, I'll stay."

He gave a nod, then the wheel began to turn.

I saw his eyes change as the trance took him, I supposed in the same way that the gold-vision took me.

The smooth stone wheel turned faster and faster, and after a while, I began to see glints of silver inside the ribbon of shadow whirling around on it. The spindle spun, too, the silver skull moving so fast I could make out no details. The pieces didn't fly apart though, the strange magnetism of the spindle keeping it all together.

Tait's fingers suddenly began to move, darting in and out toward the spindle. At first, I couldn't see what he was doing, but after a while, I realized he was plucking pieces of silver from the shadows.

I didn't know how long it took, but eventually he was holding a palmful of tiny pieces of silver metal. The wheel slowed, and he began to dart in and out again, this time depositing the pieces onto the now slower-moving skull.

I gaped as I watched. He must be seeing black runes,

ELIZA RAINE

telling him exactly when and where the flecks of silver were, and where to put them. I longed to see what he could. Did everything go dark for him the way it went gold for me? Did the passing of time morph into something intangible? *Did he get visions of monsters when he was done?*

I could have watched him for days. The wheel slowed even more, and deep furrows of concentration took his face. Yearning to see more, I stood up silently, and moved around behind him for a better look. He didn't react to my movement, so I moved closer still.

The finger he had pricked was still streaming with shadow, keeping the wheel slowly turning. His other finger flicked and jabbed at the silver on the skull, smoothing the new flecks into the body of the object.

A single black rune floated from the shadows, wrapped around the spindle.

I froze.

*I could read it.*

'Press'.

Another rune floated up.

'Catch'.

I took a step back, my heart hammering. Darkness edged my vision, a soft vignette of gloom.

*How in the name of Freya was I seeing black runes?*

I was a *gold-giver*, I shouldn't see anything other than gold runes.

I glared down at the binding mark on my wrist, refusing to look at Tait and his wheel.

It must be because of the binding, I told myself firmly. The black rune now burned into my skin couldn't be coincidence. But... Did that mean I would be able to understand what to do with shadows like I did gold?

I risked a glance back up at Tait. The shadow ribbon still flowed from his fingertip, his other hand working more gently on the silver skull now.

I shook my head hard enough for it to hurt a little. Even if being bound to the Prince of the Shadow Court had somehow made me see, and understand, black runes, it didn't mean I was a *shadow-spinner*. I couldn't prick my finger and have shadows stream out any more than I could fly!

"Whew. I have to tell you, that would have taken days if I'd needed to start again," Tait said heavily, his voice startling me.

"You're... done?" I looked at him, trying to keep my confused thoughts from showing on my face.

His shoulders were sagging and the wheel had stopped turning. No shadows flowed from his hands.

"I am done with the skull, yes. I need to add and repair the thorns, then fix it to a new staff rod." He squinted at me. "You know, I'd love to see how you do what you do."

I looked away awkwardly. "It's erm, just the same as normal smithing of metal. Just... more delicate."

I was not about to invite him to watch me work. Not with what followed. Looking back at him, I wondered how I might ask him if anything odd happened to him after shadow-spinning. "*Gold-givers* get very tired after working," I said, casually.

He gave me a wry nod. "So did I, once. But I'm old. My stamina grew with age."

"How long have you been doing this?"

He smiled. "Too long. And for too many that are not what the Prince is."

I cocked my head. "And what is that?"

His eyes flashed with emotion. "A lie."

"What do you mean?" He waved away my question.

"I say too much to whom I shouldn't - a bad habit of mine." He gave me a genuine smile, moving away from the wheel and gesturing at the skull. "Would you care to admire my handiwork? An old man always loves to have his ego massaged."

I stood warily, then moved to inspect the skull. I would never have known it had been damaged. "Like new," I said.

"Indeed. Another few hours, and Mazrith will have his magic back."

"And he'll be able to heal that wound?"

The *shadow-spinner* turned serious again. "I hope so. But never permanently. Not while he is ailed so."

"Ailed so?" I looked intently at Tait. "You mean his curse?"

Tait nodded. "He told me that he made you aware of it."

"He didn't have much choice," I muttered, remembering the glowing wound. *And the scars.* "Was it a gold-fae who cursed him?"

"My overactive lips are done for the day," he said. "The Prince's secrets are his own. Now, if you would be so kind as to ask the others to send in some rabbit stew, I have more work to do." He gestured toward the door.

# 13

## REYNA

I refused the offer of one of the guest bedrooms in the Prince's suite, opting instead to stay in the big chair in front of fireplace when everyone else retired. A restless energy made the thought of lying in a bed for hours intolerable. There was something calming about the low heat coming from the orange embers in the colossal fireplace, and sitting in the padded chair felt safe.

But it wasn't quite enough to still my thoughts. I had decided to say nothing to Lhoris about the black runes. He was fiercely opposed to any notion of helping the shadow-fae and I didn't want him think I had an affiliation with them now. But aside from my rune-marked mentor, I didn't know who else to ask. It seemed unlikely Voror would know much about the rune-marked.

The Prince?

My eyes flicked to the closed door of the Prince's bedroom for what must been the hundredth time.

I dismissed the idea. I didn't want him to think I was moving any closer to the shadow-fae any more than I did Lhoris.

Eventually, the warmth of the room and the quiet crackling of the fire lulled me into a doze.

The nightmares came almost instantly, fear causing my eyes to burst open every time I drifted off. Over and over, I entered a place where liquid gold engulfed the world, and swirling shadows, carrying rotten body parts and sewn-together faces swam before me to the tune of the Elder's song.

"You know, you were unconscious for a day. You probably don't need much more sleep." Frima's soft voice came from behind my chair, after I'd jerked awake again, swatting at the non-existent scene in front of my face.

I leaned forward, rubbing my hands over my sweaty face, cursing the fact that she was seeing me weak. "It's the snake venom," I lied quietly.

She stepped around my chair as I dropped my hands. "Uh-huh. Want a drink? There's a few hours until the day starts."

Deciding that anything was better than the dreams, I followed her into the room with the big table.

She closed the door behind us, and I couldn't help relaxing a little. It was brighter than the sitting room, the grey walls lit by sconces and the view from the huge window at the end of the room still sparkling. It felt further from the darkness of the dreamworld I was trying to avoid.

Frima moved to a row of shelves and picked up a jug. "Nettle tea," she said.

"I've never tried it."

"It's bitter, but it makes you strong."

"Then I'll take it." I eased myself into a chair in front of the map. "Thanks."

She poured the drinks, then set one down in front of me. "Actually, it sounds as though you are owed the thanks." She stared down at me, the beads in her braids glinting.

"Huh?"

"Maz would have died if you'd left him in the forest. The Queen, or the Starved Ones, would have killed him."

I picked up my tea awkwardly. "He saved me. Felt wrong to leave him to die."

"He kidnapped you and threatened to kill your friends. I wouldn't have saved him."

I scowled up at her. "Maybe I shouldn't have."

"But you did, because you know."

"Know what?"

"That he is not the monster the world needs him to be."

I turned back to my tea, unable to hold her gaze and unwilling to answer her.

She said nothing, and the silence stretched.

"Is this a map?" I said eventually, pointing at the papers neatly laid across the table and weighted down with carved figures. Now I was close, I could see that they were indeed chess pieces but painted in five colors. Most of the pieces were black, but I could see the odd blue and green pieces.

She nodded, sitting down next to me. "Yes. This is what we call the war room. Where we strategize. Blue are the ice-fae we know are here, and the green are the earth-fae."

I scanned for gold or red, finding none. In answer to my

un-voiced question, Frima shrugged. "The fire-fae have not been seen in decades. And no gold-fae would be allowed to stay here."

"Why do you let the others stay?"

"They cause no harm. And the Queen does not know of them. This is our problem right now." She pointed to a small group of pieces that had no color, just the pale wood of the piece.

There were a number of groups of them, I realized, all around the edges of the Shadow Court.

"Starved Ones," I murmured.

"Yes. We have never seen them gather like this."

"Are they attacking people?"

"Not yet. Which means they are not attempting to swell their ranks. Nor are they advancing on the mountain. We have no idea why they are gathering."

"Why are you telling me this?"

She laughed softly. "What would you do with the information? You will never return to the Gold Court. And even if you did, why would they care that we face a gathering army of undead? They hate us."

I had nothing to say to that, so I sipped my tea. She was right, it was bitter. But there was something fortifying about it. I sipped some more.

"I came in here because I couldn't sleep," I murmured quietly, staring at the groups of colorless pieces.

"And now I've given you more fuel for your nightmares?"

"I fear so. Will you fight them?"

Her face hardened. "We sure as Odin won't let them take the Court. But they are hard to kill." Her gaze moved to the pieces. "Impossible to kill, in fact. Only Maz can come close." Her eyes snapped back to mine. "Please tell me that is what he needs you for? Something to help rid our world of these blighted creatures? I know he found something under the mountain, I know he has searched for you for years." Her voice was eager, and I couldn't hold her intense look.

"I can't tell you anything he won't, you know that."

I wouldn't have told her even if I could. She probably knew that too. But seeing the intensity of her motivation, and that it was directed at ridding the world of Starved Ones made me warm to her a little.

Her shoulders drooped. "I do not understand why he does not talk to me about you. He tells me everything else."

I was surprised to hear the fierce female's defeated tone.

"Are you..." I forced out the next word, not understanding why it tasted so unpleasant in my mouth. "Lovers?"

She let out a snort. "That would be like fucking my brother." She pulled a face. "I heard the fire-fae are into that, but not here, thank you very much."

Silently cursing the relief I felt, I changed the subject. "Has the Queen returned from the forest?"

"Yes. That is why we're all in the Serpent Suites tonight. If she gets word that Maz has no magic, it would take all of us to even have a shot at protecting him."

"She's powerful then?"

Frima's eyebrows lifted. "Incredibly," she said resignedly. "Her real name is Lasta, but we are only allowed to call her 'the Queen'. Odin-cursed infernal fucking female."

"What's the story with Mazrith's real mother?" I asked.

"Nuhuh," Frima said, shaking her head. "If you want to get personal with the Prince, you ask him, not me."

It had been worth a try.

Tait tiptoed into the room, waving a staff, complete with rod, snake and thorns. He looked exhausted, but he was beaming. "It's ready."

# 14

## REYNA

Frima leaped up, and together they hurried off to the Prince's bedroom, leaving me sitting in the war room alone.

I fiddled absent-mindedly with a black-painted figure, until Brynja came into the room carrying a tray covered in pastries and cheese. "Good morning, my lady."

"Oh, Brynja. Hello."

"I heard a rumor, and I wanted you to know first," she said, her voice hushed. "The Queen is going to make an announcement today."

My stomach tightened. "About what?"

"I don't know, but the rumors are that riders were sent to all the Courts a few days ago, and the last returned just this last hour. Oh, and it's something to do with the Prince's birthday."

I relaxed a little. "Probably some pretentious ball."

She shook her head. "The Shadow Court hasn't sent

emissaries to the other Courts since the King was alive, apparently." She glanced over at the door. "She even sent someone to the Gold Court."

My uneasy stomach returned. The Shadow Court had just raided the Gold Court palace and stole three *gold-givers*. What could she be planning that would be worth risking sending an emissary?

"How is your foot, Reyna?" Kara's voice filled the room as she came in, clapping her hands at the sight of the pastries.

"It's good, thank you. Did you sleep well?"

I let myself fall into easy conversation with Kara as we ate breakfast, trying not to let my nerves get the best of me. I longed to ask how Prince Mazrith was, but I refrained. I had no idea how long it would take to heal himself using his magic, but I suspected he would not want me there when he did so.

Ellisar produced a chessboard from one of the large bookcases in the sitting room, and Kara and I spent the best part of a few hours playing on the fur rug in front of the fire, Svangrior pacing and Lhoris scowling the entire time.

I was listening intently for any sounds from the Prince's bedroom, so a loud knock on the door made me start.

Svangrior strode over, cracking it open an inch. "Rang-vald," he growled.

"I bring a message from the Queen to her *son*."

"Speak."

"I would rather deliver the message in person."

"And I would rather you didn't," Svangrior retorted.

The bedroom door swung open, and Prince Mazrith

strode out, staff in hand. His face was no longer pale, and he was dressed as a Prince should be, in leather trousers, a fine black linen shirt and his thick fur cloak.

Svangrior stepped to the side, but not far enough that the Queen's advisor would be able to see how many people were in his rooms. Mazrith's large form filled the gap immediately.

"What do you want?"

"Not me, your highness. It is the Queen who wants you." He gave a small, obsequious chuckle. "Your presence is required at high tea, mid-afternoon today."

"Tell her that I politely decline."

"No, no, Prince Mazrith. This is a Court affair. All courtiers must be present, and you must attend with your betrothed. The Queen has been planning something very special, and it is all for you."

My heart skipped. This must be what Brynja had heard about.

"What time?" Mazrith gritted out.

"Two after midday. Farewell." Mazrith slammed the door closed, then turned.

I tried not to hold my breath as his eyes fell on me. Shadows rolled across his irises, his repaired staff in his hand. The Prince's magic was back.

"How is your foot?"

"How is your chest?"

We both spoke at the same time.

Silence followed the jumbled questions, then everyone else in the room began to move, apparently in a sudden hurry to leave.

Mazrith strode over to where I was sitting cross-legged in front of the game board. "My foot is fine, thank you," I said stiffly.

"My chest is mostly healed," he answered, equally terse. "Thank you." He cast his gaze over my head. "Keep that headband on during this high tea, whatever happens. I will make sure your friends stay under guard here."

A wash of genuine gratitude that he had thought of Lhoris and Kara made me soften. "There are rumors that the Queen sent riders to the other Courts, and now they are all back."

He frowned. "Where did you hear that?"

"It doesn't matter."

"Your maid. Nobody else has left this room since we returned."

I took a turn to scowl. "Fine. Yes, it was my maid. What do you think the Queen is up to?"

"I suppose we'll find out shortly." Anger, rather than nerves flashed in his eyes.

"What happens at a high tea?"

"In normal tradition, cake and wine. In my stepmother's world, Odin only knows."

"Well, at least you are facing her with your magic back."

He gave a snort, his braids falling over his shoulder. "If I had to face her without it, I would be dead." He turned as the door to the to the other room opened and Frima stepped through, her half-skull mask on and staff in hand.

"You need to go and get dressed," Frima said to me.

I frowned down at myself. "I am dressed."

"Not fit for a Prince's betrothed at a Court affair, you're

not."

Frima escorted me back to my rooms with Brynja, checking the room thoroughly for snakes before leaving us. I hoped Voror had managed to follow us and checked the room for threats too.

Once alone, Brynja spent, to my mind, an excessive amount of time going through the dresses that had apparently multiplied inside the huge wardrobe. The long dressing table was adorned with jewelry now, too, large red and navy stones set in silver bangles, necklaces, hair pins and brooches.

"Where did these come from?" I asked, gaping down at the gems. Their value would have been enough to bribe the Gold Court guards a hundred times over.

"They were all sent up by the seamstress the morning you, erm, *left*, my lady."

"Huh."

Once a dress had been selected and I'd been laced into it, she applied powders and presses to my face until I assumed I looked like I belonged in fae-royalty's company. Other than my hair, of course. That would never look like it belonged anywhere. She managed to style it elaborately around the spelled headband though, and tucked Voror's feather discreetly inside it.

The dress was deep purple, had long, scooped sleeves, laced down the front, and was cut low over my chest. A necklace with a deep ruby stone in the middle of it sat over my sternum, and I reluctantly put on the matching serpent ring. I glared at it as I slid it onto my finger.

It represented my lack of freedom so perfectly. A venomous snake had tried to take my life, and now I wore one on my finger that would forever give my location to my captor.

"You look lovely, my lady."

"Thanks, Brynja."

I didn't particularly want to look in the mirror, but I couldn't leave the room without catching a glimpse of my reflection.

I looked taller. Elegant. Older somehow, the make-up deliberately accentuating my cheeks and my eyes.

I let out a long breath. "Let's get this over with."

Hopefully this time I could get through a meal with the Queen without being force-fed or having someone else's blood dripping on me.

I saw the Prince's jaw twitch when he saw me. His eyes flicked to the ring on my hand when Frima and I reached him outside his rooms with Svangrior.

"You look... appropriate," he said, and I was sure his gaze was a little too low.

"Thanks, I think. Is Ellisar staying with my friends?" I asked.

He gave me a curt nod, and we began moving down the gloomy maroon corridors. "As a human, he is not welcome at Court."

I rolled my eyes.

"Do not speak unless the Queen speaks to you."

"I remember the last time I had to eat a meal with the Queen," I said. "Don't worry. I plan to do my best to go unnoticed."

He shot me a sideways look, and I just caught him muttering something that sounded like 'little chance'.

I kept my mouth shut, unwilling to start a fight. I was too apprehensive about this high tea. Being around the crazy Queen was unsettling enough, let alone not knowing what new horseshit she was about to throw at us.

*Us.*

The word rang in my head, and I wondered when I had started to see the Prince and I as an 'us'.

It was when I accepted that my fate was tied with his, by something older and more important than the Shadow Court Prince's problems, I told myself firmly.

It definitely wasn't when I'd seen those scars on his face that he kept hidden. Or when he had promised to stay out of my head. *Absolutely not.*

To my relief we veered away from the throne room when we reached the bottom of the grand staircase, instead heading for the courtyard where the ball had been. Two guards threw open the door as the Prince put on his skull mask.

I took a deep breath, and followed him into the courtyard.

# 15

## REYNA

The space looked nothing like it had for the masked dance. I hesitated, my steps faltering.

The edges of the courtyard were now a moat of thick black sludge, gently moving in a never-ending circle. A black, swirling fog spun around the monolithic walls above it, rising with the spires spearing the sky around us. Tiny red and orange lights danced in the fog, looking unnervingly like eyes and only just providing enough light to allow an ominous atmosphere to seep through the charged air.

Four long, black marble tables were set in the middle of the courtyard in a row, and the Queen sat in the center of a head table that spanned them all. Fae guests filled every seat, all dressed in dark robes and glittering silver jewelry.

The Queen stood when she saw us and gestured at the two empty seats at either end of her table. Rangvald occupied the seat on her left, and a figure wearing a deep hooded cloak was in the chair to her right.

I froze, memories of the figure who had pushed me from the shrine flooding my thoughts. But this cloak was incredibly ornate, covered in glinting gems and fine metal wire, nothing like the plain one my assailant had worn.

I forced my feet to move again, following the Prince, aware that every eye in the place was on me. Gnarled, twisted trees dotted the flagstones, their branches looking like they could wrap around a victim at any moment and fling them into the bog that bordered the courtyard. I gathered my courage as Frima and Svangrior slipped into seats at the guest tables, and we reached the head table.

Mazrith pulled out my seat and waited whilst I lowered myself into it, my heart hammering. He took his own seat, all the way at the other end of the long table. I couldn't talk to him, but I could see him clearly.

Between silver candelabras holding black-wax candles were platters of finger sandwiches and cakes covering the center of the table. A crystal plate, teacup and wineglass were set at my place, and on my plate was a cake with black and red frosting. It was in the shape of a tiny person, curled in the fetal position.

I looked away, my stomach tightening. A faint smell of something rotten drifted past me, and I swallowed hard.

"Welcome, my darling courtiers, and honored family," the Queen said, sickly sweet voice filling every corner of the courtyard. She was wearing a long, sleeveless, green gown of shimmering silk that clung to her body, and an enormous ruby at her throat, so large it made mine look like a toy. Her bone crown was perched on a large twist of braids, more sparkling rubies set into her black hair.

She spread her arms wide, her staff in the hand closest to me. The skull on the end of the staff had color in its eyes, I noticed. I tried to look closer, but she swished it out of my view, raising it high above her head. A slow smile spread across her face, showing her black teeth, and her dreamy gaze fell on Mazrith. "Welcome, my son." He didn't move or speak. "My dear boy, I have a gift for you. Something to celebrate your thirtieth year."

Shadow began to trickle from the end of her staff, pooling first on the table in front of her, then pouring off the edge onto the floor. I moved my head, trying to see more, but it was too dark, and my view was too obstructed.

"But we must first partake in the delicious feast that I have laid for you all." She gestured around the courtyard, and the fae all burst into beaming applause, murmurs of thanks rustling across the tables. "A toast, followed by a delicious sampling," she said, reaching forward and picking up a glass of the fizzy wine. I looked at my own glass but made no move to pick it up.

"Do as she says." Mazrith's voice entered my head. I threw him a glare, then picked up the wine.

I would only have a sip.

I could feel eyes on me, and I looked at the hooded figure next to the Queen. They were wearing a mask under the hood, I realized, but it was too dark to see any details, other than the fact that it seemed focused on me.

"To the Shadow Court," the Queen said, before sipping from her glass.

"To the Shadow Court," the rest of the fae said, doing the same. I sipped when they did, trying to distract myself from the hooded person.

All around me, people bit into the cakes from their plates. I picked up my own piece, looking surreptitiously for somewhere to get rid of it.

Coughing started at another table, and the Queen's eyes flashed with delight. " Aha!"

I turned to see a male pushing his chair back from the table, clutching his throat. The fae seated either side of him looked unsure what to do, one leaning over to thump his back.

"You have found my special prize!" A ribbon of shadow burst from her staff, straight to the fae's mouth, and he jerked as it entered him. Less than a second later it was out again, flying back to the Queen. The male sucked in breaths, shoulders heaving, as the ribbon of shadow deposited something in the Queen's hand. She held it up with a smile.

It was a tooth.

My face screwed up in disgust. Had she put a tooth in the cake to choke him?

"Do you know who this belonged to, Lord Tyr?"

All the color drained from the fae's face as she addressed him. "N-n-o, your highness," he choked out.

Her voice dropped low, the sickly tone remaining. "It belonged to the man you had follow mine to the Gold Court."

The male stiffened, his breath held. "I don't know what you're talking about, your highness."

It was a clear lie. Her face flushed with rage, then the

smile returned. "He was called Rolf, I'm told. I have also been informed that you disapprove of my sending an emissary to the Gold Court."

The male's eyes moved to me. Hatred shone in them, and my breath caught. "My Queen, I just wished to make sure that our enemies were not taking advantage of us." His eyes narrowed at me. "Or infiltrating our palace."

"You think I am corruptible?" The Queen's voice was quiet. Dangerous.

"No, my Queen."

"You think I am unable to run this Court?"

"N-no, my Queen. I was just trying to—."

"Interfere where you were not welcome? Undermine me? Distrust me?"

There was a hissing, snarling sound from the ground, and instinct made my whole body tighten. With a crash, something black and huge leaped up from by the Queen's feet, onto the table between Mazrith and me.

Fear had me halfway out of my chair before Mazrith's voice sounded loudly in my head. "Don't move!"

The thing on the table was like nothing I'd ever seen, even in my dreams. Made completely of shadow, it best mimicked a hound of some sort. But everything about it was out of proportion; its limbs were too long, its body too tall, its black teeth too big for its jaw. Its long tail was barbed, and its eyes were as red as the Queen's were.

It turned its face toward the now trembling fae, jaws snapping silently.

"Tyr, your lack of faith in me is very upsetting." The

Queen's smile vanished, her voice becoming a hiss. "You are a fool. A fool unworthy of the palace, and my Court." She gestured, and the shadow-beast launched itself over my head.

I suppressed a shriek, ducking low in my chair and swiveling in time to see it sprint at the male, crashing into him and knocking him clear from his chair. He didn't even have time to reach for his staff. The creature clamped its jaws around his throat and snapped its head back.

I turned back as soon as the blood began to gush. I tried to fix my eyes on Mazrith, tried to keep my roiling fear under control as the awful sounds of the creature devouring its prey behind me carried across the silence. But his glinting mask made it worse.

The skull loomed out of the darkness and panic began to flood me, an overwhelming feeling of being completely trapped making my head swim and my eyes dart everywhere, looking for escape.

I couldn't leave this place.

I could never be anywhere else.

*Forever.*

My hands shook as the panic spread.

"Look at me." Mazrith's hand lifted and in one smooth movement, he removed his mask.

My eyes locked on his face.

"It's her magic. It instills fear. You are not weak." His voice was clear and deep in my mind.

I stared at him.

*It wasn't real.*

The male being eaten by a fucking shadow creature was

real. But staring at Mazrith's bright, intense eyes, I felt some control seep back.

"Now that unpleasant business has been dealt with," the Queen said, clapping her hands together and making me jolt in surprise. "We can move on with my gift to my son."

She waved her staff, and shadows rushed back to it. I refused to turn and see what carnage was left.

I heard chairs scraping, and relieved murmurs.

The Queen looked at Mazrith, and he slowly moved his eyes from me to her. "Dear son. It has been centuries since royalty celebrated their birthdays as they should. So, in a revival of ancient tradition, I have arranged a most special celebration."

Excited murmurs replaced the nervous ones.

"How interesting," Mazrith said flatly.

Her eyes flashed. "Oh, I think it will be very interesting indeed. I have organized, especially for you, a *Leikmot*."

There was a collective gasp, then an enthusiastic hammering of applause.

I searched through my head, trying to remember what the ancient word meant, and came up with nothing.

The Prince stood up slowly. "A games festival is a very thoughtful gift," he said, bowing his head. "Thank you."

*Leikmot* was a games festival?

"I thought so," the Queen beamed at him.

"How and when will it be played?"

The Queen gave him a delighted smile. "I sent invitations to all the other Courts, and all but the Fire Court agreed to take part."

Mazrith's amiable smile slipped. "You invited the other Courts?"

"Indeed," she beamed.

"Including the Gold Court?"

"Including the Gold Court."

Mazrith's eyes flicked almost imperceptibly to me before he spoke. "We have forcibly taken their rune-marked, amid much bloodshed." A small cheer went up from the guests as my own skin felt tight. "I am surprised they did not kill your emissary on the spot."

The figure next to the Queen rose slowly. "The thing about the Gold Court," he said, his hood tipping back to reveal a glittering mask and straight white hair. "Is that we are less barbaric than you have been led to believe."

My blood turned to ice in my veins as recognition smashed into me. *No. It couldn't be. Not here in the Shadow Court.*

The shining gold mask turned my way. "Isn't that right, Reyna?"

The vision he had sent me, of myself tied to a bed, bleeding and beaten, burst into my head, as Lord Orm let out a long, low laugh.

# 16

## REYNA

I was vaguely aware of muttering and whispering all around me, but none of the words were penetrating my skull.

*Lord Orm was here in the Shadow Court.*

*How?*

*Why?*

Fear, and the desire to run, welled up again inside me.

"Who, pray tell, is our guest?" Mazrith's voice was icy cold and hard as steel. I tore my eyes from the gold-fae, looking at the Prince instead.

"I am Lord Orm," he said, bowing his head. "And I am here at your mother's invitation."

There was another round of gasps and murmurs, but they died out quickly. The courtiers were staring at a member of their sworn enemy standing in their own palace, but given what the Queen's shadow creature had done to the last person who had questioned her decisions, I couldn't see any of them objecting aloud.

*Why?* Why had she invited a gold-fae to the Shadow Court? *And of all the fae, why him?*

"My dear son, I have taken my cue from you!" the Queen said, red eyes glinting cruelly. "You have embraced our enemy, you assure me for our mutual benefit. Lord Orm here responded to my emissary, and we realized we too can mutually benefit one another."

She turned to the rest of the fae. "We will host the first round of the *Leikmot*, beginning tomorrow. You, as my closest courtiers, are all welcome."

The guests at every table leaped to their feet, clapping and cheering. Through the commotion, I found the Prince's face just soon enough to see the flash of fury before he schooled his expression.

"Once again, I thank you," he said to the Queen, loud enough to carry over the elated crowd. "I must make my preparations and ensure the security of the Court for our guests."

A hush fell over the courtyard. "Indeed," the Queen said. "Prepare yourself for a most spectacular celebration."

I hurried to keep up with the Prince and his warriors as they marched through the main hall and up the grand stairs.

All of them looked ready to kill with one glare, and none of them had said a word since we left the courtyard.

The shock at seeing the cruel gold-fae began to lessen once I was out of his presence, allowing all the questions I had to bubble to the surface.

The Shadow Court had raided the Gold Court palace, resulting in the deaths of scores of human guards, and the kidnap of three of the gold-fae's precious *gold-givers*. Why in the name of Odin would they agree to a games festival?

There had to be an ulterior motive, a reason for them to want access to the Shadow Court. Would they try to recover what had been taken from them? Fear made my legs slow, and Frima threw me a look as I fell behind their long strides. I quickened my pace, tension washing through the corridors as we hurried on.

The second we reached the Prince's rooms, Frima began to talk, Svangrior banging the door closed behind him hard enough to make me jump.

"Maz, she's going to nominate you to take part in the games. She may not know what happened in the forest but if she found the remains of Starved Ones she will know what it cost you to take out that many. She knows you are not at full strength."

Mazrith moved straight to the cabinet on the left wall and poured himself a drink. "This goes beyond me," he said darkly.

Svangrior made a hissing sound. "She despises the Gold Court, and her sister. Why would she invite one of them here?"

"All of you, out," Mazrith said.

Everyone stilled. "Maz, we need to—," Frima started.

"I said, out!"

The two fae spun toward the war room, and I hurried after them.

"Not you." His voice was in my head, and I halted. Letting out a long breath, I turned slowly toward him.

The moment we were alone, he closed the distance between us.

"The gold-fae knew you."

I nodded. "Yes."

"How." It was a demand, not a question.

"He is a prominent courtier, who lived in the palace. He has a reputation for cruelty."

"None of that answers my question."

I couldn't hold his gaze. "He also has a reputation for hurting women."

Darkness fell over the room, and when I looked up there were shadows filling Mazrith's irises. "Has he ever hurt you?" he growled.

I shook my head. "No. But the day you came to the palace..." I faltered. How much did I want to tell him?

"Don't make me take what I need to know from you." Mazrith hissed warningly.

I took a step back, frowning. "You promised you wouldn't enter my head without permission." *That I would never give.*

"That was before I saw him, felt what he was thinking about you," he spat. "I need to know, Reyna. What is your past with this fae?"

4

ELIZA RAINE

Powerful rage spilled from his every pore, feral fury etched into every line on his face.

Making my decision, I spoke. "He chose me as his next bound concubine. I was planning to escape the palace, and the Gold Court, the night you came."

"You... you were going to run?"

"Yes."

"Where would you have gone? Any Court would kill a rune-marked from another."

I squared my shoulders, looking at him defiantly. "I would take death over a life bound to that male in a heartbeat."

"You told me you would take death over being bound to me." His words were a murmur, almost to himself.

"And I would have. But you threatened my friends." His eyes moved, roving over my hair. I frowned as they found mine again. "What are you looking at?"

His gaze intensified, before he shook his head. He held out the glass of liquid to me. "This will make you feel better."

I paused, then took it.

He was right. It tasted like fennel and burned all the way down my throat, but the fire it left was better than the uneasy fear. "Do you think they wish to attack from the inside? Are they here to steal their rune-marked back?" I asked the Prince hesitantly.

"The motives of the gold-fae are easier to guess at than those of the Queen. I do not know why my stepmother has formed an alliance with a gold-fae Lord," Mazrith growled. "She may want him to take you from me. Or she may have

110

concocted a plan as crazy as she is. She is playing a game, and we do not yet know the rules."

Mazrith reached out, taking the glass from me, then draining it. "What I do know is that you will not leave my sight."

"But—"

"You. Will. Not. Leave. My. Sight." His fierce, bright eyes burned into mine, and the resistance I should have felt didn't come.

Mazrith hadn't hurt me. And he needed me alive.

But back in the Gold Court... Lord Orm had chosen me, purely to hurt me. A shudder rippled over my skin. Standing naked on that carpet in the bright, glittering hall of the Gold Court palace felt like a lifetime ago.

"If you believe I am not safe, then my friends are not safe, either. They must be protected too," I said, on deep breath.

"Agreed," he said.

My ready argument died on my lips. I had expected a fight.

"They will stay in the Serpent Suites and be watched at all times."

"Thank you," I whispered.

I knew he was keeping Lhoris and Kara safe because they were an asset to him. Because they were leverage over me.

But the longer those deep, tortured eyes stayed fixed on mine, the more I wanted to believe he was keeping them safe because it was important to me.

Mazrith still didn't take his eyes from mine as he called in his warriors.

"Frima, go the thrall quarters. Find out anything you can. All gossip might be helpful," he commanded the female fae.

She nodded. "Yes, Maz."

"Svangrior, go to the armory. If the *Leikmot* is modeled on the ancient games, then there will be challenges of strength, wit, and speed. Find anything that might give us an edge."

Svangrior banged his staff on the ground, then whirled from the room. Frima rolled her eyes at his back, gave Maz a last worried look, then followed him out of the room.

"We have work to do."

It took me a second to work out what he meant. We were going back to the shrine.

# 17

# REYNA

"You should have let me talk to my friends before we came here." I glared at the Prince as the tiny boat was propelled toward the shrine cavern by the gentle push of shadow magic.

He glanced down at me, then back up at the cavern. "They will have reactions to the gold-fae being present in the Shadow Court that would have taken up your time. Time we do not have."

"Charming," I muttered.

There was a short silence, and I turned over the gold-working toolkit in my hands.

"Do you believe your friends will hope to be returned to the service of the Gold Court?"

"Via bloodshed? No." I looked down at the clear water we were drifting over. "Although I believe they both miss working with gold. A rune-marked who doesn't craft staffs has a lack of purpose.

"Do you miss working with gold?"

I turned to glance at him. "I have worked with gold since coming here." Unease rolled through me. *And this time, he would be there when the visions came.*

I had no intention of telling him about them, but I couldn't hide the physical reaction they caused, and he had made it clear he was not going to let me out of his sight. Given that somebody had tried to kill me last time I was alone in the shrine, I wasn't sure I wanted him to.

"After I've fixed the staff, I will need some space," I said, as casually as I could.

"That will not be possible."

I frowned at him. "It's part of being a rune-marked. I have a very visceral response to the work when it is finished. And I need space for it."

His eyes bore into mine, bright and intense. "There is no space in the shrine. It will not be possible."

My frown turned into a glare. "All I'm asking is for you to leave me alone for a few minutes. You don't have to leave completely, just..." I waved my hand. "Go back up the wrist-bridge and give me a little privacy."

He shook his head, eyes narrowing. "You are lying to me again, little *gold-giver*." I felt wisps of cold around the base of my skull, and fear trickled through me.

"Stop it."

"Stop lying."

"I do not owe you any truth." I spat the words, my fear forcing me into anger, forcing me to defend myself.

"The answer is no."

"It wasn't a question."

"Then the statement is no."

I hissed, thumping my palm against the side of the little boat, making it rock in the gentle water. He was infuriating. "Fine. If you are going to insist on me making a spectacle of myself, then don't talk to me, touch me, or ask me anything about it."

"You believe your work making you tired is embarrassing?" He sounded genuinely confused, rather than mocking.

The soul-deep belief that nobody but I could know about my visions surged through me, and I scrabbled to find something believable to say. He had promised not to get in my head, but if he was convinced the cause was strong enough, I suspected he would renege on his word.

"Every rune-marked reacts differently. I experience..." I tried to imagine what me experiencing the visions would look like to an outsider. "A few intense waves of pain. I am not embarrassed, I just don't like exposing myself as vulnerable."

It was partly true.

The Prince said nothing and we lapsed back into tense silence.

When our little boat reached the base of the wrist, the Prince stepped from it onto the stone. I followed him, but when I reached the part of the wrist that crossed the chasm, I faltered.

The muscles of my thighs began to tremble, and I swore viciously. *Get a grip, Reyna.*

But every time I made to take a step, the tremble returned.

My cheeks burned with shame. I was stronger than this, I wasn't afraid of heights.

The memory of my weightless legs dangling over the edge of the chasm filled my head, then plunging through the air. I dropped to my knees, planting my hands on the stone, drawing reassurance that it was there.

Refusing to look up at the Prince, I moved so that I was on my backside, and began to shuffle along the bridge. I didn't look up from the stone once until I had reached the hand and the statues.

My face so hot it hurt, I crawled awkwardly into the center of the palm, my arms now trembling too. I was aware of the Prince's fur-cloaked form close to me, but I refused to look at him.

"It's adrenaline," I snapped, unable to bear his silence. "I'm human, and we have chemicals in our body that make our bodies react in a way we don't want them to."

I yearned for fresh air, and my head was beginning to pound.

"Fae have adrenaline too."

My head jerked up involuntarily at his quiet response. His eyes were bright, and I glared at him. "Let me guess, you mighty fae are strong enough to overcome it?"

"Not always. No." His soft words took the fight from me.

He held out a hand. My immediate instinct was to bat it away, but my angry swat froze midway.

The truth was, a steady hand to help me to my feet was exactly what I needed. I could see no judgment in his eyes, and it was too late to hide my vulnerability.

I took his hand, and let him pull me slowly to my feet. He cocked his head when I was upright, a silent question.

I nodded, and he let go, moving to the statue with the broken staff. Slowly, steadily, I followed him.

Once I was standing in front of the damaged statue, I took a deep breath, the tremble ebbing away. Setting the broken staff-top back in its place, I felt a pull, like a magnet. The gold vision descended immediately, and more runes than usual flowed quickly from the place the rod had met the top. I scrambled to pull a scalpel and thick brush from my kit, then began to work, blending the gold back together seamlessly.

When the runes stopped flowing, the intricate, beautiful instructions ending, I stepped back, and the gold-tint covering my sight lifted.

I took a few long breaths, aware of Mazrith just behind me.

How long until the visions started? I usually had a few minutes.

A loud grating sound made every muscle in my body freeze.

"What—?" Mazrith started, but a cracking sound echoed through the cavern, cutting him off.

I took two more hasty steps backward, into the middle of the palm, as the stone making up the fae statue started to crack apart, dark veins threading their way across the stone. Then the cracking stone began to fall away completely, and my hands flew to my mouth in surprise.

Under the grey granite was... *gold*. The same beautiful fae woman holding her staff, but made from solid gold.

The stone continued to tumble away, until just the gleaming metal remained.

"What in the name of Freya..." I took a tentative step toward the gold statue, unable to resist the draw of so much of the precious metal. But as I did, the statue's arm moved.

I froze.

She was lifting her staff. More movement caught my eye, and I held my breath in astonishment as her lips parted.

"While he is more than ten feet tall,

Even in death he shall never fall.

Aided by golden touch and darkest night,

Prize from the steel his greatest delight.

Only this may be used here to repair,

Nobles and royals with secrets to share."

As she finished speaking, her staff dropped gently back to the ground, and her mouth closed.

# 18

## REYNA

**S**ilence, so thick it was deafening, descended over the cavern.

"You... You heard that, right?" I didn't look at Mazrith as I spoke, my eyes glued to the statue.

"Yes. I must write it down, now."

I turned to him as he began to pull things from a pouch on his belt. I saw him unroll a small piece of parchment just before a wave of darkness washed over me.

"Horseshit," I swore, moving swiftly onto my backside, placing my hands flat against the stone palm as I had before.

"What is wrong?"

"The pain I told you about. It's starting," I said fast. "Don't talk to me, don't touch me."

"As you wish," he replied, but his last word was a distant whisper.

The laugh was starting in the background. The unease,

the sense of wrongness. Then the smell filled my nostrils, and fear bolted through me. The smell was supposed to come on the second vision. Not the first.

"Reyna."

For a beat I was sure my heart had stopped completely.

It was her. The Elder.

The darkness lifted, and I sucked in air, wishing I wasn't underground. Sweat had pooled at the base of my neck, and my hands were damp on the cold stone.

"Reyna, you are pale, let me-"

"Leave me alone!" I half-yelled at the Prince. The second wave started, and my fingertips scraped across the stone as my hands curled involuntarily.

She was laughing, It was her. Had it always been her?

"Reyna. The copper-haired gold-giver."

Light fell over the red-tinged scene. Body parts. Legs here, arms there, bones picked clean.

Bile rose in my throat as a figure limped into view.

"We'll give you back when we're done with you."

Bone-deep terror coursed through me, and I felt my eyes burning as the vision lifted.

I ground my teeth together hard, forcing myself to contain the fear. It wasn't real. It was a vision. I had managed visions of the Starved Ones my whole life. This was no different.

Except, *it was*. I knew it was. Could she see me? Was she communicating with me?

The next wave came, and I drew on all my resolve, on all my courage.

"He can't help you." She was limping closer, and deep red light was illuminating the scattered remains surrounding her. She was underground too, in a cave or burrow. "He may have saved you once, but he intends to kill you. We will give you new life. Eternal life."

A flash of light fell on her face as she grinned at me, half her jaw missing, a black void where one eye should be, and strings of hair hanging from a patch of skull. I heard the gasp leave my own lips as the vision lifted.

"Reyna, what is happening?" Mazrith's voice came to me as I squeezed my eyes shut.

"It's nearly done, just leave me alone."

I wrapped my arms around my knees, trying to fill my lungs, trying to prepare for the fourth vision.

It didn't come.

Slowly, suspiciously, I dropped my arms and opened my eyes.

Was it really not coming?

"Thank Odin," I whispered.

"What are you thanking the gods for?" Mazrith's voice was tight. I took another long breath, then moved my head to look up at his pinched, angry face.

"Sometimes there are four waves of pain," I said quietly. "Today, only three."

"Why do you work with gold, if this is the consequence? You are white and shaking and sweating and—" He broke off, shaking his head, his hand flexing around his staff.

My brows drew together. "I'm okay. It passes quickly."

The truth was that if the visions were going to get worse

ELIZA RAINE

since my encounter with the Elder, perhaps I wouldn't be so willing to work with gold.

*She had been talking to me.* It was as though the visions before had been taunting, searching. Now, they were aimed, direct.

"That was more than pain," Mazrith said. "I know fear when I see it." His eyes bore into mine, and I felt the wisps of cold at the base of my skull.

"Don't you dare," I hissed.

He held my gaze a second longer, then narrowed his eyes and lifted the parchment that I hadn't seen him screw up.

Smoothing it out, he swore. "I don't remember the wording of what the gold statue said."

I swallowed, relieved he had changed the subject. "Something about returning here with something."

"That is not enough." His voice was tight.

I closed my eyes and sighed. "Do I need to try to make her speak again?" I wanted nothing less than to risk the visions again. But I sure as Odin wasn't going through all of that for nothing.

"No." Mazrith stepped forward, his tone harsh. "Absolutely not."

I gave him a look. "I'm not that fragile," I muttered, unsure how true it was.

"We will come back later, when you have rested."

"I thought we didn't have time?"

Anger, or frustration, flickered over his features.

"I remember what she said. Quite the riddle, it was." A haughty male voice floated into my head, and a weak smile took my lips.

122

"Voror." I looked at the Prince, then up at the ceiling of the cavern. "Voror heard the riddle," I told him as I searched for the bird.

My heart lifted as I watched him swoop from the darkness, coming to land beside me.

"You look unwell," he said, blinking at me.

"I just worked with gold. What did the statue say? How well do you remember?"

Mazrith moved closer, parchment and a small charcoal stick in hand.

"I remember it perfectly," the owl said, tipping up his beak. "She said: While he is more than ten feet tall,

Even in death he shall never fall.

Aided by golden touch and darkest night,

Prize from the steel his greatest delight.

Only this may be used here to repair,

Nobles and royals with secrets to share." As Voror repeated, verbatim, what the statue had said, I relayed his words to Mazrith, who wrote them down on his paper. When he was done, he scowled down at his writing.

"Does that mean anything to you?" I asked him.

"Perhaps." He looked at the other statues in turn, then to me. "We have to get something to fix these other statues? 'Only this may be used here to repair nobles and royals with secrets to share'," he read again.

My brows lifted. "If the other staffs are broken, then you're going to need to find rune-marked for all of them."

He stepped toward the nearest stone figure, reaching out to touch it. "This one is shadow. But I don't think the staff is made from the same silver mine is."

I got cautiously to my feet, my palms still damp. Moving to join him, I brushed away some of the stone on the top of the staff, just as I had with the gold one. To my surprise, yellow metal gleamed back at me. "More gold?"

"More gold," Mazrith agreed tightly.

I picked at the stone, exposing the top of the staff. It was beautiful. A snake wound around itself in a figure eight, and its body was set with a series of green stones, all different shades and types.

"Do you know what needs repairing?"

I squinted at it, reluctant to touch it - reluctant to risk triggering the gold-vision again.

A single black rune floated up from the staff tip.

I wasn't able to stop my gasp of astonishment. *I knew what the rune meant.*

"What is it?" Shadows sprang from Mazrith's own staff, ready to fight. Or protect.

"We need to find some jade," I whispered. "To repair this staff, we need to find a piece of jade." I knew in the same way that I knew what to do from the gold runes I saw. I leaned close to the statue and saw a small indentation in the bottom part of the snake's body that clearly had a gemstone missing. "There." I pointed.

Mazrith gave me a long, suspicious look. "How do you know it needs to be jade?"

I thought about lying to him. But I glanced down at the inscription that named me as the key to all this and changed my mind.

"I just saw a rune. And it meant jade."

The Prince stared at me, and I stared back. Eventually he took his eyes from my face and looked back down at his parchment. "So, this ten-foot-tall figure will give us the jade?"

Voror fluttered over and landed on top of the statues head. "Aided by golden touch and darkest night," he said.

I repeated the owl's words to Mazrith, who looked sideways at the beautiful white bird with lingering suspicion. "What does that mean?"

"I do not know," Voror replied.

"Do you know any ten-foot-tall figures?" I asked.

"Not living ones."

"So... You think it means another statue?"

"It must do."

I bit my lip, thinking. "The statues we saw inside *Yggdrasil*," I said, my cheeks reddening at the thought of the inside of the ethereal tree. *The location my fae-wine-addled brain had chosen for my obscene dream.* Mazrith didn't know that, though, and I forced myself to concentrate. "They were tall."

"Far taller than ten feet," he replied. We all fell silent again.

"We must think on this," Mazrith said after a few minutes. "But let us do so with warmth and food. You need to rest."

He was right. I felt exhausted.

I was grateful for the silence as we made the journey out of the cavern and back to the Prince's rooms. His reaction to my pain confused me, and my bleary thoughts were struggling to untangle my questions. *And feelings.* Accursed feelings snaking their way in and muddling things even more.

Why was he so protective of me?

*Because I'm an asset. He needs me to get his Court back from the crazy fae currently on the throne,* I told myself.

*Not because he likes me.*

I closed my eyes as we bobbed along the water. *Get a grip, Reyna. A firm one. One that won't keep slipping.*

"You still look unwell." Voror's voice was a welcome relief from my own stern reprimands.

"I'm just tired."

"The effects of the poison have not worn off, yet."

I nodded. "Perhaps not fully."

"You are talking to your bird?" Mazrith's deep voice said from behind me in the little boat.

"Yes." I answered him without turning.

"I will ponder on this riddle while you rest," Voror said.

"Why do you call it a riddle?"

"It rhymes."

"That makes it a poem, doesn't it?"

"Only if you are stupid. Which, to be fair to you, you often are."

My shoulders slumped as I gave him a look. "Fine. Maybe we should give it to Kara, since she's the smartest person I know."

"What?" Mazrith's words were sharp enough that this time I did turn.

"Voror thinks the poem is a riddle. And my friend, Kara, is very well read. She's smart. She may be able to help."

"Out of the question. Nobody must know of this but us."

I stared at him in the gloom. "How long until your birthday?" He glared back at me and said nothing. I shrugged. "Fine. Then work it out on your own. Apparently, I'm too stupid."

"The last thing you are, is stupid," he muttered as I turned away again.

# 19

## REYNA

"All is well?" Frima asked, scanning us both as we entered Mazrith's rooms.

"Yes. And with you?" He looked from her to Svangrior, who was leaning against the mantelpiece. The door to the hallway opened, and Ellisar poked his head around the frame. On seeing the Prince, he came into the room.

"The earth-fae and the ice-fae will arrive at dawn, and there will be a welcoming ceremony outside the front gates of the palace. I believe that is when she will choose the champion to represent the Shadow Court," Frima said. She looked as though she wished she were taking on the challenge herself.

"So, you think she will choose the Prince?" I asked.

"I can't see any other reason the other Courts would come, if not for a chance to publicly best a rival fae. I think the Queen has been planning this for some time."

I glanced at the Prince. "So, it is just bad luck that she chose the moment that he is injured to announce it?"

"Perhaps."

Svangrior banged his fist on the mantelpiece, cutting into the conversation. He looked at the Prince. "Let me fight in your stead."

Mazrith moved toward him, and to my surprise gave him a mighty clap on the shoulder, hard enough to make the fierce fae stumble forward. "Thank you, friend, but no. I cannot risk showing any weakness. That is what she wants. For me to show myself as unworthy of ruling the Court." Mazrith raised his staff a few inches, light gleaming brightly in his eyes before shadows swirled through them. "And do not underestimate my strength, friend. I am feeling better by the hour." A ghost of a smile crossed his lips. "In fact, I'm starting to look forward to the games."

Svangrior didn't argue, just scowled some more. Mazrith turned to me. "You should get some sleep."

I shouldn't have been surprised that I was to sleep in the Prince's bedroom. Mazrith had told me I wasn't leaving his sight, so I supposed I should have been grateful that he wasn't in there with me. He assured me there were other beds in the Serpent Suites, and that I would be left undisturbed.

"Sleep, Reyna," I muttered, quieting the frisky burst of imagination that accompanied the thought of the Prince disturbing me in bed. Turning and twisting under the mountain of luxuriously soft furs, the blend of warm comfort and exertions of the day lulled me into a deep sleep within minutes.

When a loud knock, followed by someone tugging on the covers, dragged me from blissful oblivion, I moaned. "Why?" I mumbled thickly.

"Dawn. Other fae to greet. Prince's betrothed has to be there. Get up."

It was Frima's voice, and I forced myself to sit up, rubbing my eyes. "I could have slept for another day at least," I groaned.

"Well, you can't. Get dressed."

I leaned over the side of the bed to grab my trousers, but Frima kicked them away.

"No, in a dress. This is a formal event."

I scowled at her. "I don't know how to get dressed in a dress."

At that exact moment, as if on cue, Brynja came into the room, carrying a tray with a mug of something steaming, a huge hunk of bread, some cheese, and what looked like wine.

"Oh, good," Frima said. "Dress her. Fit for receiving royal guests."

Brynja nodded, setting down the tray. "Of course, my lady." She passed me the steaming mug, and I sniffed. It smelled like chocolate, a delicacy I had only tried once many years ago.

"No Court has hosted fae from another in three hundred years," Frima said. Her eyes darkened a moment, sadness crossing her features. "It is a shame, in many ways," she said quietly.

"What is?"

"That it is the Queen who hosts such a momentous occasion. Maz's mother..." She trailed off, then met my eyes. "Mazrith's mother wanted to host the earth-fae, once."

"Why didn't she?"

"His father disallowed it."

"Why?"

"Because he was——" She cut off the sentence abruptly, glancing at the closed door. "He just did. Now, hurry up."

As she left the room, a slight figure appeared on the other side of the door. Frima shook her head but let her enter.

"Kara," I smiled, as she moved straight to bed to hug me. "Did you hear about the *Leikmot*?"

She nodded, sitting down on the edge of the bed. "Yes. It sounds like the Queen has a plan."

"My lady, which dress?" Brynja held up a long-sleeved black lace dress and a deep green dress that had a very firm bodice. It looked incredibly uncomfortable, so I pointed to the black one. "Long sleeves please."

I chatted with Kara as Brynja laced me into the dress and tried to sort out the tangled mess my hair had somehow become overnight.

"How is Lhoris today?"

"Good. I wish he would relax a bit."

I raised an eyebrow. "Relax? He's a captive in an enemy court! That's hardly conducive to relaxing." I cocked my head. "Are you relaxed?"

Color sprang to her cheeks. "Well, no, obviously. But... Well... I haven't been whipped or chased once since being here. The food is good, and there are books." She shrugged, looking guilty. "The thing is, I don't actually feel scared. Not in these rooms, with these warriors."

Brynja nodded. "They do treat us well. It can't be denied my lady. I haven't been beaten either."

"That's good," I said. I wondered if I should tell Kara they had been treated so well because they were leverage over me, and I was crucial in fixing Maz's life-threatening predicament. But I didn't want her to be scared, and if she felt safe in these rooms, then surely that was a good thing?

Lord Orm on the other hand... He should scare her. Scare all of the *gold-givers*. Me included.

"Just do not leave these rooms. Or the sight of the Prince's warriors."

She shook her head vigorously. "Of course not. I know who is out there."

Brynja nodded. "It's not just the Queen or her shadow-fae you need to worry about now. Any member of the other Courts would be hard-pressed to resist killing you," she said matter-of-factly, before her eyes widened and her fingers flew to her mouth. "I didn't mean to speak so callously, forgive me," she said to Kara.

Kara shrugged again. "Reyna has taught me not to be sensitive to things like that," she said. "I know where we are safe, and where we are not."

I felt a surge of pride for the young girl, along with a fierce longing to tell her about the riddle, but Frima opened the door before I could break my promise to the Prince.

"You look the part," she said, taking me in. "Are you ready? The strongest fae royalty in *Yggdrasil* has chosen a human thrall as his betrothed. I am willing to bet that will be as much of a topic of discussion as this meeting of the Courts. You are about to be the bearer of much scrutiny."

I hesitated, then nodded. "Let's go."

Are we late?" I asked as we reached the bottom of the grand staircase and turned in a direction I hadn't been in before. The hall was empty, unlike last time I'd been there, when guests had been trickling in as we arrived.

"Yes," Mazrith answered.

"Oh. Will that not make the Queen mad?"

"I wish her to be mad. I wish her to make an error, to demonstrate to all that she is unfit for rule."

"Right. Well, don't use me to make her mad. I reckon I could take her in a fist fight, but I can't see it coming to that."

The Prince's pace slowed for a beat, and I was almost sure I heard him laugh. "I would give my right eye to see my stepmother in a fist fight," he said. "But you are correct. It would not be her style."

"That awful shadow thing would tear anyone's limbs off before they got close." When he didn't answer, I spoke again. "Can you make creatures like that with your shadows?"

"I have no need to," he said, all the humor gone from his voice.

"Okay. It looked like a neat trick, though, just in case—"

He whirled suddenly, spinning me by the elbow to face him, eyes intent. "You are safe with me. As long as you are by my side, she will not hurt you."

I blinked at him. "Okay," I stuttered. He spun back, resuming his stamp across the hall tiles.

The part of me that would usually have protested that I didn't need looking after was silent, and I noticed its absence.

Had I accepted his protection?

Against his stepmother, I would accept anybody's protection. She terrified me. And against the Starved Ones too, I thought with a shudder.

But I couldn't forget the cost of that protection.

I glanced down at my wrist as we hurried along, the black rune clear, then at the snake ring.

He had bound me to him by force, and made sure I could never leave him, never be free.

I would let him protect me here, where so many forces would strive to harm me. But I would not allow myself to forget the cost.

# 20

## REYNA

The four of us made our way across the gleaming checkerboard tiles of the main entrance, toward the colossal palace doors. I realized as we got near that I had never actually been through them. Every time I had entered the palace, it had been through one of the Prince's secret entrances.

They were massive, their curved sides meeting in a point at the top while they were closed. They were ornately carved in much the same way the other doors I had seen in the palace, with battle scenes depicting glorious, bloody victories by the shadow-fae.

Mazrith flicked his staff, and shadows rushed toward the doors. When they met the rich dark wood, they flew open with more force than I expected.

The Prince strode through, but I paused, taking in what I could see before me.

I had already known that the palace was surrounded by the

weird, eerie forest we had ridden through to Tait's workshop. But down a set of wide steps made of the same shining, inky rock the palace was hewn from, a clearing had been made in the dense foliage. Sand had been spread on the ground to make a long oval-shaped stage area. An arena. Tall spires covered in winding vines were dotted around it, burning balls of bright light atop them that cast clear illumination over the sand.

The arena was surrounded on all sides by seats. On the two short, curved sides of the oval were rows of benches filled with courtiers. From my distant, but raised, viewpoint, I could see they were all wearing black and silver, making them likely all members of the Shadow Court.

On the side of the arena facing the palace were three empty ornate chairs, upholstered in fine silver fabric. They were flanked by a series of simpler chairs, and behind that more rows of long wooden benches.

On the side of the arena closest to the palace, between us and the sand, there were only ten chairs, and at their center, a throne, all facing the sandy stage.

I swallowed as I recognized the back of the Queen's head.

Steeling myself, I followed the Prince down the steps, unable to help myself from looking over my shoulder at the palace when I heard the doors slam behind me. I stifled a gasp of awe. From the outside, the doors were impressive. Almost a twin of the gates in the trunk of *Yggdrasil*, I realized as I stared. Fire burned in braziers flanking their sides, casting unnerving, red-tinged shadows over me as I turned and hurried after the Prince.

At the slamming of the doors closing, there had been a brief dip in the excited chatter of the gathered crowd. On seeing us descending the steps though, it quickly restarted, louder than before. I found my gaze drawn inexorably toward the three empty seats on the other side. Presumably, they were for the ice, earth and gold-fae.

As we got closer to the Queen's row of seats, I noticed that only three were empty, including the one immediately to her right.

Mazrith rounded the end of the row and strode nonchalantly toward his stepmother. Frima and I were behind him, Svangrior behind us. The Queen had not turned to look at us as we approached, though Rangvald had leaned in from his seat to her left and spoken with her a number of times. Everyone we passed fell silent, and just as Mazrith reached her, she stood up.

"Shadow Court!" she called out, spreading her arms wide and turning to the fae seated on the curved benches. "You join your Queen on a special day indeed." The entire crowd fell completely silent. "We are here to celebrate my son's thirtieth birthday with an unprecedented event."

"I am not your son, and it is not unprecedented," Mazrith said. Everybody froze, eyes flicking between the now rigid Queen, and Mazrith, standing before her. He stared out at everyone lazily.

What was he doing? In the time I had been in the Shadow Court, and in the conversations I had had with him about his stepmother, he had said he would toe the line to avoid disruption in his Court. But... hadn't she opened the door to that disruption already? Or was there another reason he would so publicly goad her?

The thought of her shadow creature made my skin cold.

"But anyway. Please, continue," Mazrith said into the heavy silence, waving a dismissive hand in the Queen's direction.

When she spoke again there was an evident hiss competing with the sweetness in her tone. "Hosting a *Leikmot* involving all the Courts of *Yggdrasil* is unprecedented in our lifetime, Mazrith dear."

He looked at her. "Oh, you managed to persuade the fire-fae to come?"

Her eyes narrowed. "You know nobody has seen a fire-fae outside of their own Court in centuries."

He shrugged. "*Nearly* all the Courts of *Yggdrasil*, then," he corrected her.

She glared at him, the two locking eyes in a battle of wills. Shadows swirled around the tops of both staffs, and Rangvald gave an almost inaudible cough.

The Queen snapped her gaze from Mazrith back to the crowd. "Before we welcome our visitors, we must nominate a champion for our Court to take part in the games that make up the *Leikmot*."

Voices muttered and chattered all around, the words 'Prince' and 'Mazrith' easily discernible in most conversations.

"It is a most honored position, since the games festivals can sometimes be dangerous."

My stomach twisted. Frima had been right. She was going to try to get him killed in the *Leikmot*.

"Now, the closer members of my Court and I have discussed it in depth and have already reached a decision."

There was a brief smattering of disappointed mumbles, that died out fast when the Queen's cool glare swept the crowd.

"I trust my son, Prince Mazrith, entirely." She said each word slowly and clearly. "We all know that he would do a fine job of representing our Court." Though Mazrith still looked relaxed, I could feel tension rolling from him. It seeped into my own skin, the feeling that something was wrong taking over.

"And it is because of that trust that we have decided to make another our champion. The very being he has decided to place his own trust in."

Oh no.

Oh no, no, no.

"My dear boy, what more could you or your Court ask for than a chance to show them all that they can trust your judgement? It is with great pleasure that I give you the opportunity to prove to them that you were justified in breaking centuries of tradition by choosing a human from another Court as your betrothed."

The Queen's eyes moved from Mazrith, to me. "Reyna Thorvald, future Shadow Court princess, you will be our champion in the *Leikmot*. It is up to you to demonstrate that the Prince of this Court is sound of mind and fit to rule. And if you fail, then devastated as of course I will be, we will all know that Mazrith Andask made a terrible mistake. One he will pay the price for."

# 21

## REYNA

"You can not do this," Mazrith hissed, whirling to face her, his mask of indifference crumbling. My heart was beating too hard in my chest.

"I am the Queen of this Court, and I can do as I wish," she whispered back.

"And I am the Shadow Court champion we need, you know that. Stop this madness, or you will make our whole Court look weak," he replied more calmy, still quietly enough that only those close could hear.

My stomach was twisting, my eyes flicking to the empty seats on the other side of the sand.

Three fae. Including Lord Orm. And I was expected to take them on?

Not knowing what the game would be was making my head spin and fear churn up my insides. A fist-fight? A race? A test of magic? I would fail them all. I was a human with no magic. I didn't stand a chance, and the Queen knew it. Mazrith knew it. She had cornered him.

Fury engulfed his features, dark shadows storming through his eyes.

"And we begin with the first game right now!" The Queen announced, turning from Mazrith back to the crowd. They cheered as one, excited faces lighting up in the benches.

My knees felt weak.

"No," said Mazrith, his body rigid.

She stared at him a beat, her red eyes gleaming, then spoke even more loudly to the crowd. "May I present Lord Dokkar, the earth-fae champion, and his courtiers, Lady Kaldar the ice-fae, and her courtiers, and Lord Orm the gold-fae, and his courtiers!"

Scores of fae emerged from the forest edge opposite us, taking seats on the benches on the other side of the arena, while the Shadow Court spectators both jeered and whooped. Three fae made their way past the benches and stopped at the edge of the sand. One I recognized instantly. Lord Orm, white hair gleaming under the artificial light, golden armor sparkling. His staff pulsed with a power that called to me, as though it knew its maker.

Next to him was a woman, seven feet tall with skin the color of the sky on a cloudy day, the palest of blue-greys. Her hair was as vivid as any blue I'd seen, braided into one thick plait that fell down her back. She wore white warrior garb and white war paint on her cheeks, a gleaming sapphire at her throat the only indication she was anything other than a warrior. Her staff I could not make out clearly, just that it had a similar sapphire catching the light atop a very straight rod.

The earth-fae beside her had skin the color of treebark, a rich warm brown. His eyes were black, as was his hair, but streaks of bright green ran through it, and there were hundreds of beads and leaves woven into his many braids. He wore loose-fitting clothes made from a patchwork of materials, and his staff was made from organic-looking wood, bent at all angles and glowing green at the top.

"Reyna? Take your place." The Queen gestured toward the arena.

"I will not allow this," Mazrith barked, but she leaned forward, seizing his arm and smiling serenely.

"You have underestimated me, Mazrith," she spat through her smile. "The Court needs to see why you chose her. It is too late for you to change this."

For a moment I thought Mazrith was going to hit her. But instead he gave a bark of fury, and slammed himself down in the seat next to her.

Frima looked between him and me, then slowly moved to one of the other empty seats. Svangrior did the same.

Only I remained standing.

She was right. It was too late to change this.

Nothing was valued higher in *Yggdrasil* than honor, pride, and courage. If the Prince's betrothed would not fight, she was not fit. And the Queen had done a fine job of convincing everyone that meant Mazrith was not fit either.

I took a step toward the arena, refusing to look at the three fae on the other side. My blood was rushing so loudly in my ears that the sounds from the crowd were blurring into a distant buzz.

Mazrith's voice cut through the haze, clear inside my head. "Do exactly as I tell you. Once this first game is over, we shall find a way to get you out of this."

I didn't want to give away that he could speak to me in my head, so I didn't react to his words at all. But I clung to them. I needed all the help I could get.

"Good fae, I welcome you to our Court, and I thank you for attending," the Queen sang out. "We shall begin the *Leikmot* immediately! Over the course of the festival, there will be three games held in each Court, as chosen by the host fae. The first game the Shadow Court presents is tug of war!"

Tug of war? As in, pulling on a rope?

A mix of relief and worry washed through me. It wasn't a test of magic or axe-skills, - which was good. On the downside, there was no way I was physically stronger than any of the fae. And I reckoned I weighed half what they did. I couldn't win, obviously. But I could survive, and in a best-case scenario, not look completely pathetic.

The unfairness of the fight lent strength to my anger, and I drew on it, gathering it around me like armor.

Armor. Another thing all the fae warriors had that I did not. I looked down at the long sleeve dress, my anger rocking toward rage.

There was no denying that the Queen had won this particular round of her fucked up game, but I would do whatever I could not to give her any more satisfaction.

Four thralls ran out onto the sand carrying heavy

looking ropes and laying them on the ground. Four others were fixing large poles at opposite ends of the sandy arena and drawing triangles around their bases with long charcoal sticks.

I forced my legs to move as the other three fae walked onto the sand amid raucous cheering.

"You must pull your opponents across the sand into the target triangles and attach them to the posts," the Queen called over the crowd. "The last fae standing will win. Let the challenge begin!"

The last *fae* standing.

I embraced my fury. We all knew I couldn't win, but to not even acknowledge the chance?

The cheering turned to a dull roar as all three fae moved fast, advancing on the ropes laid on the sand.

"Don't choose the rope Orm has," Mazrith's voice barked in my head, and I stopped myself throwing a glare his way. As if in a million years I'd choose to go against the male who already hated me.

Orm and Kaldar, the ice-fae, had already picked up each end of one rope anyway, so I was left with little choice in who I would be facing. The earth-fae gave me a grin that I couldn't tell was genuine or not.

"Not in any rush?" he asked me, dark eyes alive with specks of green.

"I'm human," I called back. "Want to play without your staff? Make it a fair fight?"

He glanced at the staff in his hand, then back at me. He flashed me another grin. Before he could speak, there was a roar from the crowd, and we both looked to our left. Searing light flowed from Orm's staff, and my mouth fell open as sparking blue ice whipped its way down the rope, making Orm drop it with a shout, before scooping it back up again with a snarl.

"No thanks, little human. I think I'll take what I've got," Dokkar said as he looked back at me. His accent was lilting, singsong almost, his tone impossibly relaxed.

I ground my teeth together as he lifted his end of the rope like it weighed nothing. The end of his staff glowed, and vines curled out from the gem on top, snaking toward the rope. I looked over my shoulder at the pole I was supposed to drag him to.

Not a chance. Not with a million prayers to Odin.

I bent, picking up the rope and widening my stance. Dokkar tugged experimentally with another grin, and I stumbled. Heat flamed into my cheeks.

I was going to look pathetic. There was nothing I could do about it. I had no leverage. Nothing the others had, not a single advantage. I was wearing a dress, for fuck's sake.

Another cry from the crowd made me look left. Orm was dragging the ice-fae towards his post, picking up speed as he got closer to the triangle. When he was only a few feet from his goal, the fae went completely limp. The rope pulled taut, and Lord Orm tumbled forward onto the ground.

The crowd laughed. I turned back to Dokkar, and the sight of his broad smile made me frown. A cool vine wrapped around my wrist. I yanked my hand back, but the vine was too strong. It had curled all the way around the rope and showed no signs of slowing.

"Sorry, little human," Dokkar said with a shrug, and

then I was off my feet completely. The combined power of muscle and earth magic was enough to move me twenty feet over the sand, before landing on my side, hard, only inches from the post.

I scrabbled on the sand, trying to get back to my feet, but the vine was moving up my arm and a peculiar numbness was coming with it, making my fingers hard to control.

"Let go of the rope," Mazrith's voice sounded in my head.

But I couldn't.

Dokkar was tying the other end of the rope around the post as though he had all the time in the world, and fury at my helplessness made me cry out. "You think winning an unfair fight makes you strong?"

Dokkar glanced at me. "No, I don't. I must beat one of them now." He nodded his head at the other end of the arena, where Orm's bright light hid most of what was happening. "That is what makes me strong." He moved to me, shortening the rope and tugging me into the triangle. I fought against him, kicking out, but he stepped easily out of the way every time I tried. His vines tightened around my arm, making it jerk out. Leisurely, he began to tie the other end of the rope around my now paralyzed limb. I beat at his side with my other fist, but he didn't even flinch.

"The paralysis is not permanent," he said cheerfully.

"You're making me look like a fool," I hissed, still smacking my fist into his ribs pointlessly.

"I'm not the one who entered you as my opponent. Remember that, little human. Plus, I could have tied you against the post. This gives you a little more freedom," he grinned, before dropping my numb arm. There was just enough rope between me and the post to keep me firmly inside the triangle.

I bared my teeth at him, but he just strode away to watch the other two. Putting one hand on his hip, he banged his staff on the ground and his vines immediately retracted, leaving a shining red mark where they had wound around my skin.

The crowd roared suddenly, and the light from Orm's staff dimmed enough that I could see his triumphant face, and the ice-fae tied to the post.

Anger that Orm had not been beaten made me pull against my bindings.

Two thralls ran out carrying a new rope, laying it across the center of the arena.

Slowly, Dokkar and Orm moved to either end, watching each other. Dokkar's easy smile stayed on his weathered face, just as Orm's sneer seemed fixed on his.

Together, they lifted the rope, immediately pulling it taut.

Dokkar got the edge early, his vines coiling down the rope as they had against me, whilst he smiled broadly. Orm's staff directed a beam of light at the earth-fae, but his careful inching toward his target didn't slow.

Pain cut into my neck and jerked me upright, my free hand jumping to my throat.

*Rope.* The loose end of the rope was around my neck.

Blind panic took me, and I yelled when it tightened.

I turned my head from side to side, looking for my assailant. But there was nobody there. I looked for shadows as I gasped for air, looked for any trace of magic that could be causing the rope to strangle me, but could see nothing.

"Reyna!" Mazrith's voice was in my head, and then I heard him shout out loud. I dropped to my knees, clawing at the rope until my fingers hurt, but it wouldn't loosen.

"Who is doing this!" roared Mazrith. I tried to look in his direction, but my eyes were streaming, my vision blurring. The rope cut my skin, and a garbled scream left my lips. Fresh pain added to the agony of my windpipe being crushed.

Black filled my vision, and then shadows were whirling around me, blocking out everything. There was an icy sear of pain around my hand and my throat, and then the pressure was gone. I fell forward, gasping for air. The shadows around me dissipated, and I was sure I saw the wisp of a green vine in my tear-filled peripheral vision.

Then, Mazrith was crouching in front of me, his furs shaking with rage. Gently, he lifted me to my feet, tilting my chin to look at my neck. For a second, I saw his eyes turn black, but then he scooped me up and spun around. He was moving too fast for me to see much, and my burning lungs and pounding head made it hard to concentrate.

I thought I heard the Queen protesting as we passed her throne, but Mazrith didn't stop moving.

# 22

## REYNA

I stared at the wall as I lay in the Prince's bed, listening to the voices of Mazrith and his warriors beyond the ajar door.

"Odin's raven, she nearly died!"

"A human against three fae. What the fuck did you expect?"

"It wasn't the competition that nearly killed her, it was whoever was controlling that rope."

"How would a fae do that? I saw nothing. It was as though it had a life of its own."

"Rope is a natural material, perhaps it was an earth-fae?"

Rolling over, I dragged one of the thick feather-stuffed pillows over my head.

I could never leave this room again.

Shame burned through me, almost as painful as the

fierce bruise around my throat that Kara had treated, as gently as she could, horror in her eyes the entire time.

The earth-fae had practically picked me up like I was a toy. The whole crowd, the most important members of Courts from all over *Yggdrasil*, had seen me look as weak as child.

And just to really ensure I was having a shit day, a rope came to life and tried to choke me to death. The memory made my throat constrict painfully. Mazrith, carrying me over the sand like a helpless maiden, had done nothing to help my shameful presentation to the world. But would I be here without him? No. He'd saved my life again.

I was so out of my depth it was laughable.

How in the name of Freya was I going to compete in more games?

I couldn't. *I wouldn't.*

The fact was that there was no way I could win. And then Mazrith would lose his Court.

I screwed my face up under the soft material of the pillow.

Since when did I care about Mazrith's accursed throne?

"Is it true that you were almost choked to death by magic?"

The voice was Voror's, and I reluctantly pulled the pillow from my face. He was perched on the end of the bed.

"Yes." My voice was hoarse and croaky, but it didn't hurt very much to speak.

"I did not realize this event was happening so early. I left to hunt." He blinked slowly, lifting one claw slightly from the wood. "I am sorry."

My shoulders slumped. "Don't worry about it. You couldn't have done anything anyway."

"The Prince saved your life?"

I nodded. "Again. I'm too weak and pathetic to save my own accursed life."

The owl tilted his head slowly. "For your species, you are not weak."

"Species?"

"You are human. For a human, you are not particularly weak. You are actually quite resourceful, if not as wise I am."

I sighed. "But I'm not fighting humans. I may as well be a fucking kitten in a den of lions."

"Then you are using the wrong words. You are not weak. You are the wrong species for your circumstances."

I stared at him. "How is that supposed to help?"

"If I were to fight three forest-mice and win, would that make the mice weak?" I shook my head, sighing.

"No. I get what you're saying, but it doesn't help. I'm the only human in a Court filled with fae. If I can't match them, it's over."

"That may be true, but there is no benefit in calling yourself weak, or belittling what you do have. You are damaging your self-confidence by telling yourself false truths, and that is one of the few things you do have. And besides, you have some attributes your opponents do not."

I looked at him. "Like what?"

"You are not as fast or strong as a fae, and you do not have wealth or magic—"

"Listing what I don't have is not helping, Voror."

He blinked at me slowly. "They are not all intelligent.

They do not have a wise and magical owl. They do not have the protection of the most powerful shadow-fae in history. They have not been named in ancient prophecy as key to the fate of the *Yggdrasil*."

"The fate of *Yggdrasil*..." I murmured, putting my face in my hands. "Whoever chose me, they chose wrong."

"Well, it's too late to change it now," the owl said matter-of-factly. "Who tried to choke you to death?"

I dropped my hands from my face and looked at him. "I don't know."

"Tell me what happened."

Begrudgingly, I relayed the first game of the *Leikmot* to the bird. "I thought I saw a vine, before Mazrith carried me back here," I said, the memory floating back to me after reliving the experience.

His beak clicked. "Somebody has tried to kill you twice before the earth-fae arrived," he said. "It is unlikely to be him."

"But there were no shadows around the rope to indicate it was a shadow-fae. When Mazrith and the Queen use their shadows, you can see them. I don't think they can make them invisible."

Voror blinked. "The Queen's magic is... wrong. It tastes wrong in the air."

"Do you think it was her?"

"I believe she has the power."

I took a deep breath, and flopped back on the pillows, wincing at the pain the movement caused in my neck. "How am I going to get through the games festival?" I asked quietly.

"It sounds like the shadow-fae beyond that door are working to answer the same question. They are stronger than you. Let them help."

"Everybody is stronger than me."

"Fae are stronger than you," he corrected me.

"Fucking fae."

"Hey, I didn't throw you to the lions." Frima's voice made me sit up quickly. She was standing in the doorframe, leaning against the wood, and my mouth fell open at what she was wearing.

"Frima, you look..." I wasn't sure how to find a way of saying sexy that wasn't weird.

She smiled and pointed a toe, lifting her scarlet red, skin-tight skirt and showing off her leg provocatively. "Tonight, I have a quest that requires a set of skills you haven't seen me use before. But have no fear, I'm as good with these as I am with an axe." She pushed her chest out, showing her deeper-than-expected cleavage.

"Huh," I said, unsure what the correct response was.

"One of the Queen's courtiers has a soft spot for me. I am going to try to get him to tell me what the next two challenges are. At least if we have some idea we can try to prepare."

"That's... That's good of you. Thank you." *We both know I still won't be able to win.* The unsaid words hung in the air. My cheeks grew hot again, and I wished I could banish the shame I felt at being so publicly pathetic.

Her eyes flicked to my neck, then to Voror who was stock still at the end of the bed.

"There's an owl in your room."

"Yeah."

"Okay. How are you feeling?"

"It hurts when I swallow, but fine otherwise."

"Maz wants to talk to you."

I frowned. "Then why doesn't he?"

A ghost of a smile crossed her lips. "He wouldn't enter your bedroom without me checking you were dressed first."

My eyebrows rose. The gold-fae burned women's clothing off for fun. "He could have knocked."

"That's what I told him, but he sent me."

"He's giving me a chance to say no," I realized slowly.

"Or go to him," she shrugged, eyeing me shrewdly. "If you're up for getting out of bed?" The challenge in her voice was clear, and a welcome spark of defiance fired inside me.

"Of course I can get out of bed," I spat. "I may not be as strong as a fae, but I'm not an invalid."

"Pleased to hear it. You realize nobody was watching you today until the rope tried to kill you? You did what you could, but it wasn't you they were interested in. You're human. They wrote you off before the game even started."

I felt myself tensing, but the meaning of her words penetrated the rage.

Nobody who saw how easily I was defeated in that arena would have been surprised. Or have even cared.

Voror was right.

I wasn't a fae, so comparing myself to them was worse than pointless. It was downright damaging.

And the owl was right about one more thing. I *did* have something they didn't.

My self-pity evaporated.

"Where's Mazrith?"

Frima smiled. "In the war room."

# 23

## REYNA

When I pushed the door open, Mazrith was sitting at the huge table, staring at the map. Plates of bread, meats, pastries, and cheese covered the other side of the table. "You wanted me?" I said, instantly regretting my word choice when he snapped his head round to face me.

He looked at my neck first, then at my face. "Are you able to eat?"

"I don't know. But I am hungry." He stood up, resting his staff against his chair before picking up and passing me a plate. His furs were gone, just a simple dark shirt covering his huge torso. He gestured at the food, then moved to the cabinet that held the tumblers and drinks.

I moved along the platters, choosing foods that I hoped wouldn't hurt my throat, then chose a seat a few along from the one he had been sitting in. The fireplace was lit and the curtains open, and the combination of the warm glowing

156

firelight and the sparkling sky outside was surprisingly cozy.

"Your rooms aren't like the rest of the palace," I said.

He didn't answer until he had poured the drinks and brought them over. "Mead," he said.

I took it from him gratefully. It was like drinking liquid comfort, the pleasant sensation numbing my throat and warming my chest.

"I believe it was my stepmother's magic controlling the rope today," he said tightly as he sat down.

"So does Voror." I picked at a piece of bread, then chewed experimentally. It didn't hurt too much when I swallowed, so I tucked into the rest of the food on my plate with more enthusiasm.

"We need to find a way of keeping you alive."

I could help my snorted laugh. "Through more of those? Good luck with that."

His eyes darkened. "I do not need luck," he growled.

I closed my eyes a moment, then opened them again. "Look, the faster we solve your riddle, the faster I can serve my purpose to you."

He frowned, looking down at my hand. Looking for the ring I wasn't wearing. "At which point you will attempt to escape our betrothal," he said quietly.

That wasn't the response I had expected. He was absolutely right, but it wasn't the direction I needed this conversation to go.

"At which point, you can overthrow the Queen and end the games," I said firmly. "Or at least choose a better champion."

"I told you I would help you and I was unable to," he said, still staring at my ringless hand.

Was his anger giving way to guilt? I stared at him. The more I looked, the more I was sure I could see the scars lining his face.

Memories flooded me in a rush, most of them from those two nights in the mountain. Him, under whatever glamor he used, covered in scars from head to foot; the huge wound on his chest; the vision of him and his mother. I rubbed my hands over my face, trying to snap out of the thoughts.

"You did help me. You saved my life, again."

His eyes lost focus a moment, then snapped back to mine with an intensity that made my palms sweat around the butter knife I was holding. "No."

"What... what do you mean, no? Those were your shadows that removed the rope, weren't they?"

"The rope should never have been around your neck. I failed. You should never even have been in that arena." Shadows that looked like storm clouds churned through his eyes, deep wells filled with a language I simply couldn't translate.

Emotion surged through me, making my face hot. "Why do you care?" I whispered. He stared at me for so long I thought I might never escape his mesmerizing, constantly-moving irises.

"The Queen outsmarted me." His tone was cool, and he dropped my transfixed gaze. My stomach lurched, and I bit the inside of my cheek to force my emotion down, forced myself to keep my face neutral. "She outsmarted me in public and has me exactly where she wants me." His fingers moved to one of a few amulets around his neck, and he turned it over in his hands, staring at the map. "We are being attacked on all sides, and now she is a step ahead. I can't see the way out."

I closed my eyes.

*He's lying.*

This wasn't just about the Queen. I'd seen it in his eyes, I could feel it rolling off him. He cared about me. I just couldn't work out why. Outright, greedy fae possessiveness? Or something more?

I took a breath.

Whatever was going on inside that mysterious, intense brain of his didn't change what needed to be done.

"If I lose, which I certainly will, you will lose credibility in your Court."

"Yes."

I opened my eyes. "Unless you publicly cut ties with me."

"I can't do that."

"Why not?" Something that was either relief or surprise accompanied my demand.

"Bound betrothals are unbreakable by anything other than death." He didn't look at me as he spoke.

I clenched my jaw, preparing to say what I knew I had to. "And you are not willing to kill me?"

"No," he answered softly, still not making eye contact.

As I had hoped, but it was still good to hear it. "So, I am to continue to play the role of your betrothed."

"Yes. And you must do exactly as you are told, by me and

my warriors. The world must believe that I chose well in you, and we will have to find a way to do that outside of the *Leikmot.*"

"Fine." He fingers stilled around the amulet, and he looked sideways at me. I shrugged. "You expected an argument?"

"Yes."

"What would be the point?"

Slowly, he turned his head to me. "You have lost your fight?"

My eyes narrowed instinctively. "I have been made to look weak, and a fool. But, as my learned bird friend pointed out, this is not a fair fight."

Mazrith tilted his head. "Indeed. I would like to see Dokkar beat you at working with gold."

I nodded, straightening a little. "I have something they don't." I held his gaze. "You."

He said nothing, but his eyes were bright.

"They are scared of you. Everyone in the Five Courts is scared of you. And they all saw you save me today. If they believe that you will hurt them, if they hurt me, they may take it easier on me."

Mazrith continued to stare. "You do not wish to be dependent on another's strength. You have made that clear many times."

"Yes." My face was so hot it hurt. "But as I said before, this is not a fair fight. *You* are a match for them, not me. There is nothing else I can do, and despite any earlier impressions I may have given, I do value my life." I stood up. "And in the meantime, there is no question that our best, and likely only, chance to depose your stepmother and break your curse is by solving the riddle. Have you had any more ideas?"

"No." His face darkened. "I have been somewhat distracted."

"Then let me give it to Kara. She has nothing to distract her, and she is smarter with words than anyone else I know."

His jaw tightened. "You can't tell her any more than she needs to know."

"I won't."

He nodded. "Fine. Give her the riddle." He fished the piece of parchment from the pouch on his belt and passed it across the table to me. "Frima is trying to find out what the next two games will be, so that we can get a headstart."

"It can't hurt to know more," I said, tucking the paper into my trouser pocket.

"Is there anything you are exceptionally skilled at?"

I couldn't help a grin of satisfaction as I remembered the alehouse in Upper Krossa, and my many victories at the gameboards. "I'm not as stupid as I keep being accused of. I'm pretty good at chess."

He cocked his head. "There were definitely games of intellectual skill in the ancient *Leikmots*. Let us hope that is repeated. Anything else?"

"Erm. I'm smaller than the other fae. Could that help?"

He shook his head. "I doubt it."

There was a knock at the door. "Enter," the Prince said. Ellisar poked his head in.

"Sorry to bother you, Maz, but I had an idea, and Svangrior and Kara said I should tell you right away."

My brows raised at the mention of Kara. "Tell me," Mazrith said.

"Well, it occurred to me that if we could make your magic invisible, just like whoever manipulated that rope did, then you might be able to help Reyna in the games without anyone knowing. Or at least, without anyone being able to prove that you were helping."

Hope, actual real hope, fired through my chest. Mazrith looked between me and Ellisar. "We need to talk to Tait. Go and get him, bring him to the palace."

"Of course, Maz," the huge human nodded, then backed out of the room again.

"Do you think you could do that?" I asked excitedly.

"If I could, it could be of great help."

"That's an understatement."

He gave me a look. "You were hungry," he said, glancing at my empty plate.

"Yes."

"And thirsty." He scooped up my empty glass. "More?"

"Do you have something that will help me sleep?" The nightmares would come tonight, for sure.

"I have something for everything," he muttered, quietly enough I only just caught it.

He returned a moment later with two glasses of what I assumed was red wine. "So," I said, taking the glass and deciding to be bold. "We are working together, and now drinking together."

"So it seems." He sat down, and my eyes flicked to the

amulet he had been holding. Most of the jewelry he wore looked regal, but that one was different. It was teardrop shaped and plain, no shiny gemstones in it like the other, and it hung on leather, not chain. And it didn't have a snake on it. The metal was worn in places but I could make out a raven in the center, carefully hammered into the surface.

"Where did that come from?" I pointed at it.

"My mother."

"She gave it to you?" My pulse quickened. Could this be the way into the conversation I was so desperate to have with him?

"I do not wish to speak of her. Or my father, or my curse, before you start."

I sighed. "Fine." I took a long sip of the red wine. It was delicious, like plums and spices and a hint of smoke.

"Instead of assailing me with questions, why don't you tell me something?" Mazrith said.

I glanced at him, and he leaned back in his chair, crossing his ankle over his knee and taking a sip of his own wine.

"What do you want to know?"

"Your owl."

I paused. "What about him?"

"Where did he come from?"

"I don't know."

"Liar."

I didn't answer him, sipping more wine instead.

"You test me," he said, his voice a low growl. "I regret telling you I would not look inside your head more every second we spend together."

"Do you regret me saving your life too, as that was what led to that promise?" I set my glass down and folded my arms over my chest.

"It would not surprise me if you end up the death of me regardless."

"Hey, you started all this! I was minding my own accursed business when you showed up!"

"We've been through this. There was as much chance of a creature like you living your life in that shithole as there is of Ellisar bedding the goddess Freya."

"A creature like me? What does that mean?"

He bared his teeth at me as he sat up straight in his chair. "It means a woman with whatever it is you have inside you that drives me to fucking distraction!"

I stared at him, pulse racing at his words. "You said I was bored to tears in my old life. That I was meant for something else," I said quietly.

"All true. Though I am painfully aware that truth is not a concept you are familiar or comfortable with."

"You're hardly forthcoming with your own infernal truths."

"I do not lie."

"Refusing to say anything isn't much better."

"It is infinitely better."

I tilted my chin, fixing my glare on him. "Did you ever plan to kill me?"

He held my gaze. "No."

"And my friends? Did you plan to kill them?" My voice was hoarse, and I realized why I had asked the question. *Because I knew the answer.*

His eyes dropped from mine, and all the remaining warmth left the room.

"Refusing to say anything is better than a lie, huh?" I said quietly. Still, he said nothing, glaring down at his lap.

I stood up, grabbing my glass. "I am tired. Good night." I turned, and the Prince did nothing to stop me leaving.

Once alone in my room, I buried myself under the blankets, leaving one arm free to gulp down the wine.

I had been moving dangerously close to trusting him. To wanting him. *Worse, to wanting him to want me.*

That was why I had asked the question. To force me back to reality. To take me back to that day he had broken into the workshop and dragged Kara from the pantry. Threatened to slit my friends' throats.

And then bound me to him by force.

I drained the glass of wine.

I may have need of him now. But I sure as Odin did not want Prince Mazrith.

# 24

## MAZRITH

A tiny figure representing a Starved One danced in my hands as I turned it over and over.

They were coming.

And they wanted Reyna. The infuriating red-haired human was the key. *To everything.*

What would she do when she found out? She didn't trust me, as much as I didn't trust her.

But blessed Odin, I wanted her.

As deep as my soul had ever allowed me to feel, she was there.

Her courage astounded me. She burned brighter and hotter than anybody who had ever crossed my path. I couldn't stand it.

I dropped the wooden piece on the map with a hiss and scooped up my wine. But it wasn't strong enough to obliterate the thoughts consuming me. Nothing was.

Fates have mercy on me, I missed my life before her

endless domination of my mind. A domination I was destined to endure for eternity.

She already wanted to escape.

If she ever saw the real me, she would not be able to move fast enough.

# 25

## REYNA

"Rise and shine." The sing-song voice dragged me from sleep.

"I hate you," I said, keeping my eyes closed.

"Charming." Frima sat down hard on the end of my bed, jolting my covers from me.

"Why is it always you who wakes me up?" I groaned.

"I come bearing chocolate, pastry, and good news," she said. I opened my eyes to see her holding out a steaming mug and a plate with a chocolate covered pastry on it. She was back in warrior garb and had a gleam in her shrewd eyes.

I sat up, taking the mug from her, then the pastry. "Thanks."

"I was able to get the information from the Queen's guard. And a mighty fine shag, much to my surprise. He didn't look like he had it in him." She grinned at me, and my face flushed. "The next two challenges are a rock-throwing competition, and a horserace."

I stared blankly at her. "How is that good news? I will definitely not be able to throw a rock as far as the others, and I can't ride a horse."

"Well," she said, folding her arms. "Rock-throwing is a lost cause, I agree. But you can learn to ride."

I blinked. "How long do we have?"

"Rock-throwing is after lunch tomorrow, and horse racing is the following night."

"I can learn to ride that quickly?"

"Maybe not, no. But you can learn to hold on and go fast. There's no magic or strength needed to win a horse race."

She had a point. I chewed my pastry.

"And before that, I'm going to teach you a few moves."

I paused my chewing. "Moves?"

"You can take a staff into the challenges, just like the fae champions. And you may not have magic in yours, but I can teach you to do some damage with one all the same." Her eyes sparked fiercely, and once again, against all my will, I warmed to her.

"Enough damage they won't be able to just pick me up like a toy?" I asked hopefully.

"Enough damage that they won't be able to get within three feet of you without using both hands to defend their baby-makers," she said wickedly.

"When do we start?"

"Now. Well, in ten minutes. Get dressed in proper clothes—no accursed dresses—and we'll go to the training room."

I scrambled out of bed. Energy was rushing through me, all remnants of the previous day's helplessness evaporating.

This time, when I faced off against those *veslingrs*, I would have a weapon. Not a magic one, but at least I wouldn't be defenseless. Frima was Mazrith's right-hand woman, a well-respected and feared warrior. I would learn everything I could from her, in as much time as I could take.

"Please could I speak with Kara while I'm getting ready?" I said as I hurried to the wardrobe. "It's important."

Frima nodded, then left the room, Kara slipping through the door a moment later.

"Morning. How are you feeling?" Her wide eyes were filled with worry and her eyes moved quickly to the ugly bruise around my neck, then flicked down to my foot.

The skin was a normal color, and the two dots where the fangs had pierced my skin looked more like normal scabs now.

"I'm fine, Kara," I said as she came toward me. I pulled my leather body wrap around my middle, over my shirt. "How are you?"

"Good," she said absently, moving to me and lifting my tangled hair so that she could peer closer at the mark. "Does it still hurt? Your voice sounds a little croaky."

"No. Whatever you gave me worked great."

Her face brightened. "More stuff from Ellisar's dad."

"Who knew an animal healer could be so helpful," I said.

She crouched down, inspecting my foot. I stayed silent, tying my wrap tightly, then securing my belt.

"It looks a lot better. Does it hurt?"

"No."

I took the piece of parchment with the Prince's neat handwriting from where I'd hidden it under my pillow and gave it to her. "I need your help."

"While he is more than ten feet tall,
Even in death he shall never fall.
Aided by golden touch and darkest night,
Prize from the steel his greatest delight.
Only this may be used here to repair,
Nobles and royals with secrets to share." She read the whole thing aloud before looking at me. "What is this?"

"I, erm... I can't really tell you," I said apologetically. "But I think it's a riddle."

"Mmm, sounds like it." She looked at me quizzically. "You need help solving it?"

"Yes," I nodded.

She looked back down at the paper, sharp eyes moving quickly as she read. "Given that there aren't any ten-feet-tall fae that I know of, it must be talking about a statue," she murmured.

"That's what Mazrith thought," I said without thinking.

Her eyes snapped back to mine. "The Prince gave you this?"

"Yeah, sort of. Look, I'll be able to tell you more soon. But at the moment, with the Queen and the other fae here, it's honestly safer that you don't know."

"Okay," she said. "I'll do my best." She sounded a little doubtful, but I beamed at her.

"Thank you, Kara. If anyone can crack it, you can. But please, don't let anyone else see it. Even Lhoris."

"Okay. Are you leaving the Prince's rooms?"

"Yes. Frima is teaching me to fight with a staff."

"Oh. That sounds like a good idea. Reyna, be careful out there."

I squeezed her shoulder. "I won't be alone, or going far. Don't worry."

The training room was in the same wing of the palace as the Prince's rooms, and I was happy to see that the walls were not painted maroon.

Thin furs covered the central part of the wooden floor, and the walls of the large square room were lined with weapons.

Frima moved straight to the staffs. "Choose one."

"Anything I should be looking for in particular?"

"No, just go on instinct."

There were at least ten of them, all different lengths and thicknesses, made of metal or wood.

Metal would do more damage, wouldn't it? But it was heavier to wield. My hand moved between them as I pondered the merits of each.

"You're not using instinct. You're trying to think your way to a result. Look at me."

I looked away from the staffs and at Frima's face. She tilted her head slightly, and then her eyes lit up. She moved, heading for a low cabinet on the other wall that had a display of small daggers and throwing stars on it. She pulled open a drawer, then made a triumphant sound before heading back to me, holding something small in her hand.

I peered curiously as she opened her palm.

A small tin of dark oil paint.

My brows raised. "I can't wear warpaint. I don't have any braids."

"You don't need braids to wear warpaint. If you are fighting, you need paint."

I looked at the black marks that were so often smeared on her cheeks. "I'm not of the shadow Court."

"You're representing them." I scowled at her and she laughed. "It's not black."

I leaned forward, looking. She was right. It was blue. The color humans wore, but much darker, like Ellisar's paint.

When I still didn't move, she sighed. "Wear it now, at least. You can decide whether to wear it for the *Leikmot* later."

"Why should I wear it now?"

"Because right now, I need you to be a warrior. And warriors wear warpaint." She thrust the tin at me again.

Uncertainly, I took it.

"On your cheeks," she encouraged.

With a resigned sigh, I smeared some across both of my cheeks.

It was smooth and cool, and I was almost sure I felt a small tingle.

"Good. Now, choose a weapon, and try not to think about it. Just run your hand over them all, and see where you stop. Let the fates decide for you."

"The fates have decided enough for me already," I muttered, turning back to the staffs.

"I'm sure they have their reasons."

"Yeah? I think they've been misinformed."

"Reyna, you've as much courage in you as any fae."

Much as I didn't like to be compared to a fae, I knew the words were a compliment coming from her. I looked sideways at her. "Thanks."

"Choose a staff," she said.

"Fine." If I was going to learn from her, I would do it properly.

*Let the fates decide.*

I closed my eyes and tried to picture myself as a warrior. Reaching out but keeping my eyes shut, I brushed my fingertips across the stacked staffs, letting my hand close when it felt right.

Opening my eyes, I pulled a sturdy, if a little short, wooden staff away from the wall.

"Excellent," Frima said, selecting a long metal one and tossing it into her other hand as though it weighed nothing. "Let's begin."

"If we keep going like this, I'm going to be too exhausted to even attempt to compete," I panted.

Frima twirled her staff in her hand as we circled each other, darting it out at my knee lightning fast. I managed to block her, but only just.

"We have restoratives," she grinned dismissively. "I'm just worried what Maz will do to me when he finds out I'm responsible for all the bruises you have."

I bared my teeth defiantly. "What bruises? You've only hit me twice."

It was sort of true. She'd only hit me *hard* twice.

She laughed. "So far." She straightened suddenly, standing her staff up on the floor. I didn't move from my protective stance, suspicious. "Your aptitude and reflexes are better than I had hoped, so let's move on to technique. I wasn't joking earlier when I mentioned baby-makers."

Slowly, I straightened. "Okay. I'm listening."

"Good. And watch, too." She moved to the other end of the room and dragged over a straw-stuffed dummy that had a target tied around his chest and three small axes embedded in it. She untied the target, then gently *thunk*ed her staff against the dummy's chest. "Ignore this whole area."

I frowned. "But isn't that where all the stuff you want to damage is? Heart, lungs, and so on?"

"Yup. But against a fae, you're never going to damage their vital organs. Your goal is to inconvenience and disable them."

I didn't like the thought of aiming small, but I could see she had a point. "Okay."

"So, you'll be wanting to go here,"—she smacked the staff with a satisfying thud into the crotch area of the dummy— "here,"—she thwacked it fast into the front of its throat—"or here." With a deft movement, she dropped into a crouch and swung the staff, hard at the back of the dummy's legs. Straw burst out of the weaker part of the model with the force.

My fingers flexed around my own staff. I could see how

all of those moves would be effective, even on a fae. "I'm a little short to reach the throat on the other fae in the *Leikmot*," I said.

"Then we'll adapt it. She stood in front of the dummy and crouched until it was about a foot taller than her. Then she stabbed her staff upwards, ramming the end into the part of its neck that met the chin. The straw head lolled slightly.

"That'll do it," I said, suppressing a smile.

"Sure as Freya it will," she said, jumping back to her full height and turning to me. "Right, your turn. We do it over and over, until I think you can't do it any better."

# 26

## REYNA

y the time we returned to the Prince's rooms, I was oscillating between barely able to lift my arms and positively vibrating with energy.

We had trained all day, only stopping for a short time to eat the lunch that Brynja had delivered to the training room. Although my thighs burned from crouching so much and my arms ached from wielding the weapon, I felt stronger, not weaker.

I'd wiped the warpaint off before we left the training room, unwilling to let anyone else see me wearing it. I wasn't a warrior, and it didn't feel right to display warpaint. But I couldn't deny it had felt right when I was wielding the staff.

Brynja had a hot bath ready for me when I got back, and as I sank into the large copper tub, she passed me a tumbler of mead. It took no time at all for the fire to burn in my chest and the aches to recede a little.

A knock on the door made me startle, but it was Kara who poked her head around the door.

"How did it go?" I asked her, relaxing back into the hot water. "Any luck with the riddle?"

"No, not yet. Did you learn how to hit somebody with a staff?"

"Sure did," I smiled at her.

She beamed back. "Good."

"Do you want to eat in my room and play a game of chess tonight?" I asked Kara. "I wanted to ask you what you knew about horses."

*And I wanted to avoid Mazrith a little longer.*

"Yes, of course. I'll go get the board, and some bread and cheese."

When I entered the bedroom, Kara had set the board up on the rug in the front of the fireplace, a small picnic of bread, fruit and cheese laid out to one side.

She beat me twice, but I didn't care. A sort of relaxed fatigue was washing over me, the ache in my muscles and the warm fire a strangely satisfying combination.

Kara didn't know much about horses, but before she left my room, she promised she would look for anything useful on the Prince's shelves to read before I had to run in the race.

I half fell into the luxurious bed, and before I even had time to worry about nightmares, I was asleep.

I slept soundly, right through night, Brynja waking me with a large breakfast an hour before the rock-throwing challenge was to begin. When I'd eaten and then washed, I emerged from the bathing chamber to see the maid sorting through a large bundle of material on the end of the bed.

"Ah, my lady," she said, an unusually flustered tone to her voice. "Frima dropped off some fighting garb for you. But I, erm, don't know what all of it is for."

"I may be able to help," I said. "Is this... chainmail?" I held up a sheet of metal interlocking rings. I'd seen it on palace warriors and guards before, but it was expensive.

"Yes. I think so."

I looked at her, then at the pile of armor and clothing. We had no idea what we were doing, I conceded. "I'll go and ask her to help," I said.

Still only wearing a toweling sheet and a thick black robe, I pushed the bedroom door open and peered around the frame. "Frima?" I called, seeing nobody. I didn't want to go looking around the suites, dressed as I was.

Mazrith rose from the large seat by the fire.

*How the fates had I missed him there?*

His eyes flared when he saw me, and I gulped, our conversation from the previous night still fresh in my mind.

"Frima is not here. What do you require?" His words were tight.

"Never mind. We'll work it out," I said quickly.

He took a step toward me. "What is it you require?" he repeated.

"We, erm, don't know what all the stuff she gave me is for. But as I said, we'll work it out."

But he was already striding toward me. "We have little time before we leave for the challenge. I will help."

Brynja looked at Mazrith as he entered, then at me, her eyes wide. "I'll leave you to it, my lady" she said, then bolted from the room.

I rubbed my hand over my face.

Mazrith stared at the bed. "Dressing. You need help dressing?" he asked quietly.

"I need help with armor," I snapped, though the truth was that I didn't know what most of the garments were, either.

For a moment, I thought he was going to leave, but then he picked up a white cotton item. "This first. Then the shirt and the trousers." He thrust those at me too, and I took them. "For the love of Odin, do not remove that robe in this room while I am in it." His words were a rasp.

Swallowing hard, I hurried to the bathing chamber with the clothes, pushing the door tightly closed behind me.

*He did want me.*

The memory of the fae-wine dream caused heat to wash through me, along with a tiny flicker of regret that I'd left the bedroom so quickly.

*Don't be a heimskr, Reyna! You would not let him touch you.*

Shaking my head hard, I finished fastening the trousers and tucking my shirt in, then pushed the bathing chamber door open and stepped back into the room.

Noticing that he was wearing warrior garb, I tried to act as casually as I could. I pointed to the multitude of leather straps running over his tight black shirt. "You must be taught to do this as a kid," I said.

Mazrith held out a leather strap with a few silver rings on it, and a belt. "These next," was all he said, tightly.

I secured the belt around my waist, but when I took the leather strap from him, I faltered. "Erm..."

Jaw tensing, he stepped forward and lowered it over my head. "Lift your arm."

I did, and barely stifled a sharp breath as his finger brushed down the side of my ribs. It only took him half a minute to fix the strapping, but my accursed lungs failed to work the entire time.

Next, he held out a black leather wrap, half the size of my gold one and designed to go under my bust, around my navel.

I took it, winding it around me and tying the laces at the front. When I looked up, he was holding the chainmail out like a net, and I saw the hole in the top. Slowly, he lowered it over my head, then fixed it at various points to the leather straps underneath. Again, with his head bent close to mine and his fingers so close to my skin, I found myself unable to breathe properly.

When he stepped back, his eyes were dark. "This collar protects your neck when you fall," he grunted, and fixed something to the back of the chainmail.

He handed me two smaller pieces of leather with ties. "These go around your shins."

I crouched, the weight of the chainmail making me awkward. As I tied the shin guards on, he spoke again. "Where is your staff? This strap goes over your hips and has a sheath for it." I pointed to the dressing table, and he moved to get it. "This has a good weight," he said, almost to himself.

"I like it," I answered.

"Then you must name it. Weapons should have names."

I stood up, our eyes locking as he passed me the staff. "I'll think on it," I said.

"What about your hair?"

"What about my hair?"

"How will you fight with it like that?"

I couldn't help smiling. Lhoris had given me grief for years about managing my wayward hair when I worked. I moved to the dresser, trying to get used to the weight of the armor, and roughly shoved my red curls into the magicked headband, ensuring Voror's feather was safely and securely tucked inside it.

I turned back to the Prince. "Better?"

"Functional," he said. "You look uncomfortable in the chainmail."

"It's a little heavy."

"Yes. It is made for fae, who have more muscle."

I resisted scowling at him. "Do you have any made for humans?"

He blinked at me. "I shall source something more appropriate as soon as possible. But now, we must leave."

I had assumed that we would be going back to the arena in front of the palace gates, but I had been wrong. Frima and Svangrior met us in the grand hall, and when the huge doors were opened the sandy space below was empty. We made our way down the grand steps swiftly, and I shrugged my shoulders, trying to make the chain mail more comfortable.

"Where are we going?"

"The forest."

"The creepy forest you said never to linger in?"

"The one and the same," Frima grinned at me.

"Great."

We walked in silence, all three fae faster than me, so my legs were doing far more work. There was no path through the gnarled, creepy trees, but the undergrowth we moved over had clearly been trodden on before. When we slowed slightly to move through a denser patch, I saw a ribbon hanging from a branch, the fabric the same dried-blood color so common in the palace. At the end of the ribbon was an eyeball.

"Is that glass?" I asked, then immediately wished I hadn't.

Svangrior snorted as he looked over at me. "Does it look like glass?"

Despite myself, I peered at it. The whites were blood-shot, the pupils wide, and bits of deep red sinew stuck to the back of it.

I swallowed down bile. "No."

There were more ribbons as we went, and I realized

somewhat belatedly that we were following them. They were morbid signposts.

After another five minutes, I decided that the trees were actually worse than the eyeballs on ribbons.

If I looked at any area of bark for more than a couple of seconds, faces began to form. Twisted, tortured faces, with eyes that wept black ooze. The branches overhead ended in sharp, abnormally twisted points that could have swooped down and gouged people's eyes out to decorate more ribbons.

"Are the trees alive?" I murmured as I ducked low to avoid a particularly vicious-looking branch and was almost certain I heard a whispered hiss of disappointment from the leaves.

"Some say the ancestors of the shadow-fae have spirits that reside in the trees," Svangrior said.

I looked at him in mild horror. "Their spirits didn't end up in *Hel* or *Valhalla*?" I hadn't heard of such a thing.

He shook his head. "No. Their crimes were suitable for neither, so—" He glanced at Mazrith's back. "So the King banished them here. Or so the rumors go."

"The King? Mazrith's dad, or a previous King?"

"My father made this forest what it is," Mazrith said from ahead of us. "And I do not wish to speak of it. I believe we are almost there. Prepare yourself."

# 27

## REYNA

We emerged into a clearing that the forest looked like it had been reluctant to create. Whilst the floor was dirty, dusty soil, the trees overhead were all bending over the space, hovering like waiting predators.

There was no breeze at all, yet the twisty branch ends moved almost imperceptibly. If they were given the go ahead, or whatever was keeping them back was released, then I was sure the restless haunted forest would descend upon its prey instantly.

And there was plenty of prey. As before, there was a throne clearly meant for the Queen, with a few benches for her Court around it, and rows of chairs and benches surrounding the rest of the stage for everyone else. The clearing was a perfect circle, and had markings on it in dark chalk, like a clockface.

Orm, Dokkar, and Kaldar were all standing at the edge of the circle, and there was no sign of the Queen.

A hush fell over the crowd when they spotted us. Then a low chorus of mixed booing and cheering began.

"You should go and stand with the other champions," Mazrith said quietly, turning to me.

I nodded, nerves firing. Frima gave me a gentle punch on the arm. "Don't forget, you're armed this time."

I tightened my grip on the staff. "No chance of me forgetting," I told her.

"Good luck."

Svangrior grunted, and the three of them made their way to their seats as I moved to the other champions. Orm was at one end of the line, Kaldar in the middle, and Dokkar at the other end. I stepped into line next to the earth-fae.

He gave me a sidelong look, his lazy grin already in place. "You look better prepared today," he said.

I lifted my staff. "Yes."

He gave a small shrug. "Try not to get yourself killed."

My instinct was to retort with something about him worrying about his own life, but I bit my tongue. I had enemies here. Plenty. I didn't need to defend myself with words in this arena. I had armor, and a weapon.

"I'll do my best," I answered.

"Can't ask more than that."

"I am here, watching, *heimskr.*" Voror's welcome voice floated through my head. "I wish you to know that this forest has some very severe issues. It has no manners at all, and it does not seem to recognize my greatness one bit."

I suppressed a smile. As long as the forest didn't hurt

him, I couldn't help enjoying the idea of the uptight owl being affronted by a haunted tree.

"It appears you are about to have unwelcome company," he said gravely.

Expecting the Queen to arrive, I looked over at her throne, but Orm sauntered into view instead. Taking a place on the other end of the line, next to me, he leaned on his staff.

His armor gleamed, and he smelled like weapon oil. "How are you enjoying your time in the Shadow Court?"

His voice made my skin crawl, and I refused to look at his piercing, cruel eyes. "Just fine, thank you for asking," I said.

"Shame, as you will not be here much longer."

"I am betrothed to shadow-fae royalty," I said, almost choking on the words as I said them. "I will be here as long as I wish to be."

"Look at me, little human."

I gritted my teeth, steeled my nerves, and turned my head slowly, trying to keep as imperious a look as I could manage on my face.

His eyes roved over my every feature, firing with an emotion I recognized.

I was a challenge to him.

"Yes. Yes, I can see what he sees in you. What you could be." The same image he had shown me before scraped into my mind, only now I was wearing a black-and-ivory crown as he whipped my naked body. He laughed when I broke eye contact, the image fading away. "They will turn on you, you stupid little *veslingr*, and then you will beg me to take you back the Gold Court."

Dokkar coughed loudly from my other side, then leaned out of the line on his staff. "You two know each other?"

"This pathetic little human was supposed to be bound to me."

Dokkar raised one eyebrow. "And now she is bound to the Prince of Snakes."

Orm spat on the dirt, and Dokkar gave me a curious look. "Rune-marked are treated well in my Court, but not fought over as you appear to be."

Grateful for the earth-fae's interruption and keen to keep him talking, I kept my gaze fixed on him and floundered for something to say. "I think it must be the hair," I said eventually, shrugging and flicking a loose tendril of my red hair as casually as I could.

He gave a small laugh that cut off abruptly when Orm grabbed my shoulder, spinning me back to him. Before I could stop myself, the training I had repeated a hundred times kicked in.

I crashed my staff straight up between his legs.

The sound of wood on metal rang through the clearing, and Orm let go of my shoulder, staring at me in disbelief.

Armor.

He had defensive armor between his legs, I realized through my own shock at what I had just done.

"You dare to strike a fae Lord?" he hissed, his alabaster face darkening to an ugly shade of purple. "You? A pathetic human?"

I thought of the fierce human warrior woman he had

struck down dead, and rather than shrink back, my shoulders seemed to widen, to square up. Movement in my periphery caught my attention, and I turned slightly. Shadows. Snakes made of shadows swirling and winding across the dirt. Waiting.

"Say my name and I will tear his fucking throat out," Mazrith's voice sounded in my head.

The 'M' was already forming on my lips; the desire to see Orm dealt what he deserved was overwhelming. But he couldn't hurt me here. Not in front of everyone. This was my chance to do what I had wanted to do back in the Gold Court. *Stand up to him.* Lifting one palm in a 'stop' motion to the advancing snakes, but drawing courage from their presence, I spoke.

"I am promised to royalty and I absolutely dare to strike you," I said, my voice only quavering a little. "I did not give you permission to touch me, and I am your equal in this competition."

The purple of his face deepened, spittle forming at the corner of his mouth when he replied. "I will not kill you when you belong to me. I will keep you alive as long as is possible. Know that."

A massive cheer erupted from the crowd, and we both snapped our heads to the source of the commotion.

The Queen had arrived.

Mazrith's snakes turned a few times on the ground, but when Orm reluctantly stepped back into line, they slithered away.

"Welcome, all!" The Queen's high-pitched voice sang

out over the space and the crowd clapped. I couldn't see clearly from across the dirt circle, but her black dress didn't look quite as perfect as usual, and her red eyes were not quite so bright. Rangvald hurried along beside her looking unusually wild-eyed.

"As you all know, Lord Dokkar of the Earth Court won the last game."

I didn't know that. It hadn't even occurred to me to ask what happened after I was carried away by Mazrith. But then, the winner of these games didn't interest me, I just wanted to survive.

The Queen sat in her throne and swept one arm out in his general direction, but her beady gaze fixed on me. "Let us see who can best him this time. Each of you, choose a position in the ring."

The other three moved immediately, and both Voror and Mazrith spoke in my mind at the same time.

"Do not stand next to Lord Orm," said the owl, as Mazrith commanded,

"Next to Dokkar."

"Fuck that," I muttered. Frima had said that this was a rock throwing competition - and given that the arena was round, not long and thin, I was fearing the worst. This was set up so that we would be throwing rocks at each other. And I did not want to be opposite Orm.

Trusting my instincts, I jogged across the dirt, tracking Dokkar. I wanted to be opposite him. He would take me out of the competition, the same as the others, but I was pretty sure he wouldn't deliberately try to kill me in the process.

Kaldar had taken the position right in front of the

Shadow Court Queen, and Dokkar had moved to her left. I positioned myself quickly on her right side. Orm took the last space with what seemed a slightly forced swagger.

He was furious. I could see it in his tense, rigid movement.

*Oh Reyna, pissing him off right before the game was perhaps not smart.*

But instinct had taken over. Frima had done her job well, it seemed. And being able to fight back with something more useful than taunts and bravado?

That had felt pretty fucking good.

There was a loud clap, and then shadows swooped in over the arena, making me jump in surprise. Boulders rumbled across the ground, emerging from the trees, rolling and veering, guided by slender tendrils of inky shadow, until they stopped in piles beside each of us. When they had finished depositing rocks varying from fist-sized to head-sized, the shadowy ribbons swirled around each of the champions' feet, creating a ring a few feet wide.

"Last champion standing wins. If you leave your shadow-ring, then you forfeit." The Queen paused to chuckle cruelly, "and believe me, you'll wish you'd been hit by the rock instead. Commence!"

# 28

## REYNA

Before I even had time to think, Orm was moving. To my surprise, though, the enormous boulder he launched through the air wasn't headed for me.

Dokkar threw up his staff, his vines shooting out to try and block, or reroute, Orm's massive rock. But he had reacted too late. The rock didn't hit him square on, the vines catching it in time to shift its trajectory, but it crashed hard into his side, hitting both his jaw and shoulder. The earth-fae flew backward onto the dirt with the force of the rock, and Orm's face lit up with glee. Blood began to darken the dirt around the fallen earth-fae, and somebody yelled from beyond the arena edge.

"Forfeit! Earth forfeits!"

The black shadow ring around Dokkar vanished as the fae tried to groggily sit up, blood pouring from a wound on his jaw and his shoulder hanging far too low. Two fae with

COURT OF GREED AND GOLD

bark-colored skin like his own ran onto the dirt and began to drag him away.

"Strike now, while Orm is distracted," Mazrith said in my head.

I may not have been as strong as the fae, but I could be accurate. I scooped up a rock that I could lift comfortably. Focusing on his disgusting grin of glee, I aimed at Orm's mouth. As the rock left my hand, I realized Kaldar had taken advantage of the gold-fae's distraction too.

There was a satisfying thwack, then a wail of pain as her larger rock hit him in the gut, and mine crashed into his nose. Blood immediately began to seep down from his nostrils.

His rage-filled eyes snapped to mine, and he lifted a rock as big as my head at the same time as his staff. As he hefted the boulder in his hand, gleaming white light burst from his staff, dominating my vision. I screwed my face up as my eyes were forced closed in response.

The boulder was coming my way and I couldn't see to dodge it. Panic swamped me. I ducked down blindly, then gasped.

An image was coming into focus against the backs of my shut eyelids.

*An image of me.*

I could see myself crouching, but from where Orm was standing. I felt a surge of triumphant glee that didn't belong to me, then saw the rock heading fast toward my slight form.

Seeing exactly where it was going to land, and exactly

where the black ring was, I leaped to my feet, jumping to the right just in time to avoid the boulder landing.

The vision vanished, and I opened one eye as Orm howled with indignation.

"What the —?" I started, but then another vision covered my eyes, replacing what I could see in front of me.

This time I was seeing through Kaldar's eyes. Cold hatred for every individual around me overwhelmed my senses, followed by a determination to remove Orm from the fight, however necessary. Disinterested disdain was all I felt about the pathetic human rival in the competition. She could be dealt with later.

The vision lifted as Ice threw a hefty rock at Orm's middle.

I didn't have time to work out how the fuck I had just seen through my opponent's eyes, but I could use what I had learned. She was going to throw everything she had at Orm because I was no threat.

If Kaldar was going after Orm, then there was no point bringing her attention back to me. Picking up a rock, I threw it as hard as I could at Orm's face.

Between us, we pelted Orm with everything we had; Kaldar with large rocks that he had to concentrate on deflecting from his torso and legs, and me with smaller rocks, all aimed for his stupid, perfect, fae face.

Finally, a rock struck him squarely in the temple and his ferocious efforts to block the larger rocks faltered. His eyes rolled in his head. Ice gave a triumphant bark and hurled a big boulder at his middle.

He made a clumsy attempt to block it but failed. It

powered him to the ground, rolling off him as he tumbled backward. One of his arms fell out of the black ring as he tried to roll back to his feet, and he gave a shriek of pain.

"Forfeit!" yelled a gold-fae from the side of the arena.

The black ring unwound, and the shadow swept back toward the Queen. The gold-fae ran to help Orm up, but as soon as he reached him the Lord cuffed him hard enough across the head to knock him backward.

"I did not tell you to forfeit for me!" he roared.

"But my Lord, you were in pain."

"Reyna!" Voror and Maz both yelled my name in my head, and I whirled from Orm's display just in time to see a rock hurtling toward me. I lifted my staff instinctively, managing to smack the rock away but leaving an alarming bend in the wood.

I looked at Kaldar, wondering if I could talk to her like I had Dokkar. But the disdain I had felt from her seemed to have turned to something deeper.

There was no cruel smile, no berserker-style rage, just hatred in her eyes. She picked up a much a larger boulder, and fear washed through me as her staff glowed and lethal spikes of ice grew all around the rock, swelling its size. She lifted it with both arms. It was wider than she was.

My staff couldn't deal with that. Nothing but magic could deal with that. She was taking the chance to get me out of the competition for good.

"You won't survive that rock," Voror said in my head.

"No shit," I muttered, my pulse racing so fast I felt dizzy.

The rock left Kaldar's hands, and her aim was true. It was going to hit me.

"Don't leave the ring unless you have no choice," said Mazrith, his mental voice a rasp.

Time seemed to slow as the rock completed its arc and began its descent.

Letting instinct take over, I threw myself out of the way.

I did what I could to stay inside the ring, but her aim with the enormous rock was too good.

Just about all of my body ended up outside of the circle of shadows.

Pain that felt nothing like normal pain seeped into every fiber of my body. It was hot and cold at the same time, inside my body, then inside my blood, rushing through me, burning me from the inside out.

"Forfeit!"

I heard the shout, but the pain continued. I was vaguely aware that I had curled up, and that the ground felt like it was moving, but when I tried to concentrate the freezing fire inside me seared hotter.

"I said *forfeit!*"

The pain vanished.

Trying desperately to stay conscious, I rolled onto my back. The fresh air and clear skies I craved weren't there, just the trembling branches of the trees that would tear me apart given the briefest of chances.

"Reyna?"

"I think I might be sick," I mumbled, not really sure what was happening.

Frima appeared, dropping to a crouch and expertly tipping me over onto my hands and knees just in time for me to vomit onto the dirt.

I heard the crowd laughing and jeering behind me.

"This human bested a gold-fae in battle today," Mazrith's voice boomed. "For that, she deserves your cheers. Unless you would like to endure the pain she just has?"

I blinked but stayed on my hands and knees, willing the nausea to subside.

Someone began a slow clap, and a few more joined in. The smattering of applause died out a mere moment later.

"Fuck them," Frima whispered. "Can you stand on your own?"

"Yes."

I took one more deep breath, then got to my feet as steadily as I could.

"The winner is Kaldar," said the Queen as soon as I was upright. I avoided looking at her as the crowd exploded into genuine applause, but I was unable to avoid the gaze of Lord Orm. Drawn like a moth to flame, my eyes fell on his. And they were murderous.

# 29

## REYNA

Mazrith and Frima stood each side of me, each clearly shortening their stride as we made our way in silence back through the forest. Svangrior was behind us, muttering curses regularly.

We had waited until everyone else had left, and although Frima said it was because they wanted to avoid any altercations in the forest, I suspected it was to allow me time to recover.

What they didn't know was that my brain was in a turmoil of its own that had little to do with falling out of the shadow ring.

How in the name of Odin's arse I had been able to see through the eyes of Orm and Kaldar? And not just see, but feel, too. Not every thought, not physically what they were experiencing, but a definite sense of their overriding emotion.

*How*

How was that possible?

*You've had visions that don't belong to you your whole life, Reyna.*

Could I have been seeing through another's eyes all those times I'd had the gold-induced visions? Through a Starved One's eyes?

But the vision I had of Mazrith and his mother was in the past—a memory at best. This... This was real-time, live, and without being anywhere near gold.

The thought of telling anyone about the visions made my stomach constrict, the bone-deep sense that it was a secret I must keep warring with my growing need to know more. When we were back in the palace, I would find time alone to talk to Voror. He was the only one I could trust to talk to about this.

We entered the imposing doors to the palace, mercifully clear of fae, then headed quickly to the Serpent Suites.

"Frima, could you..." I pointed at my chainmail once we were in the sitting room and the doors were closed behind us. "Help me?"

She nodded, and I stepped into the bedroom, bending to untie the shin guards.

When I straightened, though, it wasn't Frima who had followed me into the room.

The door clicked closed behind Mazrith's large frame.

"Orm is ready to up the stakes. You should have let me kill him." Shadows swirled out of the top of his staff, spinning around us both. He was a few steps below me, making our faces level for a change, and the fury dancing in his eyes made my breath catch. For the wrong reasons. It was terrifying, but it was beautiful. Compelling. Right, somehow.

*All fae are beautiful, and all fae are deadly.*

Remembering that the cause of the agonizing pain I had just experienced was shadow magic forced me to recover my senses. That they were created by the gods with the capability to do that to a living being...? It was just wrong.

"I wanted to stand up for myself," I said, as indifferently as I could. "And besides, the Queen would have been given a legitimate reason to punish you. Say you started a war." I shrugged. "I was doing you a favor."

His face twitched, then the shadows rushed back to his staff. His eyes didn't soften, though. "Perhaps. That man hates you with a vehemence. Why?"

My brows lifted in surprise. "You really don't know?"

He bared his teeth. "Do not play games with me, *gildi*."

"You got the toy he wanted."

Mazrith's eyes narrowed. "That... That is it?"

"Yes. He wanted me as his concubine, and for free labor on his staff, and you got me instead. Now he has a point to prove."

"Not because... Because he is infatuated with you?"

My mouth fell open. "In what world do you look at him and think he is infatuated with me? He is a greedy, power-hungry, deranged psychopath, who doesn't like having his things taken away. Simple as that."

"Greed," Mazrith repeated, almost to himself.

"Yeah. Greed. Pretty standard with your kind."

He glared at me. "You believe your kind are not greedy?"

"Not compared to the fae," I snorted.

"You are naive."

"Says the male who didn't know why the other boy was mad at him," I shot back.

To my surprise, Mazrith gave a low, humorless laugh. "Oh, *gildi*. You must never, ever compare me to a child."

The words Orm had said on the carpet swam back to me.

*"Playthings are for children. I am a fully grown male, which you would find out on entering my bedchamber."*

Two fae saying something so similar, yet there was absolutely nothing about the way they said it that was the same. Orm's words had been a promise of pain and torture, an immature boast of power and prowess.

Mazrith's words were loaded with a different kind of promise altogether.

I swallowed. "Fine. Maybe we are both a little... under-experienced in some areas."

Mazrith tilted his chin back, eyeing me. "For you, that is a most reasonable observation."

I ground my teeth. "You realize I'm only *un*reasonable when I'm kidnapped, forced into marriage, and my life is being threatened?"

"Frima believes so. I am still not sure."

I sighed, rolling my eyes, and trying to squash the unexpected stab of happiness that Frima believed I wasn't a total *heimskr*. "Are we done here? I'd like to remove this armor."

"I will talk you through it. First, unclip the chainmail at the neck."

I did as he said, feeling for the clasps. When I got to the chainmail, he moved to help me, but I stopped him.

"Let me see if I can do it myself," I said. He had already

told me where to unfasten all the clips, and I wiggled my shoulders, checking it was loose.

"Fine. You know, it was your rock that took Orm out?" I looked up at Mazrith, my fumbling fingers pausing.

"Huh? I think the fucking great boulder Kaldar threw at him had something to do with it," I said, wishing what he was saying was true.

"It finished him off, perhaps, but it only hit him because your rock hitting his temple caused him to fall. You, a human, took out a fae Lord."

I lifted the chainmail over my head carefully, and wondered if he could be right. I had seen Orm's eyes roll when my rock hit him.

"If you win one of these games, you will earn a braid."

I dropped the chainmail to the floor with a jangle. "A braid?"

"Yes. Honor means braids." Mazrith frowned. "This is the same in your court, is it not? Lhoris has a braid."

"Yes, of course it is, but... I never thought I would earn a braid fighting."

"But you did believe you would earn one?"

"Yes," I started, then trailed off. I may have told Skegin in the alehouse that I would earn a braid before he did, but that had been a bluff. The *Yggdrasil* way was to fight with words when you had no weapons. *My* way was to fight with words. But had I ever actually believed I would wear a braid in my hair? I had believed my future was hiding in another Court somewhere, belonging to nobody. Free. Alone, disguised, but surviving.

"Actually, no," I admitted. I glanced at him, wondering

COURT OF GREED AND GOLD

why I was telling him this at all. "Braids are earned with public acts of valor or great victories. Bravery and courage and ingenuity, recognized by your clan or Court." I shrugged. "None of that could be achieved in hiding."

"You believed you would hide for your whole life?"

"How else could I escape the Gold Court?"

He opened his mouth, an indecipherable look on his face as he shook his head, as though unsure what to say. "A life in hiding... No. No, you could not earn braids. Nor could you —" He stopped speaking, shaking his head again. "It is irrelevant what you cannot do in hiding, as you will soon be the most recognizable human in the five Courts."

My stomach turned over at his words.

They were true. Hiding was impossible now, from the Prince, Lord Orm, or the rest of the world. They had all seen me. I was being used as a fucking spectacle.

*And the Starved Ones are after you too. How could you hide from them?* The voice in the back of my head made me shudder.

"Fine," I said, squaring my shoulders and forcing out the unwelcome thoughts. "I'll win the horserace, and earn a braid."

Mazrith cocked his head at me. "Good. Are you tired, or in pain?"

"No," I shook my head. The pain from training with the staff had been eased with the baths and mead, and the pain from the shadow-ring appeared to have no lingering or lasting effect. I felt surprisingly good.

"I'll have food sent to your friends' room. Take an hour to eat and rest. Then we go to the stables."

# 30

## REYNA

I met Brynja outside my room, carrying a tray laden with food and a basket hanging under her arms filled with bottles and glasses.

"Ah, my lady, thank you. Follow me." She smiled as I took the basket from her.

It turned out the room my friends were staying in was around the bend in the hallway, past the war room. The hallway forked left, where I could see more closed doors, but the door on the right revealed Kara curled up on a chaise, a book in her hands, and Lhoris half upright in a large armchair, piles of furs arranged around him, dozing. The room was decorated like others in the Prince's suites, though this one had no fireplace or window, and a large tapestry of a wyvern on the far wall. A large bed was against one wall, and a small table and bookshelf lined the other.

"Reyna!" Kara rushed to me as I came in the room and enveloped me in a hug.

"Brynja and I bring food," I said loudly, before whispering in her ear. "Any luck with the riddle?"

"Not yet," she whispered into my shoulder, before releasing me. Brynja transferred the food on to the small table, and I joined her with the basket of drinks.

My stomach rumbled loudly as I looked at all the bread, cheese and cold meat cuts, and the handmaid passed me a plate.

"Thanks, Brynja."

"My lady," she nodded, then left the room, pulling the door closed behind her.

I began to load up my plate, ravenous after the amount I'd put my body through in one day, then poured myself a healthy measure of mead to go with it.

"Frima just told us about the second *leikmot* game," Lhoris said, sitting up straight in his chair.

"Did you really hit Lord Orm in the you-know-where?" Kara said, wide-eyed.

I moved to sit next to her on the chaise, setting my drink down on the floorboards. "I did, yeah. He had armor on, so all it did was piss him off, but..." I was unable to keep the glee from my voice. "I did throw the rock that knocked him out long enough for Kaldar to land a big one."

"Freya and the fates, I can't believe it!" Kara clapped her hands together.

"It felt good to have something heavy in my hands," I smiled at her, before chewing on a hunk of bread. "And now, I'm learning to ride a horse."

Lhoris' deep voice sounded guarded. "It is good you are learning to ride. It could enormously aid your escape." His dark eyes bored into mine when I looked at him, and I knew what he was trying to do. He was trying to get me to confirm that was still my goal.

I nodded at him. "For tomorrow, it will help me stay alive. Maybe even..." I trailed off, suddenly feeling vain.

"Maybe even what?" said Kara.

"Well, Mazrith says if I win tomorrow, it would be enough to earn me a braid."

Kara's fingers flew to her mouth. "You've always wanted a braid!"

"I know. And I could never have earned one in hiding."

"Reyna." Lhoris' tone was filled with warning, and I looked at him. "Do not let your motivations change with the lure of things you do not need. Remember why we are here."

"I know, Lhoris. But when I was trapped in the mountain with the Prince, I... I learned more about him. And I don't know why yet, but I am connected to his fate somehow."

Lhoris tilted his head, shifting further forward in his chair. "That does not mean you can trust him. I know you can't run from your own fate, Reyna, but you can stay in control of it."

"What did you learn?" asked Kara.

Discomfort made my stomach squirm, and I put my food down, grabbing the mead instead. I hated lying to them. They were my family. But I daren't risk sharing too much with them. "If I could tell you, I would."

Lhoris scowled, and Kara patted me on the shoulder. "Well, if we're all stuck here until the Prince doesn't need you anymore and we can escape, surely it's not so bad if you earn a braid on the way?" Kara looked innocently at Lhoris, and if I hadn't had a plate of food on my lap, I would have hugged her.

"Escape is harder with every single soul who recognizes your face," Lhoris answered gruffly.

"Escape isn't harder. Staying free is," I said.

He shook his head. "Ever you argue with sense."

"Look, this is out of my hands now. Someone has tried to kill me, more than once, and there's a good chance it's the Queen. I'm concentrating on staying alive and learning what I can while we're here."

"I'm learning too," Kara said. "Ellisar has been teaching me animal medicine."

I glanced at her. "Really?"

"Yes. He's quite a good teacher, actually."

Lhoris glared between us. "Do not lull yourself into believing these fae are your friends, both of you. You are *gold-givers*, the tool of their sworn enemies. They will not hesitate to end you when you have served your purpose."

I swallowed some more mead. He was right. Of course he was right. "We will not forget, Lhoris," I told him, holding his dark-eyed gaze a beat, before turning back to Kara. "Now, tell me everything you have read about horses."

All too soon, Brynja knocked on the door to tell me the Prince was waiting for me in the sitting room. With more hugs and promises to be careful, I left my friends to find Mazrith standing by the door to the Serpent Suites, dressed in leather trousers, fur-topped boots, and a plain linen shirt open low down his chest. My eyes flicked involuntarily over his exposed skin.

"Admiring my amulets?" His tone was deep, silky smooth, and my face heated. Saving me from responding, he lifted his arm and I saw he was holding a leather belt and my staff. "Put this on. I want you to get used to moving around the palace armed, and you will learn to ride with it."

I took it from him, frowning at the staff. "Something is different."

"Yes. While you ate, Tait altered it so that it can be folded. He also fixed the bend the rock caused."

I peered at the middle of the staff and saw a shining silver bracket. It was concealing a tiny hinge, I realized, folding the staff in half. Instantly, the heavy wooden weight of the weapon changed.

I gaped at Mazrith. "It's so light!"

"Yes. I also made some alterations myself."

"You can magically make it lighter?"

"Only when it is folded. It is the same magic used on fae staffs, when they are retracted."

I strapped the belt on, marveling at how much easier it was to stow the staff in the sheath.

"Thank you. And please tell Tait thank you."

"I will."

We made our way to the stables in silence, and I did my best to remember the route whilst adjusting the staff sheath as I walked, finding the most comfortable place for it.

Lhoris' plea to remember that we were amongst
enemies had been swiftly doused by my delight at the staff-
alterations, and I tried to play his words in my head,
bringing back my grip on my situation. But I found myself
struggling. Enemies didn't arm you with magical weapons
or teach you to fight and ride. They didn't tell you that you
could earn braids, or make your sense abandon you when
they exposed too much hard, naked muscle.

*Get a grip, Reyna.*

When we reached the stables, I took in a few deep
breaths, enjoying the smell of hay and the warm tempera-
ture. The large space was brightly lit, and the high ceilings
were much less oppressive than the corridors and rooms of
the castle.

"The stablehand will be here momentarily, with Jarl and
Idunn," Mazrith said, coming to a stop at a large oval-
shaped clearing between a few stalls.

"Idunn is Frima's horse?"

"Yes. You will be riding her today."

"How does Frima feel about that?"

"She suggested it after training you with the staff. She
trusts your instincts."

*Odin curse this woman's effect on me!* Pride swelled every
time I learned of any respect Frima had for me, and it was
dangerous. Almost as dangerous as letting my guard down
around the Prince.

"You must know that horses are sensitive creatures."
Mazrith drew my attention back to him. "They respond to
your feelings and the atmosphere of their environment. You
must be calm and confident. Speak to them as you would a

friend." I nodded, as he continued speaking. "It's important to approach them from the side, so that they can see you. Do not move too quickly, and always let them smell you before you touch them."

A snickering drew our attention to the approaching stablehand, a horse's reins in each hand.

Nerves fired through me.

They were beautiful. Sleek, powerful, and *huge*.

Mazrith took Jarl's reins, stroking him along his snout and muttering quietly to him. The horse snickered happily as the Prince tied him to the wooden post of a nearby stall, before going back to the stable hand and taking Idunn's reins. The stablehand bowed, then hurried away.

Mazrith led the big black mare over to me, her tail swishing, dark eyes flashing.

I took a deep breath. "Okay. Calm, confident, slow."

"If you are nervous, she will feel it," Mazrith said quietly.

"Yes, I got that when you told me the first time."

"Then calm down."

"I'm trying to. She's just so..." Idunn rocked her head from side to side, baring her teeth and stomping her front hooves on the dirt ground.

"Powerful? You can learn to harness that power for yourself, Reyna. Calm, and confident."

I remembered the rush of powering through the forest on Jarl, and a thrill of excitement replaced some of the nerves. I drew a calming breath, forcing my shoulders to relax. Idunn's swishing tail slowed, but she still swung her head and tapped her hooves.

"Step forward. To her side." I did as he bid, keeping my

breathing slow as I approached her. One knock from her huge swinging head would have me on my backside. "Place your hand on her neck." I bit the inside of my cheek and pressed my hand to her sleek black coat. She instantly stopped moving, her swishing head coming to a stop where her huge dark eye could see me. I felt the powerful muscles tense, then relax, and she dipped her head. Her hooves stilled.

"Good. We are ready."

Over the next few hours, Mazrith spoke more than I had ever heard him. He showed me how to hold the horse's reins, and where to place my hands when leading a horse, as well as how to rub them down and groom them with a brush and comb.

When he was happy I was no longer twitchy around the huge creature, we went through mounting. I was not about to try vaulting up onto Idunn's back like Frima did, so the Prince called up a shadowy step from his staff. I put one boot on it, gripped the saddle, and heaved myself up as gracefully as I could manage.

Once I was in the saddle, the Prince mounted Jarl and showed me how to sit comfortably with my back straight, how to hold the reins, and where to put my feet in the stirrups.

Next, we went through how to control the horse with my body, using my legs to ask her to walk or stop, along with the commands most of the horses in the stables were trained in.

After an hour of riding Idunn up and down the stable yard at a gentle pace, and according to frequent corrections from Mazrith, my confidence swelled.

"Can we leave the stable soon?" I asked as I brought Idunn to a stop right next to Jarl and Mazrith. He gave a nod that I was coming to recognize as an acknowledgment of a job well done.

"Yes. We need to practice faster movement, which has to be done outside. But we can't linger in the forest, so I will tell you what you need to know here, first." He moved his mount closer to me, lifting his reins so I could see them and explained how to use them along with shifting my weight in the saddle to control the horse's speed. He went over using my knees and weight to stay on the horse by standing and lowering myself if she was moving fast, and how to use my feet to stop her in a hurry if I had to.

The nerves I had felt earlier had shifted to apprehensive excitement. I wanted to feel what Idunn could do, the power beneath me burning with restless promise.

"What if I get lost?"

"Idunn will follow Jarl, so you will not get lost. You will not even need to steer her, though your steering seems good so far."

"So you'll be in front when we go through the forest?"

"Yes. When we come out of the other side, we will ride through the town to a small wood that has what we need to practice jumping."

"What if I fall off? If you're ahead of me you won't see me."

His grey eyes bore into mine. "If you fall, the forest will take you."

I swallowed. "So, don't fall off?"

"Don't fall off."

# 31

## REYNA

As soon as we emerged from the safety of the palace, I dug my heels in, gripped Idunn's back between my thighs, and gave the command Mazrith had taught me.

"Yaa!"

Idunn took off instantly. My breath caught as wind whipped over my body, and I tilted alarmingly to the right. Idunn neighed loudly as she veered off, the black of Jarl and Mazrith heading one way, as we went the other.

"No!" I moved the reins, shifting my weight, trying to stand higher in the stirrups as Mazrith had shown me. Idunn corrected course as I regained my balance, and relief was fast replaced with concentration as I tried to move in rhythm with her. Blocking out everything, even the Prince in front, I focused on feeling the horse, understanding how she was moving and trying to move with her.

It was hard, with the forest streaming past at a dizzying

pace, but the more I responded to the horse, the smoother we moved.

And faster, I realized, finally confident enough to look up.

We had gained on Jarl and Mazrith significantly, only a few feet behind. Mazrith cast a look at me, and for the first time, I thought I saw a flicker of joy in the serious fae prince's face.

"Yaa!" Idunn sped up, and the instant feeling of power fed my racing heart even more courage. The horse was doing my bidding, moving me over land in a way I could never move myself. I could fly through the forest, fly through the mountain, fly through the whole Court, if I wanted to.

I drew level with Mazrith, twisted trees whipping past on either side. Aware that if I got ahead of him I wouldn't know where to go, I forced my excitement down, instead trying to exert more control. I used my feet and the reins to slow Idunn down, the delight at her response not as adrenaline-fueled as the speeding up, but satisfying nonetheless.

I almost found myself disappointed when we burst out of the forest and onto the cobbled stone path to the town.

"Whoa," Mazrith called to Jarl, and I did the same, slowing Idunn to a walk.

"I didn't fall," I said, beaming at the Prince.

He stiffened as he looked at me, the joy I'd seen on his face before gone. "I have never seen you smile like that," he said, voice as stiff as his face.

My smile slipped. "Well, I've never felt like that," I replied awkwardly, turning away from his intense stare. "I think Idunn likes me."

"Your motivations are true. She can feel it."

"My motivations?" His rigid expression had mercifully been replaced with his usual sternness when I looked at him again.

"You enjoy the feeling of riding her. The feeling of her power."

I tilted my chin. "Freedom. That is what I feel from her."

His eyes flashed. "Whatever you wish to call it, she feels it, and you appear to be able to respond. When your motivations align, then you ride as one. I am relieved. There are some horses that will never accept some riders."

I remembered the first time I had been in the stables. "Like Jarl's sister? You said something about your mother being the only one who could ride her."

The Prince blinked at me. "That horse is an exception to most rules."

"Why?"

"It doesn't matter." He gestured ahead as we entered the town, and I bit back a sigh.

It was late, and most of the building's lights were burning bright. I cast my eyes up at the star-sprinkled sky.

"You wouldn't think the stars were bright enough to illuminate the whole Court," I said, almost to myself. They did, though, casting a constant twilight over everything, that only dimmed at night, rather than going completely dark.

"Do you miss how the Gold Court is lit?"

I turned to Mazrith with a snort. "I miss nothing about the Gold Court."

"It is bright there. So very bright, all the time. This must seem dark to you."

I looked around again, noticing how much of the cobbled path, stonework buildings and distant trees I could make out clearly. "It's not so bad."

We only passed a few people as we made our way through the town, most of them outside the alehouse, drawn out to see who would be out on horseback so late. They all bowed their heads when they realized it was their Prince, and just about all of them followed the gesture with a distrusting glower at me. One man gave me a wink, though, when he knew his friend wasn't looking, and a large-set woman with a black eye gave me an encouraging smile.

The buildings became sparser on the other side of the town, the cobbled path ahead leading into a forest that looked significantly less twisted and dangerous than the one that surrounded the palace. A noise came from a narrow alley between a closed bakery and a row of houses. I turned, peering into the darkness.

"Leave me alone! My husband will be back from the raids any day, and he'll tear you limb from limb," a woman was saying, her shrill wobble belying her bold words.

I turned Idunn toward the alley.

"Your husband's not here now though, is he? And he'll be none the wiser when he gets home, if you know what's good for you." The man's voice was gruff and slurred.

A ringing slap sounded, and I entered the alley in time to see a tiny, curvy woman land her palm against the ruddy cheek of a large, bearded man with his trousers open. He shook his head, and then faster than I would have thought he could move, gripped her by the throat and slammed her against the bakery wall.

"Put her down!"

They both turned to me, the woman's face turning red as he pressed his large hands to her neck.

"Mind your own," the man snarled. The woman's eyes widened as she took me in.

"I said put her down." I pulled my staff from its sheath on my belt.

The man laughed, dropping the woman and turning to me. She clutched at her throat, leaning against the wall. "You may be on a horse, but you're no fae," he said, eyes roving over my hair. He wagged his finger. "You're a freak, is what you are."

"I'm not fae," I agreed. The woman had dropped to a crouch and was sidling along the wall, out of the alley. I wondered briefly where Mazrith was, but the man spoke again, drawing my attention back to him.

"Why don't you get down off that horse and we can talk about this. And by talk, I mean I can remove that expensive-looking mare you obviously stole, and teach you a lesson about interrupting me."

For a second, my stupid behind actually considered his words. I wanted to take him on, wanted to practice what Frima had taught me. But sense kicked in. The woman was away, hopefully to safety. I didn't need to spend a second longer in this vile man's company.

"She said no," I said. "Leave her the fuck alone."

He looked to where the woman had been standing,

letting out a snarl when he realized she had gone. I turned Idunn in the tight space, but then the horse neighed loudly, rearing and almost throwing me from the saddle. I clung on with my hands and knees, turning my head to see the man laughing as he yanked on Idunn's tail.

As her hooves met the ground again, I let out an unexpected roar of anger, letting go with one hand and using it to smash my staff into the man's face. He howled when it connected, dropping to the ground. I brought it around again as Idunn spun, this time across the back of his head.

"Piece of shit freak," he spat through a nose streaming blood. "You'll pay for this."

I bared my teeth at him. Idunn reared again, and I knew she needed to be out of the narrow alley. "Go, girl, do what you need to do." She shot toward the main street, almost unseating me again, but slowing as soon as she saw Mazrith and Jarl, calmly waiting on the main path.

"Whoa girl, there you go," I said soothingly rubbing her neck. "You did well." She pawed the ground but stayed still, throwing her head toward the alley every now and then. "Where were you? I could have done with some help back there," I said, looking at Mazrith as I kept stroking the back of Idunn's neck and replacing my staff with my other hand. My pulse was racing, but I stayed as calm as I could, for Idunn's sake.

"You needed no help."

Annoyingly, pride surged through me at his words. He was right. I had needed no help. "Oh. How do I calm Idunn? That *veslingr* pulled her tail."

"A gallop through the woods will help." He pointed at

the forest. "It's a clear path, until you reach a large stream. You can't get lost. Let her run as fast as she likes."

I nodded, then leaned my head low to the horse's pricked ear. "Okay, Idunn. You did great. You've earned some fun. Let's go."

# 32

## REYNA

Blasting through the woods on Idunn whilst not having to worry about the forest around us was even more fun than the first gallop. The more I felt her power and speed, the more I believed I wanted to ride forever – that maybe the fates had *meant* for me to learn to ride.

When the stream came into view, I slowed her, relieved that her restlessness seemed to have abated. My backside was aching though, and I turned to Mazrith to ask if we could dismount for a break. He was nowhere to be seen.

Panic started to bubble through me, and I spun Idunn on a circle, looking for him. Had I gotten off course?

I couldn't see how. I had followed the wide, well-worn path straight to the stream, as he had told me. I looked up at the canopy of trees the starlight was trickling through.

"Voror?" I whispered.

"You appear to like horses," the owl said, a note of

disdain in his voice. My shoulders sagged in relief at not being alone in the forest.

"Do you know where Mazrith is?"

"Not far." Almost as he replied, I heard hooves. A few moments later, Mazrith emerged from the trees into the clearing by the stream.

"Couldn't keep up?" I said, cocking my head.

He gave me a look, then vaulted easily off Jarl's back. "Your body must need a rest," he said, and magicked the step from his staff.

I eased myself gingerly off Idunn's back then walked around a bit, stretching and bending, trying to work out the stiffness. "I'm going to need a whole lot of mead," I muttered.

"Good thing I have plenty," Mazrith replied. "We are here to learn to jump." His shadows leaped from his staff, disappearing into the trees, then returning wrapped around a large log. They deposited it in the middle of the clearing, before returning to his staff.

"Your power seems fully returned," I said.

"Indeed. Now, the commands for jumping are similar, but not the same, as those we have already learned. Instinct plays a part, but so does trusting the horse."

I listened as he told me what to do with the reins and how to bend my knees when the horse took off and landed, and which commands to use. My backside and aching thighs protested when I mounted Idunn again, but I was keen to learn. There was no way the course I would be racing tomorrow would be a simple sprint, I was sure.

The first time we approached the log, I reacted too late.

Idunn skidded to a halt just before the obstacle, and everything moved in unearthly slow motion as I tipped forward in the saddle, then sideways.

I knew I was going to fall before I actually did, and threw my arm over my head, screwing my face up and bracing myself.

I let out a gasp when I hit a cushion of something freezing and soft.

Mazrith's shadows had caught me. They flurried around me, so cold my bare forearms stung, righting me on my feet again. My limbs shook a little as I turned to the Prince.

"Good," he said.

"What?"

"Good. You protected your head. You would probably have just broken a few bones. Now, try again, and tell her to jump earlier."

I gaped at him. "Just broken a few bones?"

"Try again."

Both annoyed at his cavalier attitude to the wholeness of my bones, and enormously grateful that he had caught me, I stamped on the shadow step to get back on the horse.

This time, I asked her to jump too early. She knew she wasn't going to clear the log, only half jumping and landing awkwardly. Concern for the horse flooded me and I was halfway off before Mazrith assured me she was fine.

The third time, we got it right. Idunn soared over the log, and my knees jarred as we landed on the other side. I turned in triumph to Mazrith, who gestured at the log.

"Again. Bend your knees more on the landing."

We did it again, and again, and as I improved Mazrith

used his shadows to raise the log off the ground, the jumps getting higher and higher. Idunn's leaps were so graceful, the sense of flying through the air filled me with awe, every single time.

"It is late. We must return to the palace and get rest before tomorrow." The Prince eyed me as I rounded the log, and I knew my face must have been flushed. "You have done well today."

"Will I be riding Idunn in the *Leikmot*?"

He gave me a look. "Of course. You have not spent all these hours bonding with her, just to start again tomorrow."

"I will need to thank Frima."

"Yes. You will."

We rode gently back through the forest, and I enjoyed the sway and gait of the canter.

When we reached the town, we passed a crowd of people moving toward the alehouse, all talking animatedly.

"I can't move him, I've tried. He just won't get up," a man said, shaking his head as a woman was saying to another,

"Not a word of sense from him. Not one. Just muttering about snakes."

"Well, I'm not sorry," the woman replied, her arms folded over her chest. "You know, it was about time somebody hit him hard enough to make that nasty brain of his snap."

A cold feeling swept through me, and I forced it away. Lots of people got hit hard all the time in *Yggdrasil*.

We rounded the next bend and saw a figure sitting

cross-legged by the side of the cobbled path. My heart skipped a beat as we got closer to the man I had hit in the alley. He had a stick in his hand, and he was drawing something in the dirt, scrubbing it out, then drawing it again.

We drew closer.

*Snakes.*

He was drawing snakes.

"Lovely, lovely snakes, slither, slither, slither," he muttered happily, drawing three long snakes, then enthusiastically scratching them away with his stick and starting again.

"Hey," I called as we reached him, drawing Idunn to a halt. Mazrith didn't stop.

The man blinked up at me. Drool was coming from the corner of his mouth, and dried blood crusted around his nose. There wasn't even a hint of recognition in his eyes.

"Snakes," he smiled. "Lovely, lovely snakes."

# 33

## REYNA

We rode the rest of the way through the town in silence, my heart pounding in my chest. Every sideways glance I gave Mazrith was met with no response, the Prince staring resolutely ahead.

I hadn't hit the man hard enough to do that to him. When I left the alley, he was coherent, yelling threats.

But Mazrith... He had to catch me up when I rode through the woods to the stream.

When we reached the first gnarled, horrible trees, the Prince finally looked at me. "Are you ready? Ride fast. Do not lose me or go ahead."

I nodded tersely, trying to concentrate.

"Yaa!" He shouted, and Jarl took off. I mimicked him, relishing the feel of Idunn power to life under me. For the time it took to gallop through the haunted forest, I was blessedly relieved of the confusion wracking me.

The stable doors came into view, and the horses slowed

COURT OF GREED AND GOLD

to a canter, kicking up dirt and dust as we skidded to a stop inside. Mazrith dismounted Jarl as I panted for breath, shadows flying from his staff and slamming the stable doors shut behind us.

They flowed toward me, the step to help me down materializing.

Glaring at it, I deliberately slid off Idunn's back on the other side.

Prince Mazrith's expression hardened as I stalked around the horse toward him.

"What did you do to that man?"

Mazrith's eyes flashed bright before shadows swept across them. "I ensured that he will attack no more women."

I stopped half a foot from him, staring up at his defiant chin. "Curse your height!" I snapped, my fists clenching. "You said I had it covered!"

"You did."

"Then why did you go back?"

"This is my Court. *My* people. Slaithwaite is *my* town," he snarled, tipping his face down so I could see straight into his fierce eyes. "It is my job to protect the people of that town from predators."

"By destroying their minds?"

Anger was etched into his features now, his jaw tight and his huge shoulders tense. "You believe he deserved any better? Do you know what was in his head when he was in that alleyway with that woman?"

My resolve faltered. I may not have seen inside the man's head, but I could sure as Odin guess what he had been thinking.

*And you can hardly be too judgmental about getting inside people's heads now, can you?*

I unclenched my fists.

I hadn't seen into the faes' minds on purpose during the *Leikmot*.

Mazrith had just reduced a man to a dribbling mess deliberately. "Criminals should get a fair trial," I said, but I could her the loss of conviction in my own tone.

"He had one. It was swift and conclusive. This is my Court. My justice."

"Is that how you'll keep the peace if you become King?"

"*When* I become King, yes."

"Fear is crippling, not empowering."

Something truly dark crossed his irises, darker than the swirling shadows. It was solid and black, and for a moment he had the soulless eyes of a reptile. "You do not need to tell me that."

I forced myself not to flinch. There was darkness in him, I already knew that. But there was also honesty. Integrity. And in my gut, I knew he was no danger to me. At least not until his curse was lifted.

The blackness in his eyes melted away. "His clan do not know that he was punished. I am not using fear to control them or their behavior. I am simply meting out punishment for dishonor."

"One fae should not wield that much power over their people. Why not have him brought before the Court?"

Mazrith gave a dry laugh. "And introduce him to my stepmother? He would probably be her type." He reached out, and this time I did startle, stepping back. He caught my chin though, holding me still.

My pulse raced instantly, both with fear and something else. Something deeper.

"*Gildi*, this Court is beyond fucked. You must see that. The Queen is deranged. She has killed nearly all of our rune-marked, she rewards debauchery and murder, and practices rituals other Courts would deem worthy of the god's punishment. I will not let you lecture me on how I counter her wrongs."

A single gold rune floated from his thumb, right before my face. His eyes flicked from mine to the rune, and then back.

"You will be the death of me, *gildi*."

I didn't know what he meant, and abruptly, I didn't care. Fire was surging through me from where his skin met mine, and the desire to fight it was ebbing so fast that panic was starting to creep in.

I didn't want to want him. I didn't want to trust him.

*But I did.*

He stepped into me, closing the short distance. "The death of me," he whispered, the shadows in his eyes gone, bright grey light replacing them. The faint scars on his face were visible this close, the warrior under the fae fiercely and wholly present. He bent his head, his breath whispering across my cheek as I forced myself to look away, turning my head and closing my eyes.

He wasn't using magic. I knew he wasn't. It was him. The real him was compelling me to turn, to catch his lips with mine.

*Don't do it, Reyna. He took you, and claimed you as his own. He's just like every other accursed fae in Yggdrasil.*

Except, he wasn't. He wasn't the monster he portrayed.

I felt the lightest touch along my jaw, then the press of his lips to my neck, just under my ear.

The fire in my body turned to molten liquid, a moan escaping my lips as my skin burst to life with sensation everywhere.

His lips moved against my skin, kissing and tasting as if I were a delicacy to be savored. His hands clenched in my hair, and I gasped as he turned my face to his.

His beautiful grey eyes pierced through me, burning away every logical thought in my head. With a growled breath, he tilted his head down and captured my mouth with his own.

The kiss was exquisite. Gentle and intense at once, our tongues danced together in a wild, yet melodic, harmony. With every movement of our mouths, every slide of his tongue against mine, the fear and doubt I felt faded away. All I could think about was him and the way he made me feel. Every fiber of my being felt alive, a fiery charge flowing through every nerve ending as all of the desire I'd desperately been trying to deny came bubbling to the surface.

"Maz?"

As though struck by lightning, we leaped apart. I panted for breath, my limbs shaking as I tried to recover a single sensible thought.

Svangrior came stamping into sight a beat later, Ellisar by his side.

I whirled toward the basket that had been left full of

bottles, trying to look busy, as heat continued to course through me. My desire was so strong it was making me dizzy, my movements clumsy as I picked up a random bottle in a vain effort to look like I hadn't just been kissing the Prince of the Shadow Court.

Ellisar frowned at me when the warriors reached us. "Why is your face so red?"

"We rode hard through the forest." Mazrith said before I could answer. "What is it?"

"We've had a report of Starved One sightings in two of the lower villages."

The fire in my veins cooled instantly. Memories of the Elder and her song washed through my head, and I forced them out with an effort.

Mazrith swore viciously. "Have they attacked anyone?"

"Not that we know of."

"We will convene in the war room. Gather all the information you have."

# 34

## REYNA

e all made our way back up to the Prince's rooms in silence, Ellisar swinging the basket of bottles on his arm as we went.

My legs were still unsteady from what was without a doubt the stupidest thing I had done since the Prince of Snakes had burst into my workshop and kidnapped me.

*What in the name of Odin's arse were you thinking, Reyna? Fucking heimskr!*

My silent mental reprimands were quickly drowned out by the torrent of need swamping my entire body — in a way I hadn't even known was possible.

I didn't have a lot of experience kissing to call on, but I knew enough to know that level of intensity, that level of physical reaction from my body, was not normal.

It had been a seriously long, seriously stressful day.

Not only did I have a healthy amount of adrenaline

COURT OF GREED AND GOLD

flowing through me from the exhilaration of the horse riding, but I had successfully refused to think about the fact that I saw into two faes' heads that morning.

This was definitely a case of confused emotions.

My desire for the Prince, and my fucking shocking loss of willpower, were a direct result of a very difficult day.

*Nothing more.*

I fisted and relaxed my hands repeatedly as we walked through the gloomy palace corridors, trying to work out some of my restlessness and failing. When we finally stepped inside the fire-lit Serpent Suites, the three males strode straight toward the war room. Mazrith paused before entering and turned to me.

My cheeks flamed instantly.

"I advise you rest. The race will be taxing and you will need your energy."

I nodded, searching his eyes, though I didn't know what for. Desire that matched my own? Shame?

Shadows and light flickered across his irises, as always, but he turned away before I could decipher anything. I watched him march into the war room and push the door closed behind him.

"Oh, sorry, my lady!" Brynja backed into me, pulling a cart covered in bottles and food. "I didn't see you there. I'm to take this to the fae," she whispered.

I reached out, picking up a small bunch of grapes. "I'm sure they won't miss these," I said with a forced smile. "Or this." I scooped up a small block of rich, red cheese.

Her eyes widened, but then she smiled too. "It's the

drinks I would be going for my Lady. One bottle of some of these wines is worth as much as my father's hut."

"Is there any fae wine here?" I asked before I could stop myself, the vivid memory of the wine-induced dream that I'd been trying to keep out of my head coming at me in a rush.

She raised her eyebrows, then shook her head. "No, my Lady, that's usually kept for different kind of meetings than the one I believe they are having."

"Oh, never mind. I was just curious," I said quickly.

When Brynja spoke again, her voice was low, almost a whisper. "As you're curious, the Prince usually keeps his drinks cabinet well stocked." She looked pointedly over at the huge cabinet on the other side of the fireplace, where I had seen him get mead a number of times.

"Is that right?"

"Yes, my Lady. And in case you were still curious, fae wine always has metal lacework around the neck of the bottle."

"Well, thank you for sating my curiosity," I whispered back.

She nodded, then continued maneuvering the cart toward the war room.

I looked back at the cabinet, desire pooling inside me. The thought of downing a glass of the fae-wine and falling into a dream filled with everything I wanted but shouldn't had me halfway across the room.

*Reyna, don't be so fucking stupid!*

The angry voice of reason in my head made my steps slow, then stop.

COURT OF GREED AND GOLD

I needed to go to bed. Rest. Sleep. Prepare for the race. Not indulge in fantasies about a man who fucking took me captive.

Shaking my head angrily, I turned on my heel and marched to the bedroom.


Almost as soon as I entered the room, Voror melted through the wall, perching on the bedpost.

"Hello!" Relief at the distraction from the flood of need made my voice overly enthusiastic.

The owl blinked suspiciously at me. "You smell like horse."

"Right," I said, taking off my staff-belt.

"And... lust."

I froze, staring at him. "You can smell lust?"

"Of sorts. Inform me of what I have missed."

"You saw the *Leikmot* game, yes?"

"Yes."

"And you saw the riding lesson?"

"Yes."

"Then there's nothing you don't know," I said, turning away from him under the pretense of untying my boots.

"This is not true."

"Look, it was one kiss!" I snapped, turning back to him.

He blinked at me slowly. "I was referring to how you dodged a rock with your eyes closed. But if you would rather talk about the kiss, we can. I have little to offer, though, your amorous practices are utterly baffling to me."

My cheeks heated as I turned back to my boots.

I had already accepted that I would have to talk to someone about the visions, and that I would not be discussing them with Mazrith. Voror was really my only option.

"Something, erm, happened."

"Yes, I saw. From what I understand the meeting of mouths moves onto to a practice that involves an unpleasant amount of bodily fluid and peculiar moaning-"

I waved my hands at him. "I mean the *Leikmot*! The rock dodging."

"Oh. Good." He ruffled his feathers, as though trying to dislodge something unpleasant. "Continue."

I told him about the visions from inside the two fae's heads.

"Has anything like this happened to you before?"

I took a deep breath, trying to decide how much to tell him. "Not from inside someone else's head, no."

The owl shifted his weight from talon to talon. "Very interesting."

"Do you know why it's happening?"

"No. I have no idea."

I let out a long sigh. "Curses. I had hoped you might be able to help."

"Well, you are human, yes?"

"Yes."

"So, you have no power to see inside people's heads yourself. Somebody must be doing it for you. Many fae can project images, and shadow-fae can do far more mind magic than the others."

It made sense that someone might have been trying to

help me from the sidelines that morning. But the visions of the Starved Ones, and of Mazrith's mother... Nobody was there then, and they had happened my whole life. Did that mean the two kinds of vision weren't connected?

"Are there people here who might try to help you?" Voror said when I didn't speak.

"I guess. Mazrith, or Frima, maybe?"

"And just to confirm, the visions today definitely helped you?"

"Definitely."

The owl clicked his beak. "Then embrace them, and do not worry about the source. If someone is helping you, then they will make themselves and their reasons apparent soon enough. Please remove the horse smell before I speak with you next." He took off, soaring up to the rafters.

"Wait, I—" But he was gone.

I blew out a sigh, and stared at my boots.

He was right. It seemed obvious now that somebody was helping me. And, given that I had already decided to accept any help I could get, this was no different.

I pulled off my boots in turn, a slight twinge from my injured foot easy to ignore.

Was Mazrith helping me?

No matter what Lhoris said, more and more I struggled to see him as my enemy. To see him as the monster the five Courts believed him to be.

Did monsters kiss like that?

Heat swooped through me at the memory, causing an almost painful pulse of need between my legs. Somehow I was on my feet again.

"Fuck," I swore.

My body was a mess. I was far, far too restless to sleep. The slightest break in concentration, and my mind was on him, naked and hard and dangerously close to losing control.

With a snarl, I moved to the bedroom door.

There was no way I was going to spend the entire night in this turmoil. As far as I could see I had two choices.

First, I could go and knock on Mazrith's door. And what would I do then? Demand he take that exquisite fucking kiss where I was so desperate for him to take it? To lift me from my feet, carry me to his bed, and devour me like the feast he claimed I was?

A soft moan escaped me on a heavy breath, and I gripped the door handle.

I could not go to Mazrith.

I couldn't.

So, that left the second option. The fae wine.

Opening the door a crack, I peeked out. There was nobody there.

Living out my need inside my head with him definitely didn't count as actually submitting to him, did it? The memory of the last dream, and the tangible satisfaction it provided me made my chest heave. It wasn't real. It was just a fantasy. A harmless, if vivid, release of whatever my stupid fucking head had got me fixated on.

"It's just a dream," I whispered, then tiptoed over to the drinks cabinet. As quietly as I could, I opened the cupboard door and scanned the bottles until I found one with metal lattice-work around the neck. It was a tall, thin bottle, dusty with age. I removed the glass stopper and tipped some of the liquid in a glass from the counter, before putting the bottle back.

My stolen wine in hand, I ran as quietly and quickly as I could back to my room.

# 35

## MAZRITH

I watched from the doorway of the hall as Reyna filled the glass with fae wine, then disappeared back to her room.

My cock stiffened, and I gritted my teeth.

The kiss had affected her as much as it had me, then.

I was a fucking fool. An Odin-cursed fucking heimskr.

Why had I kissed her?

I could ask all I liked, but the fact was a hundred god-spelled steeds would not have kept my lips from hers.

This was unbearable. Intolerable. Dangerous.

I took a step out of the hallway, toward her room.

I knew what would happen if I knocked on that door now. She had wanted it as much as I had. And now she was stealing my fae wine. Stealing a night lost to fantasy.

So, so, much safer than reality.

I turned to the drinks cabinet. Before I could talk myself

out of it, I poured myself a glass from the bottle she had selected.

I couldn't touch her. Couldn't kiss her. But we could both dream.

My shadows swirled around my hand, around the bottle, and I stared, my conscience warring with my desire.

I closed my eyes, submitting to my aching desire. The shadows rushed the glass, and I downed the contents.

Moving fast, I made my way to my own room.

I had precious few moments before she fell asleep, and the mind-magic would not work if I were not asleep too.

She was inside the tree in *Yggdrasil* again. This time though, she was not laid out on the stone table naked, but standing by the trunk of a beech tree in the black dress she had worn to the ball.

Her eyes widened when she saw me, and I glanced down.

I was wearing nothing, my aching cock hard and ready.

"*Gildi.*"

"This is a dream," she said in a rush, then bit down on her lower lip hard. Her eyes flicked between my cock and my face, and I let a smile take my lips.

"This is a dream," I repeated.

I moved toward her, and she backed up, her perfect backside hitting the trunk of the tree, Dappled light filtered through the leaves above us, playing over her beautiful face, her green eyes glowing.

"Are you going to let me touch you this time?"

She shook her head. "No."

"Are you sure?" I reached her and ran one finger up my length. She stared, transfixed. "Perhaps a kiss?"

I could see the lust spark in her eyes, and her tongue darted out, wetting her lips. "You said before that I would beg. I won't," she said.

"I worry that one day you will make *me* beg, *gildi*" I said, closing my hand around myself. She drew in a sharp breath. "So much fire," I breathed, moving my hand slowly up, then down. Watching her try to keep her eyes on my face instead of my cock made me throb harder.

"You would beg to kiss me?" she breathed, her eyes closing just for a moment.

"Oh, Reyna. I would beg you to fuck me. I would beg to have you on your knees for me."

She moaned softly, and one of her hands moved to her thigh, lifting her skirt, watching my hand on my cock.

She was wearing nothing under her dress, and a growl escaped me as her hand closed over herself, pressing into the soft flesh.

The sight of her touching herself was almost more than I could bear. I gripped myself so hard my knuckles turned white, and shadows rushed around me, dancing over her thighs and making her gasp. Her eyes flew to my face.

"Kiss me," she whispered, her hand moving more tightly over herself.

With a single thought, my shadows wound around her wrist. She cried out as they pulled her hand away, lifting both her arms above her head and pinning them to the tree bark.

Wild desire had me wanting to rip her dress from her, but her wide eyes and heaving chest slowed me. I stepped into her, pressing my hardness against her hip, brushing my lips over her hot cheek.

"Always," I breathed, dipping my head lower, finding her soft lips with mine. She met me with a ferocity that made me moan into her mouth, her tongue finding mine and her taste exploding through me, intoxicating. She ground her hips against me, and I moved my lips from hers, burying my face in her neck as I pulled the front of her dress open.

"So beautiful," I murmured as I took her in.

She pressed against me, her nipples hard points against my chest.

My lips fastened over her throat and her head tipped back, the move exposing more flesh to my mouth and hands.

She moaned and thrust her hips harder against me, and I wrapped my hand around her thigh, urging her forward. My hand found her heat and I groaned. She was wet, so fucking wet.

"Beg me to fuck you, Reyna." I moved back to look into her flushed, beautiful face, stilling my fingers. Her eyes flew to mine, but she didn't respond. "Beg me. Beg me to fuck you," I whispered. "And I will."

She stared at me, breathing hard.

Every part of me wanted to feel her from the inside, to

bury my fingers inside her wetness, to make her scream my name as I fulfilled the desire flowing from her.

But something stopped me.

And Odin help me, I knew what.

When I took this woman, when I finally entered her body, claimed her as my own, it would be no fucking dream.

I closed my lips over hers again before she could say a word, thrusting my tongue hard into her mouth, dominating it with my own. She moaned again, louder, and I moved my hand to her breasts. Pinching her nipple, I sent my shadows to her thighs. I felt her arch her back, pressing herself harder into me as they found their mark.

She whimpered as I pulled back, and my cock throbbed so hard it hurt. Keeping one hand teasing at her hard nipple, I moved my other back to myself, pumping hard as my shadows darted in and out of her slick sex. She ground herself against my thigh as they worked, leaving my skin wet with her desire. I leaned back, far enough to watch her body tense, back arching even further off the tree, her fingers outstretched, and her lip caught between her teeth.

Her eyes fixed on mine.

"Come for me, *gildi*."

With a long, gasping moan, I watched as she came, her body spasming and shaking, covering my thigh in her wetness. My hand sped up, the sight of her lost to pleasure a delicious torture. I was so close, unable to keep control much longer.

"Maz," she gasped, dazed eyes focusing on me as my shadows released her. Her hands dropped, tangling into my hair, and she pressed her mouth to mine, pulling me into her fiercely.

Her taste tipped me over the edge. Her body pulsed against mine with the remnants of her orgasm, her tongue exploring my mouth as though she had never tasted passion before.

I exploded, thrusting helplessly against her body as pleasure ripped through me. I groaned into her mouth as I gripped her tighter, then stilling, shaking, as the last of my release tore through me.

She pulled back, staring into my eyes.

"Are you ready to beg?" I panted, brushing my thumb across her swollen lips.

"Never," she whispered back.

# 36

## REYNA

I gasped as I awoke, rolling onto my back and blinking furiously at the ceiling.

A dream! It had been a dream. Just a dream.

I took a series of deep breaths, trying to make the room come into focus, instead of Mazrith's taut, naked body, pressed against mine.

My core pounded with need, and I let out a growl of frustration as I rolled back over, burying my face in my pillows.

What the fuck had I been thinking? How I the name of Freya was that supposed to have helped?

A soft knock at the door had me leaping from my sheets.

Could it be Mazrith? Need powered through me, and I sent a prayer to the gods that it was Mazrith.

Kara blinked at me as I threw the door open.

"Oh! I didn't mean to catch you while you were, erm, not dressed, but I need to talk to you." I looked down at myself, it belatedly occurring to me that I was only wearing a thin nightshirt.

I forced a neutral expression onto my face. "What's wrong? What time is it?"

"Dawn, and I think I've solved the riddle."

I froze, my brain finally moving away from hard male body parts, and back to reality. "Really?"

"Uhuh. It took me while to realize, and to be honest with you, there's a still a lot of it I don't understand, but I'm pretty sure I've made a breakthrough this morning."

"I'll get Mazrith."

"Maybe you should put some clothes on first? It's waited this long, I'm sure a few more minutes won't hurt."

I glanced down at myself, my face flushing. I knew what was going on under the nightshirt. "Erm, yeah. Good idea."

I took my time to wash and dress, trying to calm my raging body.

*You chose the wine, Reyna. You knew you would have to deal with the consequences.* I hadn't realized quite how intense those consequences might be, but they were better than actually going to his rooms last night.

I was a grown woman, I could deal with a vivid fantasy.

When I left my room, Mazrith was standing in the sitting room, talking quietly with Frima.

I swallowed when I saw him, noticing his powerful arms under his shirt, the way his hair fell in front of his delicately pointed ears, the tight curve of his backside in the black leather.

His head turned, and his eyes locked on mine, firing with what I was sure was desire. My face flamed.

"Kara wants to speak with us, alone," I said quickly.

"Both of you in the war room, now," he answered. "Frima, make sure we are left alone."

"Look," Kara said when we were all together at the huge table. She smoothed the paper out flat and ran her finger down the rows of text.

*While he is more than ten feet tall,*
*Even in death he shall never fall.*
*Aided by golden touch and darkest night,*
*Prize from the steel his greatest delight.*
*Only this may be used here to repair,*
*Nobles and royals with secrets to share.*

"You see?"

I shook my head but heard Mazrith hiss out a breath from where he was standing behind the chair I was sitting in. "The first letters."

"Yes! They spell the word 'weapon'." She looked up at the Prince, swallowing. "Do you know of any massive weapon statues?" I turned to look at him too, excitement thrumming through me, until I saw the expression on his face. It wasn't exactly anger, but it sure wasn't elation.

"There is one. A fallen axeman who was deemed a berserker in life."

Not wanting to sound stupid, but also not wanting to miss anything, I coughed. "A berserker is a warrior, right?"

"The definition varies in each Court," Kara nodded.

"Here in the Shadow Court, you must kill a hundred enemies before earning the honor," Mazrith said quietly.

"And you built a statue for him?"

"No." He let out a long sigh.

When he said nothing else, I turned back to Kara. "Anything else?"

"No, not really. This suggests you need to get something from the statue, then I suppose you have to repair a noble or royal." She shrugged. "But I don't know what you have to get, or who you have to repair."

*I do. A piece of jade and the shadow-fae statue.*

"We know those parts," I told her.

She looked at me, eyes bright with curiosity. "I wish I could come with you," she said.

"Out of the question," Mazrith snapped. "It is not a place I wish to visit at all, let alone with others. Kara, you must tell nobody of this, you understand? You are in danger yourself by even being aware of it."

Guilt flooded me. I had suggested involving her. "Can you give her one of these headbands?"

He glanced at my hair, then his staff. "No. They are... complicated."

"But you made me one."

He let out a small growl. "I can only sustain one at a time."

"Oh." I moved my hands to my head. "She can have mine then."

Mazrith's hand came down sharply on the back of the chair. "Do not be foolish. The Queen is far more likely to try to interrogate you than Kara."

"He's right, Reyna, I won't accept it from you," Kara said.

"I will remove it from her memory," Mazrith said.

Kara looked at him, and I leaped to my feet. "No. Absolutely not."

He glared at me. "It will not harm her."

"I don't care."

"You would rather the Queen looked inside her head for information? Do you know what that entails?"

"The Queen doesn't know that she knows anything, and besides, she's under the protection of your warriors!"

"Erm, do I get a say in this?" Kara's voice squeaked from behind me.

I turned. "Of course, but-"

She cut me off, standing to grip my shoulder, then stepping to the side to look at the Prince. "I don't want to know. Remove it."

"Kara!"

"Reyna, it's the safest thing to do. I don't want to endanger your life, and if it truly won't hurt me, then what is the harm?"

I gaped at her wide, innocent eyes. "You would let him inside your head?"

"Why wouldn't I? It makes sense."

"It's... wrong."

She shrugged. "This isn't wrong, it's helping me. I don't need to know about this riddle anymore if you aren't taking me with you, and I don't want to be of any use to that

COURT OF GREED AND GOLD

hideous Queen." She shuddered, then looked at Mazrith. "Do it, please, but..." She faltered. "You're sure you won't get rid of anything else? Or change anything?"

"You have my word," Mazrith said, not looking at her, but at me.

Kara nodded.

A helpless feeling numbed me as I watched his shadows gently swoosh from his staff and whirl around Kara's head. She showed no sign of pain, no sign that anything was happening at all.

*How could she let him inside her head?* The logic was undeniable - enough that I could not object. But I couldn't make it sit right in my own mind at all.

The shadows swooped back, leaving Kara. I gripped her wrists. "You okay?"

She smiled at me. "Yes. I know I helped you with a tricky puzzle, and that you've just removed it from my memory to keep me safe. And that you are worried about me," she said softly. "You don't need to worry. I'm fine."

"You'd better be," I growled, looking back over my shoulder at Mazrith.

"I am. Promise."

I rounded on Mazrith as soon as Kara left the war room. "Why didn't you remove the memory of the riddle altogether? Why let her remember that she helped you at all?"

He looked taken aback. "I was preparing for a temper tantrum about me entering her mind," he said drily. "Not the details of what I did in there."

"Answer the question."

"If my stepmother ever has cause to question her, Kara will be able to tell her immediately that I removed anything that she might want to know."

"But if you had removed all memory of it the Queen would get no clues at all."

"Yes."

"You chose to ensure that the Queen will abandon her questioning sooner," I said slowly.

His eyes flared brightly. I took a step closer to him. "The Queen's methods are unpleasant."

Emotion was rushing through me, a torrent of unspoken, unspent confusion tightening into a force I couldn't control. "You chose to lessen harm to my friend over keeping your secrets?"

"Stop." His word carried force, and I realized with a start that I was less than a foot from him. His body was tense, and shadows swirled around his staff. "I thought you were going to yell at me for using my magic on your friend's mind," he said, voice strained.

"You want me to yell at you?"

For a second, I thought he might say yes. "We must make for the berserker statue. Now."

"But-"

"No. We have precious few hours before the race, and we must use them." He swept from the room before I could speak.

I stared at the door he had banged closed behind him, trying to force my raging emotions under some sort of control.

The confusion, adrenaline, and that accursed kiss... It had all combined to make my brain a useless pile of mush. And mush would get me killed. I had to focus.

I forced every thought I didn't want to confront to the back of my head and followed the Prince.

We had a clue from the riddle, and that was what I needed to concentrate on.

## 37

## REYNA

"Why is everything in your Odin-cursed Court underground?" I grumbled as I followed the Prince through a narrow chamber carved out of the rock.

"It is not. But everything she is unaware of is."

"'She' being the Queen?"

He grunted what I assumed was a yes. "She married into my family and was never shown all of the Court's secrets."

My lessons with Kara had not extended to family trees or Court royalty beyond the gold-fae, so I didn't know the setup in the Shadow Court. "Your mother was descended from royalty then?"

"Yes."

"And she showed you the Court's secrets?"

He didn't reply. Unwilling to stay silent long enough for my brain to start trying to process any of the barrage of emotion I was trying to ignore, I kept talking. "I know your stepmother is the sister of the gold-fae Queen." There was still no reply, so I tried something different. "This statue. Is it far?"

"Yes and no." I rolled my eyes. "Much like the sanctuary, very few know of it."

"Why did you say you don't want to go there? Is it dangerous?"

"No. It holds... memories I do not wish to revisit."

"Oh. What is that?" We had emerged into a cave with a high ceiling, hundreds of stalactites hanging down and looking lethal, the ground ended abruptly a few feet in front of us, and in the middle of the narrow ledge was a cube that looked as though it had been hewn from the mountain itself. Shadows crawled all over the top of it, making the stone look like it was alive.

The Prince looked over his shoulder at me, tightened his furs, and headed for the cube. He held his staff up and his shadows rushed out to meet the others, mingling energetically, then descended over the whole rockface. When they reached the bottom, there was an opening in the front of the cube that hadn't been there before. Mazrith stepped inside and turned to me. "Come."

I frowned but followed. "What happens inside the cube?"

"It will take us where we need to go."

I reached the opening, the shadows now spinning around the bottom of the cube. "Will it seal us in?"

"Yes."

My footsteps faltered.

"You are scared of small spaces?"

"No, it can be the largest space in world, but if I can't get out of it, then I'd rather not be in it," I said, eyeing the thing warily.

"A fear of being trapped makes sense for someone enslaved," he muttered.

I threw him a glare. "Thanks for the validation." With an effort, I made myself step into the cube with him. As soon as I did, the opening sealed.

Before I could even mention how much worse being trapped in the dark was, the box began to move. Straight down.

We dropped so fast my stomach lurched, my breath catching before I could shriek, a strangled gurgle emerging instead.

As quickly as it had started, the cube shuddered to a halt, tipping me sideways into the wall. The opening appeared again, and I panted, looking at Mazrith in the growing light. "You could have warned me!"

"I was too distracted by your sarcasm," he said, then stepped out of the cube. "Besides, you do the opposite of what I tell you anyway."

I climbed out after him, my limbs shaking slightly from the shock of the drop.

I followed Mazrith off the new ledge we had arrived on and into another passageway in the rock. Just moments later, we entered another cave, and even if it hadn't been for the enormous statue in the center of it, I would have known this place was ancient.

The statue of the axeman was on an island in the middle of a crystal clear, totally still pool. Almost twenty feet tall, the warrior was on one knee, armored head bowed, clutching the largest axe I had ever seen. The blades resting on the ground were as large as the statue's shins, and he held the huge handle high, up near his bent head.

"Wow," I breathed. "How long has this been here?"

He gave off the same feeling as the shrine, and the statues in *Yggdrasil*. A feeling of something well beyond my understanding - beyond human understanding.

"I do not know. A very long time," Mazrith said, moving to a small boat on the tiny shore of shingle we were standing on. The light in the cave was coming from the pool, sparkling with a clear cold blue shine as the boat moved through it. "We are deep within the mountain. Nobody has built here for an age."

"We're deep within the mountain? That fast?" *The cube*, I realized putting two and two together. "That's how you got to me so fast in the forest with the Starved Ones?"

He nodded and gestured for me to get into the boat.

"Then why couldn't we use the cube to get back up?" I slapped my forehead as I climbed in. "Because you need your shadows to make it work, and your staff was broken."

"Yes. The shadows that reside in the cube are as old as the mountain itself. They belong to nobody. They were..." he trailed off, an indecisive look crossing his features as the boat began to move. "They were introduced to my shadows when I was a child, and I was accepted."

"And the Queen doesn't know of it?"

"No. I don't believe her magic would be accepted, even if she did, but I am not willing to test that theory."

We reached the banks of the statue's little island, and I

scrambled out of the boat, staring up at the berserker. The outer tips of the blades of the huge axe gleamed in the light, as though they were made from real steel, the rest of him clearly stone. Runes were etched into the shining silver, though I recognized few.

"He's incredible. But why is he shown so reverent, instead of victorious?"

Mazrith came to a stop next to me, staring up at the warrior. "The runes tell a story," he said quietly. "They speak of a warrior, a human warrior, who did as he was bid by his fae masters. He destroyed many enemies at their command. When a rival's sword finally landed true and he took a knee before the gates of *Valhalla*, he discovered that the enemies he had slain were not necessarily deserving of his ire. The axe is the same size as him to remind us that the warrior should always be larger than the weapon, or we become just a weapon ourselves."

I gaped up at the top of the helmeted head. "Was he accepted into *Valhalla*?"

"Yes, but under penance. He will return with the largest axe the world has seen, should *Ragnarök* ever befall *Yggdrasil*."

I snapped my eyes to the Prince. "*Ragnarök*? As in, the end of the world? I thought that was a myth to scare children."

He shrugged and his furs fell open slightly. "Maybe. Maybe not. The gods spoke in metaphors. The darkest night of our people will come, but I do not believe it will be the 'end of the world'. Just the world as we know it."

I looked back at the statue, something whirring in my brain. "Say that again."

He paused, then said, "I do not believe *Ragnarök* will be the end of the world. It is just a metaphor for what will likely be the self-destruction of our people."

"No, before that. You said, 'darkest night'. That's what the riddle said!" He pulled the paper he had retrieved from Kara from his belt.

"While he is more than ten feet tall,

Even in death he shall never fall.

Aided by golden touch and darkest night,

Prize from the steel his greatest delight," he read quickly. He ran toward the statue and I ran after him.

The statue was on a wide plinth covered in smaller rocks and boulders, many covered with moss and tangled vines of ivy that snaked up the side of the colossal warrior. Mazrith moved close to the statue, climbing over the boulders and waving his arm as he scanned it.

"There!" His moving arm stopped, pointing to a rune at the top of the axe's blade, almost level with his head. "That rune says *Ragnarök*, but can also be translated as 'darkest night'."

Excitement surged through me. "So, what does golden touch mean?"

"I don't know. You're the gold expert."

I gave him a look, folding my arms. "I hate to tell you this, but if we needed to bring any gold down here with us, we're in trouble. Short of breaking some off the statue I just repaired, I don't know how we can get any."

He frowned, then his expression changed. "You."

"Me?"

"Yes, you. You have the golden touch. You work with gold. And the inscription said you were the key."

"I don't know what I can do," I said doubtfully.

"Come here, and touch the darkest night rune."

I climbed up onto the plinth with him, trying to continue my even breaths when I got within a few inches of his huge body.

"I can't reach," I said, lifting one arm above my head. The rune was a foot higher than me.

Mazrith gritted his teeth, wrapped his massive hands around my waist, and lifted me clear off my feet. I gave a cry of surprise, flailing my arms.

"Touch the rune," he growled. Energy was humming from where his fingers pressed against me, and his proximity to my—

"Now, Reyna!"

I reached up, pressing my palm flat to the rune he had pointed out.

A loud whooshing sound rang through the cavern, and Mazrith set me back on my feet hurriedly. For a second, we were face to face, then bright gold light burst from the rune I had just touched.

We both gaped as each of the runes lit up in turn, all along the length of the blade, then back up along the blade on the other side of the axe.

Mazrith began to climb down from the plinth, turning to stare up at the statue.

I did the same and saw that the whole blade of the axe was changing color, a honey-gold seeping across it.

"What's happening?"

"I don't know."

The statue seemed to absorb the gold, the glow spreading first up the axe, before it moved over the figure itself.

When the whole statue had changed color, there was a rumbling sound, and a deep voice rang out from the huge, armored head.

# 38

## REYNA

"ho wakes me from my slumber?"

I clutched at my chest in surprise, sucking in a breath. I had been expecting something to happen, but not something so loud.

"Prince Mazrith Andask of the Shadow Court, and Reyna Thorvald, rune-marked of the Gold Court," Mazrith called back.

There was a grinding sound, then a long hissing breath. "Prince Mazrith Andask. You used to come here as a child, did you not?"

Mazrith tensed. "Yes."

"You would stay here for days."

"I did not know you were aware of my presence."

"You treated my island with respect," the statue said eventually. "Why do you wake me?"

"We seek a piece of jade that belongs to another statue in the mountain."

COURT OF GREED AND GOLD

A huge rumble met the Prince's words. "My jade," the statue bellowed.

I glanced sideways at Mazrith, but his gaze was fixed on the berserker's helmet. "We have been told by ancient sources that the jade must be returned."

"I got it for... I got it for her." The warrior's voice was so broken.

"For who?" I asked.

"The love of my life. I would have followed her until the end of time. She needed me to be a weapon, and for her, that is what I became."

"Who was she?"

"A goddess amongst mortals. A fearless, beautiful creature I was never worthy of."

So, the Prince's story had not quite been right. The berserker had become what he was by following the orders of a woman he loved. *Or a fae he loved.*

"We are a fae and a human too," I said, following the suspicion. Mazrith shot me a confused glance but said nothing.

"Blasphemy. That is what she told me, when others were listening. Fae and humans could not live together."

"We are betrothed."

"What?" The huge voice was soft. "Has the world changed so?"

"Fae still rule, and humans are thralls—"

I didn't finish my sentence. "Fae still rule?"

"Yes. Of course." The berserker gave a big, booming laugh, so loud the water around us vibrated and rippled. "Why is that funny?"

"Honor. Valor. Pride."

I rubbed my hand over my face, trying to be patient. The statue had been asleep for centuries, it was hardly surprising he was a touch crazy.

"If you can wrest it from my axe, you may have the jade," he said suddenly.

We both snapped our faces to the axe. "Really?"

"Yes. Prove your *drengskapr*."

"Honor," Mazrith translated, though I already knew the word.

A rune shone bright gold on the axe, then a sheen of light pulsed out from the weapon.

"A shield," he growled quietly.

"A shield indeed," the statue boomed. "The jade is in the tip of the handle. Come and get it, mighty fae Prince."

We both craned our necks to look at the tilted tip of the handle, nearly twenty feet up.

"Do you think the shield is dangerous?" I asked Mazrith.

He didn't answer me, but shadows spilled forth from his staff, swirling up and up, until they were level with the top of the handle.

The second they made contact with the shield, though, they evaporated. Mazrith hissed a curse.

Shrugging out of his fur cloak, I saw that he was shirtless beneath it, leather straps cross-crossing his muscular body. He stowed his staff in the sheath on his belt and made his way back to the plinth.

As soon as his hands touched the axe, light sparked like fire. He hissed a louder curse, but hung on anyway. Jumping, he threw one hand higher up, gripping the massive handle and swinging himself to the side. With a long stretch, he closed his other hand around the top. He wrapped his legs around the handle, sparks searing everywhere he made contact with the weapon, and began to work at the top with his hands.

"Odin's raven," he spat, as a huge spark flew up and his trouser-leg burst into flame.

For a moment I thought he would keep trying, whilst on fire, but with one smooth movement he leaped down from the top of the axe, then moved past me to the pool. He waded in far enough to extinguish his trousers, and I winced at the sear marks all over his chest.

"Did you see the jade?" I asked.

"Yes. It is well set in the top. I will need some sort of tool to pry it out."

But after three more attempts, and little of his clothing left, Mazrith was no closer to getting the precious stone.

"Do you give up, mighty fae Prince?" The berserker boomed, making me jump.

"No. I am just resting," Mazrith barked back from where he was crouching by the water, cooling his burned hands in the liquid.

"My turn," I said, looking up at the axe.

"No."

I raised my brows. "And why not?"

A flash of white caught my eye, and I looked up to see Voror swooping down toward us. "Voror?"

"You owe me an apology," the bird said in my head as he landed on the island. He sounded more annoyed than usual.

"Why?"

"What in the name of all that is good in the world was that box you entered? It has taken me hours to locate you."

"Oh, I'm sorry. I didn't know it would move us thought the mountain so fast."

The berserker's voice boomed through the cavern. "Who are you speaking with?"

"My friend, Voror. He is an owl," I said.

"I... I recognize his magic."

"He doesn't have any magic. He's an owl."

Mazrith grunted. "An owl who can talk and fly through walls? I think we can safely say he has magic."

I blinked at Voror. He had had magic bestowed upon him by a mysterious fae. Was that what the berserker recognized? But he was ancient, and Voror had met this fae just a week ago.

"Who do you recognize?"

"Those who sought to help me when others were driven by harm." The warrior's voice had turned distant and dreamy. Fearing we were about to lose him to more crazy ramblings, I coughed.

"So, then you know we are friends."

"Perhaps. Perhaps not." He fell silent again.

"Voror, do you think you could fly up there and fetch the piece of jade that is set into the top of the handle?"

The owl graced me with two slow blinks. "You wish for me to fetch you things? Like a common domestic pet?"

"No, it's really important. We need it to fix a statue in the shrine."

"Such things are beneath me, but as I have pledged to assist you, I will do it this once."

He spread his wings wide and took off, twenty feet high in a second. Suddenly panicking that he might get set on fire, I called up to him. "Be careful, there's a shield—"

In barely a few seconds he had darted over the axe handle and was on his way back to me. As he came to land, I saw a rich green stone in his beak.

"Voror, you're a hero!"

"More people should be as aware of that as I am." He dropped the stone on the ground, and I picked it up.

Jade.

I turned back to the berserker. "Thank you."

"I did nothing. Your owl proved his *drengskapr*."

Not having any idea how or why Voror hadn't set off the shield, I just nodded. "I'm sorry for the wrongs done to you and your love. If we can return the jade, we will."

"You will?"

"Yes."

Mazrith was staring at me.

"I would appreciate that."

Mazrith turned to the statue. "I..." He cast his eyes down, and when he spoke again, he was quiet. "Thank you. Not for the jade, but the many other times."

"You should step into the light, Prince Mazrith Andask."

The gold began to seep away, much faster than it had come, and within seconds, the whole statue was stone and steel again.

"What did that mean?"

"It meant he's old, and incoherent."

"Hmm." I held up the piece of jade. "Do we have time to go to the shrine now?"

"No. We barely have time for you to eat before the race."

# 39

## REYNA

"Where the fates have you been?" Frima said, descending on us as soon as we entered the Serpent Suites. "The race is in an hour, and Svangrior has gone to check..." She trailed off with a look at me. "Gone to check the validity of a very serious report."

"Starved Ones?" I said, stomach clenching.

She frowned. "Nothing for you to concern yourself with." She looked back at Mazrith. "You weren't practicing riding. That's what I thought you would be doing today."

"She showed an aptitude yesterday. Today, we had other business to attend to."

"Maz, she needs to do more than stay on the accursed horse. Surely whatever it was, it could have waited?"

"I do not need a lecture from you, Frima," he snapped. "Have lunch sent to the war room. Reyna and I will be eating al

Frima opened and closed her mouth a few times, then rolled her eyes. "Fine."

Butterflies skimmed through my stomach.

Why were we eating alone? We'd been alone all morning, if you didn't count a couple of ancient magic statues and Voror. What could he want to say to me now?

When we were seated at the table, a steaming meat pie before each of us courtesy of Brynja, the Prince pulled something from his pocket and opened his palm so I could see. Three pieces of gleaming metal, not much bigger than a feather lay in his large hand. I leaned over, looking closer.

They were feather-sized because they *were* feathers, I realized. Silver in color, not hugely detailed, but definitely feathers, with small loops at the top. I picked one up, discovering that they were made of metal, and incredibly light.

"New chainmail," Mazrith said.

"What?"

"They are test leaves for new chainmail." His grey eyes shone. "There's not much to show yet. But if the metal is strong enough, you will have new armor soon, made from these."

I turned over the feather in my hand. "Why feathers?" My voice was a little breathless and I cursed myself for it.

"Your owl."

I looked from the metal feather to him, cocking my head. "You wish to turn me into a metal bird?"

"I wish to turn you into a bird of prey."

A bird of prey.

Despite myself, I liked it. Birds were free to soar through

the air, to move from place to place, to govern their own lives.

I handed the feather back. "Thank you."

"I wanted you to know it is being worked on it. And Tait is looking through the volumes to see if he can find a way to make my shadows invisible."

I stared at him. His usual sternness was gone, something more... *open* staring back at me.

For the briefest of seconds, I considered telling him about the visions. Fates, telling him about *all* the visions I'd had, all my life. He was educated and had access to count-less more resources and knowledge about *Yggdrasil* and the five Courts than I did.

*But he's a fae.* The voice was loud and clear in my mind.

And not just a fae, a shadow-fae. The ones that sent people crazy, manipulated fear, and tortured people.

"I appreciate that," I said awkwardly. I stabbed my fork into my pie, and silence descended as we ate.

"Is there any mead?" I was starting to rely on the boost of energy and confidence the delicious liquid provided.

Mazrith stood and went to the drinks cabinet, returning with a flask a moment later.

"You would not have drunk readily from anything I passed you a few short days ago," he said as I thanked him and took it. "Less and less, you argue with me now." He sat back down in his seat. "Why?"

"I told you before, I have chosen to trust you." I didn't share that I feared it was turning from a choice into a desire.

He stared at me, intense gaze making me uncomfortable. "Because you have to? Or because... you want to?"

I swallowed hard. I had to tread carefully. Clearly, he was thinking exactly as I was. "I believe you have an integrity of your own definition."

"A definition you do not agree with?"

"It doesn't matter whether I agree with it or not. It only matters that *we* are not disagreeing so much."

He shrugged, eyes shining. "That is because you are not being so needlessly disagreeable."

Anger washed through me. "I am a human thrall, an orphan, and a freak. The *Yggdrasil* way is to fight with words and wit when you have nothing else. There is power in being able to stand up for yourself, at least in some small manner."

"You believe there is power in denying common sense, or logic? Your friend does not."

I stiffened. "My friend doesn't know how dangerous a fae inside her head can be."

"You speak as though you do." A dangerous tone had entered his voice, his eyes sparking.

"No, I just..." I trailed off.

"You have secrets to hide inside your head," he said quietly. "Kara does not. That is why she does not fear me in the same way that you do."

I stood up, restless discomfort making me need to move away from his scrutiny. "I have chosen to trust you, not divulge my secrets. There is a difference, one I think you are familiar with."

"I am not after your secrets. Not today. I am trying to understand your fire."

"My fire?" I stopped pacing and stared at him.

"You are overflowing with fire. Not bright light or dark

shadow, but furious flames that seep out of you even when you need them to remain dormant for your own survival. The fact that you still stand unscathed is nothing short of miraculous."

I wanted anger to provide me with a response, but it didn't come.

As though knowing exactly what I was thinking, Mazrith spoke again. "There is a reason, Reyna. A reason you cannot say nothing when you are treated as you are. A reason you fight when it will only make things worse."

I stared at him, hating how much I wanted to hear what he would say next. "What? What is the reason?" The whispered words escaped me.

"You were not born for the life you have led so far."

"You can't know that."

"I do. And you do too. That is why you fight. Every part of you rails against the hand you have been dealt."

Memories of the visions of the Starved Ones I had suffered my whole life washed through my head. I shook it, trying to clear it, and only succeeded in swaying a lock of my shining copper hair in front of my face.

I stilled.

"You do not know who you are."

The words were a blow to my gut, and confusion flared fast into anger. "What is it to you who I am?" I snapped. "All you need me to do is break your curse."

He stood abruptly, his movement so fast his furs fell from his shoulders. "You're wrong. I need you for so much more than that." He stared into my eyes, his blazing. "So much fire, Reyna," he murmured.

My breath caught, something slamming through the chaos in my head. "What did you just say?"

He didn't answer me, but the words from my dream were ringing through my skull.

"You were there. In my dream," I whispered. "You said those words, just like that. '*So much fire*'."

He said nothing, his gaze alight as I stared at him.

"You... You got in my head."

Still, he said nothing. A new wave of emotion was crashing over me, drowning out the others.

*Betrayal.*

"You said you wouldn't get in my head!" My words were a shout.

"I was a part of that kiss too, Reyna," he said in a low growl. "It was drink the wine and join you, or enter your bedroom. Which would have preferred?"

"You even have to ask?" Disbelief joined the growing fury. "At what point has it not been made clear to you that I don't want you in my head?"

"Reyna, we can not give in to our desires, the wine-induced dreams is safer, it's—"

But I didn't give him a chance to finish.

Embarrassment and stone-cold fury had taken over. I shoved my hand in my pocket, grabbing out the piece of jade. "You know what? You can fucking do this on your own! I thought you were honest, in your own fucked up way, but that's not true! You promised!"

Before I could stop myself, I had hurled the jade at him.

His hand shot out, and he caught it easily, eyes blazing. The second his fingers closed around it, my own vision turned dark, the war room fading away. Light began to seep in, and I saw the berserker statue, alone and solid on his island. Movement caught my eye, and I saw a small boy pulling a boat up on the shore. He ran to the statue, dwarfed by the huge axe blade he was ducking behind. He peered out, as though checking nobody had followed him, then ducked out of sight again. The vision faded, leaving me staring around the room, breathless.

Had that been Mazrith?

Before I could try and make any sense of it, though, a second wave came. The Queen, and the smell of blood. She was standing in front of a throne, the background a haze of maroon. A male, a huge bearded fae with hundreds of braids knelt before her, then held something out to her. A long thin object. A staff.

The vision lifted.

"What is happening?" Mazrith's barked words came to me before the third wave hit.

This smell was of burning leaves. All I could see was the staff. It was a powerful staff, the air around it humming with ancient energy. And every time I tried to focus on the details, mists swirled around it in sparkling, ethereal tendrils.

"Your stepmother has a mist-staff," I gasped, the vision lifting and the realization slamming into me.

I blinked, trying to clear my eyes.

Mazrith was rigid before me.

"What do you know of mist-staffs?"

Every part of me reacted to the danger in his voice. I took a step back, sweat sliding down my back and dampening my palms.

"Reyna, tell me what just happened, and what you know of mist-staffs, or Odin help me, I will get the answers myself."

He took another step forward, and I took another back.

There was too much information, too many secrets and lies. "I saw you," I blurted. "I saw you, and your mother."

All the color drained from Mazrith's face.

"Her death gave you something. Magic, I think, but it will expire. She told you that you need to find a mist-staff. And... Your father gave the Queen one?" Pieces fell into place as the words tumbled out. "That's why you can't overthrow her, why she is more powerful than you."

I panted a breath, trying to focus. But when Mazrith spoke, all my thoughts fled.

"You have the audacity to accuse me of anything, when you yourself are such a foul, dishonest creature?" Fury laced his words.

"I didn't want to see—"

He cut me off. "Accursed fucking human, what else of my secrets do you know? How long have you known?" His voice had risen to a shout, and I flinched, unable to keep myself from stepping further back.

"That's it. That's everything I know, I swear."

"Your word means nothing to me!" His face was a mask of rage. "You are a liar and a hypocrite, and I have no interest in playing your games!" One arm snapped out, punching at the air in anger, as the other slammed down on the table. "I am done with you," he spat.

Defiance finally kicked in. "Then how will you find your mist-staff?"

"Without your dishonesty."

"I saved your life."

"And I yours. We are even. And over."

"You can't do this without me."

"I refuse to do it with you."

A loud knock on the door, made him whirl, then bellow. "What?!"

Frima pushed into the room. "Maz, Svangrior has returned, wounded. There's a clan raid and another attack, possibly Starved Ones." She looked between us.

"We are done here anyway," he hissed. "Stay here. Prepare her for the race."

"But I—" Frima started.

Mazrith gave a bark of rage. "Just keep her alive until I return!" He pushed past her, out of the room.

Frima stared at me. "What the fuck did you do?"

# 40

## REYNA

I let out a bark of frustration myself, kicking at the table next to me.

It wasn't my fault I'd seen his infernal fucking secrets!

I hadn't chosen any of this, I hadn't asked to be part of some ancient inscription or fae fucking curse!

*But, I had chosen not to tell him what I knew about him.*

Embarrassment welled again as I thought about the dream, and I ground my teeth so hard my head hurt. He had betrayed my trust.

He had gotten into my head, without my knowledge, *for sex.*

Amazing sex. Sex that, in all honesty, he was right about. Had I not justified drinking the fae wine with the exact same reasoning he had?

*Would you have done a thing differently in that dream if you'd known he was truly there?*

A memory filtered through.

*Gildi.* He had told me what it meant in the first dream.

He had been there too, and as good as fucking told me.

I groaned, slapping a hand to my head.

*"You are a liar and a hypocrite."*

My stomach swooped unpleasantly as I recalled his words. If he had seen my secrets, my memories, by taking them from my head without my knowledge... I should have told him. At least, when I had decided to trust him, I should have told him.

"Reyna, I haven't seen Maz that angry in years. What did you do?" Frima repeated.

I stared at her, forcing myself to focus on her face and still my racing thoughts. "I, erm... mentioned his mother."

She pulled a face. "Ohh. Not a good idea."

And I knew why. More and more, it was looking like his mother had sacrificed herself in some way for him. And he only had a few weeks left to make that sacrifice worth it.

The memory of the newest vision forced its way through the emotion of the argument.

*Mist-staffs.*

His stepmother had one. Which explained why he needed one. What were they? Presumably, they were more powerful than a normal staff, but how could I find out more about them without letting anyone know? It wasn't like I could just go around asking people.

"You know, your timing couldn't have been worse."

I forced my attention back to Frima. "Is Svangrior okay?"

"Yeah, he'll be fine. Will you go and get ready, while I try and calm Maz down?"

I nodded. For a beat, I considered asking her to tell him I was sorry. But he had broken his promise. He was hardly blameless in this.

*"This is over. I will do it myself."*

His words punched me in the gut. He had no choice, though. He couldn't do this without me.

Could he?

A slow realization came over me. I wanted to carry on with this.

Another thing Mazrith had been right about — I didn't know who I was, but for the first time I had some solid evidence that maybe I was made for something else.

And I had to see it through.

I blew out a sigh. I was going to have to tell him about the other visions. I should have told him before. Most likely he would tell me it had been him who was responsible. But if not, he would have a good idea who would be capable of that.

"Can you..." I swallowed, and straightened. "Can you tell him I have one more thing to tell him, please?"

Hopefully he would take it as a peace offering.

Frima rolled her eyes. "Fates help me if you two get married and fight like this. I am not going to pass messages between you both for an accursed eternity." She turned and pulled the door open, then stilled.

"Fucking *heimskr*," she swore. "They've gone."

Frima swore the entire time she helped me get my armor on.

"I can't fucking believe they left me behind to babysit."

"Hey, I'm right here," I scowled at her as she tightened the leather around my shins.

"You know what this means?" She glared up at me.

"That the Prince really is done with me?" I muttered. The one thing I had that the others didn't was him.

No Prince? No protection.

And much as I tried to keep the consequences of him leaving confined to the impact on the race, it was impossible to ignore the burning sting of rejection.

He had been there, in the dreams. Burning embarrassment, but also a searing, swooping heat accompanied the thought. It didn't make it real, but it no longer made it a fantasy either. Nor did it make us any kind of couple.

So why did it hurt that he had left?

*He told me I could earn a braid today. And Freya help me, if such a thing were possible, I wanted him there to see it.*

"This means I have to save your behind, every time one of those Odin-cursed fae tries to kill you today," Frima huffed, bringing me back to the present.

I looked at her as she stood up. "Frima, could you make me see through another fae's eyes with your shadow magic?"

Her brows furrowed. "I could put as many nasty images as you like in there, or send you batshit crazy. But no, I can't put your head into another's. Only Maz or the Queen could do that. Why would you ask that? You think it would help you?"

I sighed. So, it probably had been Mazrith helping me. "Just an idea."

"Well, you'd better come up with some others. Because instead of striking down enemies on the battlefield and keeping my Prince alive, I'm stuck watching you race my fucking horse around the forest in some stupid fucking game the queen is playing."

"Frima, I'm not any less angry about him leaving than you are."

"Really?" Shadows danced over her irises, and it was strange seeing something I had gotten used to in the Prince in her eyes. "Because I really, really like killing my enemies. And I really, really don't like looking after idiotic humans who make others lose their temper."

I screwed my face up. "Do you like being kidnapped and forced to compete in completely unfair competitions with fuck all to defend yourself? Because we can swap if you like?"

She held my gaze a moment, then sighed. "He'll be back, when he's dealt with the Starved Ones. He had to go, he's the only one who can take them out for any helpful length of time."

Memories of his exploded staff and the wound in his chest caused a pang of fear for his safety, but I shook it off. Mazrith was strong, and this time, he was not alone.

"How far away were they?"

"Were what?"

"The Starved Ones."

"Closer than the last reports," she said, voice clipped.

I forced down my shudders, and closed my mind to the

Elder's song. But a doubtful voice got through. *They're after you. You know they are.*

I had to get my thoughts in order. Right now, I had the race. When Mazrith returned, hopefully he would have worked out some of his anger on those awful creatures, and he would be willing to talk to me.

"Okay. Shall we go?" I said, injecting as much enthusiasm as I could.

"Fine. And as I'm stuck watching you, you'd better fucking win."

Lhoris and Kara were waiting by the door when I left.

"Good luck. Ride well," said Lhoris.

"You'll do great, Reyna," said Kara, giving me an awkward hug around the ill-fitting chainmail.

We were almost at the great hall when my vision changed.

But it wasn't a memory vision. It was a seeing-through-another's eyes vision.

And it was Mazrith's eyes.

He was standing in Tait's workshop, the *shadow-spinner* wearing a grave expression. "Maz, if she's getting visions like that, then there is no way she is human."

My heart hammered in my chest, but I was vaguely aware that I was experiencing Mazrith's emotions too. Anger. Betrayal. And... was that hope?

"You believe she may be fae? Gold-fae?"

"No, gold-fae have the least mind magic of them all."

"What then?"

"I don't know. You need to find out who her parents were."

Mazrith growled, and through his eyes I saw him glare at the floor. "I do not wish to know more about her. She is a liar."

Tait reached out and touched his arm, and he looked up at him. "So might you be, if you were in her position."

The vision lifted and I saw Frima staring at me.

"What the fuck are you doing now?"

*"If she's getting visions like that then there's no way she's human."*

Tait's words rang through my skull, and I stared back at Frima, blinking fast.

"You're white. What's happening?" she said, stepping toward me.

*"There's no way she's human."*

I clenched my fists, trying to stop the words repeating, trying to stop my stomach from churning. "N-nothing, I felt, erm, ill. For a minute," I choked out.

"Oh fates, nerves kind of ill, or are you actually unwell? They'll rip you apart if they get even a hint of weakness."

I shook my head, forcing my feet to move. "No, no. Must have been nerves. I'm fine now."

My mind was racing as fast as my pulse as we resumed walking.

Mazrith must have stopped in the village on the way to wherever he was going to talk to Tait about me. I knew the rune-marked man was the only person who knew everything about the Prince.

But I was human. Of that I had no doubt at all.

Then who had sent the vision?

I stared at Frima's back as I followed her across the main hall. Had she lied to me about giving other's visions?

No, she didn't know what I had just experienced, I was sure. Her concern over me being ill was genuine.

Then who else was here? I turned, looking furtively around for anyone suspicious. I saw nothing.

*"If she's getting visions like that then there's no way she's human."*

Tait's accursed words crept back in, followed by the voice in the back of my head. The one that had always been there, filling me with doubt and fear. *You've had visions your whole life, Reyna. Of the Starved Ones.*

Gut-deep fear oozed through me. Not of the creatures themselves, but of what I might be to them.

# 41

## REYNA

Frima's shadows blew open the palace doors, and my tumultuous thoughts froze as I was forced to focus on what was before me.

The clearing in front of the palace was back, but it was much, much bigger than before. From the top of the steps, I could see that a winding, looping path had been made in a huge oval, and in the middle was the Queen's throne and the spectators' benches — all filled with watching fae. Trees dotted the course, along with obstacles that shimmered when I tried to look at them, clearly spelled to be hard to make out in advance. I could see patches where the air looked darker, as though inky clouds had descended over parts of the track, and areas that were dominated by trees or glinting metal.

Taking a deep breath, I corralled my chaotic brain into order.

One thing at a time. Right now, I had to survive this race.

COURT OF GREED AND GOLD

I loved riding Idunn yesterday. She would help me through this. Everything would be fine.

We descended the steps and I realized that we were the last to arrive. The other three fae were standing by a raised black flag directly in front of the Queen's throne. She was dressed in black lace today, a daring amount of her cleavage on show. She looked past me, then back at me when I reached the others. Frima hurried to a seat on the benches.

"Where is my son?"

"He'll be along shortly," I said, wishing it was true.

"We will not wait," she replied, failing to keep the note of glee from her voice. "Now, you are all experienced riders." Her voice was suddenly loud enough to carry across the crowd and she shot a nasty look at me, knowing I was not an experienced rider at all. "So I have decided to add some more difficulty to the proceedings."

My heart pounded in my chest. Whatever was coming next couldn't be good.

She stepped toward us, a bubble of shadows springing up above her palm. "Dip your hand in, see what you get," she smiled sweetly at Kaldar. The fae hesitated a moment, then did as she had been asked. She darted her pale hand into the shadow bubble and pulled out a rune. "Black," the Queen read loudly.

She turned, and a human thrall came running out of the edge of the clearing, leading a large black mare with an exotically braided mane and tail, and runes shaved into her huge hindquarters.

Panic flooded me as the Queen stepped along the line, offering the bubble to Orm. I had to ride Idunn.

"White," the Queen sang out, and a huge white stallion was led out, lithe and lean and wickedly fast looking. Orm shot me a smug look.

There was no way this would go well for me. The Queen was choosing whatever steed she liked for each of us, I was sure.

Dokkar pulled a rune that read 'Grey' and a thick, sturdy, grey warhorse appeared.

The Queen smiled apologetically at me. "I'm afraid I know what is left for you," she said as she held out the bubble. I put my hand in, flinching at the ice cold that somehow felt nothing like the Prince's shadows.

'Wild' read the rune I pulled out. The Queen turned, the bubble disappearing, and a cruel smile plastered around her black teeth. The stablehand from yesterday was backing out of the forest, leading the wildest looking horse I could possibly imagine. She was black in color, her mane and tail were uncombed, and she was kicking and bucking, an awful screeching neigh coming from her muzzled snout. Two other thralls were either side, trying to throw ropes around her to get her to move to the start line with the other horses.

"A shame my son is not here, I thought he would be happy to see his mother's horse after so long," the Queen sang, then sauntered toward her throne.

This was Mazrith's mom's horse? The one who couldn't be ridden?

Fear roiled through me. How the fates was I supposed to even mount her, let alone stay on?

Without Idunn, I had no hope of winning this, and little of surviving it.

Mazrith wasn't here to object, though, and the other three fae were moving swiftly toward their own steeds.

"Fuck," I swore under my breath, before making my way to join them.

"Black, white, grey, and wild," sang the Queen to the crowd. They cheered loudly. "Whoever is first back to the start line, will win."

The others had mounted their horses, but mine was still not even near the start line. I steeled myself before jogging over. The stablehand looked fearfully between me and the horse as she kicked and reared, trying to get free of the ropes holding her. "She is called Rasa, my lady."

"Okay. I can do this," I said quietly, clenching my jaw and rolling my shoulders.

Coming from the side, like Mazrith had shown me, I spoke loudly to the furious horse.

"I don't want to be here any more than you do, Rasa," I told her, holding my hands up and edging toward her, fixing my gaze on her huge, wild eye. "And everyone thinks I'm a massive pain in the rear, too."

The stablehand looked at me like I was crazy, but I kept edging closer. She stopped kicking, and I noticed how much sweat was pouring from her coat.

"The sooner we get this over with, the sooner they'll leave you alone." I kept my voice as soft and soothing but confident, as I could.

"And, if it makes a difference, I'm trying to help Mazrith."

The mare stopped snorting, her huge eye stilling as her head paused.

"One big ride. Let it all out. You could do with that, right?" I said, dropping my voice, now I was so close to her. I held my hand out, hoping she would sniff it. She didn't. But she didn't buck or rear either.

She looked similar to Mazrith's horse, Jarl, with silver flecks throughout her coat. There were no braids in her tangled mane or tail though, and no patterns shaved into her coat. She was larger than Idunn, her powerful shoulders broader and her haunches easily capable of knocking my head from my shoulders with one kick.

How the fuck was I going to get on her back?

At the thought, a barely visible wisp of shadow flickered up to my face, getting my attention, then flowed down, making a step. I glanced over my shoulder at Frima.

Breaking eye contact with Rasa was a bad move. As I turned back and stepped on the shadows, she gave a loud whinny, then dipped her head low, hooves pounding at the ground. Before she could rear up, I threw myself onto the saddle the poor stablehands had managed to secure.

I barely made it into the seat before she began to rock. Clinging to it for dear life, I yelled over the horse's ruckus as she did everything she could to shift me. I could hear the crowd laughing behind us. "Help me get to the end of this, and you'll be left in peace!"

She continued to bounce from back to front, the stable-hands all fleeing her lethal hooves. I tried to drop lower, but couldn't let go of the saddle long enough to lay my hand on her neck like Mazrith had shown me. I gritted my teeth, remembering what Mazrith had said about the motivations of horse and rider being one. This horse had energy. She was wild and untamable. I needed to try to use that. "Please, Rasa. Use this power in the race. You could win!"

She paused, just long enough for me to flatten my hand to her neck.

I could hear her heavy breaths, her hooves clopping. I bent low over her, praying she didn't snap her head back and break my nose. "Not long, I swear. Have the run of your life and show them all what you're made of," I said. "Then they'll leave you alone."

When she didn't move, I risked letting go of the saddle and lifting the reins. I tightened my thighs around her, and tentatively steered her toward the other three obediently lined up horses.

To my utter relief, she obliged, still snorting and huffing loudly.

Orm laughed as I passed him. "I won't let your own steed kill you, little human, don't you worry," he said. "I have other plans for you."

I ignored him. Nothing was more important than keeping my energy calm, confident, and focused. I wasn't risking getting thrown off the horse by letting that Odin-cursed *veslingr* get to me.

"Now that we are all finally ready," the Queen called. "Three, two, one... Go!"

# 42

## REYNA

Rasa must have previously been taught the word go, because at the Queen's word, she flew.

My breath caught as she raced off the start line, the only other horse keeping up with her Lord Orm's sleek white.

We were moving so fast along the hard, dirt-packed track that I barely had time to see that there was a large puddle before us, blocking the way. An acrid smell hit my nostrils and as I bent low over Rasa's neck, trying to get my movements in rhythm with hers, I saw that the puddle was black. Tar, I realized.

"Oh, I hope you know how to jump!" I called.

In answer, the horse accelerated. I clung on, trying not to alter her course of movement with any of the commands I had been taught, not wanting to squeeze hard with my thighs or dig my heels in. But as we reached the tar pit, my practice with Idunn and the jumping log kicked in. As one, I gave the command to jump, and Rasa left the ground, soaring over the pit. I bent my knees as we landed, and she barely paused before speeding along the track again.

"Rasa, that was fucking amazing!" I yelled over the whipping wind.

I could see Orm on my right, the white blur of his horse keeping pace. Flashes of metal shone ahead as we rounded a bend in the winding track, and I gasped as a series of huge metal spikes came into view. They were moving up and down, almost hidden from view completely when they were sunk into the ground, then jutting up with violent force.

Thinking as fast as I could, I tried to decide whether to let Rasa steer herself, or whether to try to control her movements.

I knew from just the few moments I had been on her back that she was different from Idunn. The jump had been so precise, so graceful, yet her wildness spoke of instinct and pure courage.

We reached the spikes, and I made my decision. I tucked one foot into her left side and tweaked the reins. She instantly veered the way I wanted her to, straight out of the path of the pistoning spike.

If I had thought that power and speed and control had been exhilarating on Idunn, by Freya, this was even better.

Rasa took the slightest movement from me to alter course, her precision and agility incredible.

"You are a hero!" I yelled to her. "We're in this together, now!"

Blasting through the other side of spikes, I risked looking behind me. Orm was still level, throwing glares at me whenever he could, Kaldar was a few feet behind, and Dokkar was last on his heavy warhorse.

A juddering in Rasa's pace made me whirl back forward, then shriek in surprise as she reared up, almost throwing me with the abrupt change of speed. Orm flew past us, straight into the massive black cloud blocking the track.

Kaldar powered past a second later.

"Come on! Please, we have to go in!"

Rasa stamped her hooves.

"Please, we're losing all our ground! Just straight through, so fast you won't even notice," I soothed.

I knew exactly why she wouldn't go into the cloud of shadow though. The evil, cold, draining feeling coming from it made me want to turn and run the other way.

"Please, we have to go through," I coaxed. A low wail came from inside the cloud, and then Dokkar pulled up beside me, his horse giving a loud neigh.

"Yaa!" he yelled, trying to spur his horse on. Rasa stopped her stamping and looked sideways at the other horse.

"Yaa!" yelled Dokkar again, kicking his heels hard into the beasts side. Reluctantly, the warhorse began to trot, then canter toward the cloud.

As if deciding that if they could do it, she could, Rasa lifted her front hooves again, then launched herself toward the cloud.

"Fuck, you're unpredictable," I gasped, clinging on.

As soon as we entered the cloud, I wished she had stayed outside. Eerie silence descended, even the thudding of hooves dulled.

But she didn't slow, and mercifully, she didn't stop. As all the happiness, hope, and even will to continue drained away from me, Rasa powered through the cloud. We burst through the other side, and all the light and hope came rushing back.

"You did good," I gasped, my eyes streaming with the sudden rush of wind. "Really good."

An awful scream rent the air, and Rasa's ears pricked forward.

"Help! Help me!"

I swiveled, trying to see where the sound was coming from. My movement threw my rhythm with Rasa off, and she slowed, shaking her head.

"Who is that?"

Voror's voice sounded in my head, loud and clear over the rush of wind and the screaming. "It is a trap. Ignore the screams. They will end when you round the next bend."

Relief washed through me, and I focused everything I had on feeling Rasa beneath me, and trying to merge my movements with hers. We careened down the relatively straight section of path we were on, and as soon as we rounded the bend, I saw Kaldar just ahead. Rasa was so much faster than her mare, and in seconds, we had overtaken her.

The Queen's plan to give me an unrideable horse had backfired.

Rasa was incredible.

Orm came into view ahead, just as the high-pitched shrieking stopped. "Let's get him, girl," I said, bending low, reducing the resistance of the air over us. But as she put on a burst of speed, my vision changed.

I was seeing through Dokkar's eyes, and he was panicking. His horse had slowed, and he was staring out into the forest on the left side.

"Help, please, you have to help me!" screamed a woman's voice.

"Tell me where you are!" the earth-fae called back.

My own vision returned, Dokkar's frustrated panic melting away, and my adrenaline-fueled excitement returning.

There was no way Frima, or Mazrith, could or would have sent that vision to me. Trickling fear coursed through me as we caught up with Orm.

*"There's no way she can be human."*

Another tar pit came into view, and I forced myself to focus, ready to jump. But just as we took off, Orm barged into us from the side.

The impact made his horse land as badly as Rasa did, but we both cleared the tar.

"Arsehole!" I bellowed at him.

"Vermin," he hissed back.

We powered on, neck and neck, until we rounded another bend, and a huge tree came into view, right in the middle of the track.

The branches were waving wildly, swiping and slamming into everything in their path, including each other.

"Can you navigate that, girl?"

In response, Rasa lowered her head and sped up. I ducked as low as I could, and this time gave my entire trust to the horse. The branches were moving too erratically for me to anticipate, so this was coming down to instinct, and speed.

She dodged the first two swiping branches with ease. I heard a thud to my right, and although I didn't risk moving and throwing Rasa off, I hoped to Odin it was Orm getting smacked. Hopefully right off his horse.

Rasa weaved in and out of the branches like she'd done it a hundred times, and when we cleared the other side I straightened, unable to stop myself whooping.

"Utter legend!" My vision clouded again. "Not now!"

I was seeing through Kaldar's eyes. Anger was coursing through me, my cheek throbbing where it had been hit by a branch. I lifted my staff and fired a shard of ice straight ahead, my target clear.

My own vision returned in time for me to pull sharply on the reins, driving Rasa to the left. The shard of ice Kaldar had just launched at me sailed past, shattering on a tree to side the of track as the path curved.

It took a moment for Rasa to get her speed back after my hurried course correction, but then we were flying around the bend once more. I hadn't seen Orm come through the other side of the tree. Praying it really had knocked him from his horse, I kept my sights forward. We were well over halfway around the track, if not more, surely.

We rounded another bend and my heart skipped as I saw another cloud of shadow. But this time, Rasa didn't hesitate. Her pace didn't falter as she plowed straight into the cloud.

We both knew something was wrong as soon as we entered. The cloud was thicker than before, and there were trees packed in tightly, dark forms looming menacingly out of the gloom.

Where had they come from?

Unlike the depressing, hopeless feeling inside the last cloud, this cloud lit up my senses like a great, burning beacon. There was danger here.

Rasa slowed right down, picking her way carefully through the trees. I heard hooves behind us, which slowed too.

Deep within the trees, something stirred. Rasa snickered, pulling to the side. An inky blackness seeped out from between the trunks ahead of us, slipping silently through the air and gathering in the darkness.

I recognized it immediately, and my skin turned to ice in my veins.

The Queen's shadow beast.

Its long, sinuous body slid effortlessly through the cloud as it stalked its prey. Us.

A horse shrieked somewhere in the cloud, and it paused, its ears pricked and alert.

Rasa had frozen, as had I.

Hooves thundered in the distance, and then the shadow creature turned and ran, no weight to its paws, as it raced off through the trees.

I let out a shaking breath, and leaned over Rasa's neck. "Let's get out of here. Now."

But as I finished speaking, my vision faded.

I was seeing through Orm's eyes. Glee flowed through me as the shadow creature launched itself at Dokkar's warhorse. The horse was frothing at the mouth, eyes huge wild with fear, and for all Dokkar tried to hold on, he stood no chance.

My vision cleared, and for a beat I didn't know what to do.

Dokkar had tried to help the fake person in the forest, calling for aid. My gut told me there was no evil in him.

*This is a competition! You are in the lead! Ride, Reyna!*

But Dokkar was at the mercy of both the shadow creature, and Orm.

Rasa made the decision for me.

Another shriek from a horse somewhere in the cloud made her startle, and then she was off. I clung on, dimly aware that there was no way I could turn her back now.

Concern for the earth-fae was hard to hang onto as Rasa blasted between the trees in the dark, and the sheer relief when we finally penetrated the edge of the cloud made my head spin.

My jaw fell open as she raced forward, and I realized what the next obstacle was.

The finish line.

I risked peeking over my shoulder, careful not to shift my weight. Orm was crashing through the side of the cloud, yelling and kicking at his horse. To my relief, I saw Dokkar on foot, limping as he tumbled out of the shadows. Other fae went running toward him.

I turned back. "Go, Rasa, go! Go!"

And she did.

With a burst of speed I couldn't believe she had left in her, she powered across the finish line.

There was no applause. Not a solitary clap. My head was spinning. I leaned over, rubbing Rasa's neck and clapping her staunch, wet shoulders, congratulating her over and over. But my voice was all that could be heard in the silent clearing. That and the thundering hooves of Lord Orm's horse.

He skidded to a halt beside me, his face a mask of fury.

"I believe that is a win for me. The pathetic little human," I said, straightening and beaming at him.

His furious face morphed into a sneering smile. "That depends on your definition."

"A win is a win, Orm. You can't argue with this, everyone saw."

Kaldar came cantering out of the shadow cloud, bleeding from several places.

Orm shrugged at me. "You won this game, yes. I find these sorts of things such good distractions, don't you?"

I stared at him.

"I see your betrothed is not here today. Was he distracted too?"

"Distracted from what? What are you saying?" Frustration was welling up, and Rasa was getting skittish beneath me, her body heaving as she breathed hard.

Lord Orm inspected his fingernails, then looked back up

COURT OF GREED AND GOLD

at me, eyes gleaming with cruelty. "She's very pretty. Your little friend."

I felt the blood drain from my face.

Without thinking, I dug my heel into Rasa, whirling her around. I galloped to the palace steps, ignoring the cries of the crowd and Frima calling my name. I leaped from Rasa's back onto the steps and ran as fast as I could across the hall and up the staircase.

I knew the corridors well enough, now, and adrenaline lent speed to my legs.

When I reached the Serpent Suites, my heart just about stopped beating.

The door was open.

The door was never open.

"Kara!" I screamed.

I ran into the room. Ellisar was on the ground, bleeding from his head. I ran past him, banging open all the doors. "Kara! Lhoris!"

"What the— Ellisar!" Frima's voice sounded from the main room, but I barely heard it. The suites were empty. Kara and Lhoris were gone.

# ANSUZ
## MESSAGE
### REVELATIONS · VISIONS · INSIGHT

# THANKS FOR READING!

Thank you so much for reading Court of Ravens and Ruin. I hope you enjoyed it! I promise you won't have to wait so long for the next one.

The story continues in the next book, Court of Monsters and Malice.

If you want to see some exclusive artwork of Maz and Reyna's dream, you can sign up to my newsletter at elizaraine.com. And maybe don't open it in company!